As Our Gears Turn

Nikki Adams

```
public class Main{

      public static void main(String[] args) {

      System.out.println("Love me like a

poem.");

      }

}
```

To you, and that one person you love more than life itself. The one you'd rather die than express your love to; the one you fear every waking day that they will never, ever reciprocate.

Introduction

Charlotte

The universe came to a standstill, and time seemed to slow to a halt. The smell of budding romance plagues the air. All I can focus on are the bright hazel eyes of the pretty face in front of me. Nothing else matters at this moment.

A hand cups my right cheek as I lose all sense of thought. My fingers wrap around the wrist holding my face as my other hand interlocks with his other hand. I can't focus on anything else; it's as if we are the only two people in the world. My heart beats fast, passionate. Nothing else matters at this moment.

"It's always been you," he mutters into my ear.

We dance. The moonlight shines above us as the stars match our movement. We dance to the rhythm of our matching heartbeats to make up for the absence of music. Slow and steady, full of teenage hormones and bliss. An off-white glow grows around us, our grip on each other's hands growing tighter as we continue to laugh and dance. I don't know where we are, where we are going, or what is going to happen. I can feel the crisp early autumnal wind flowing through my hair and the soft ground pressing against my shoes, but I can't pay attention to anything else other than him. Nothing else matters at this moment.

The dancing stops. Hand in hand, we are left to stare at nothing but each other. He looks like everything. He lets out a soft laugh, panting and sweating from all of the running around that just went on. I feel safe and secure, falling directly into his arms. He rests his head on my left shoulder, burying his face deep into my neck, still laughing. His hands let go of mine as he reaches for my waist and brings me closer to him. I can hardly breathe, partially due to the moment at hand and partially because he's grabbing me so tightly. His face is mere centimeters away from mine at this point.

"Charlotte, I can't deny it any longer," he whispers, "I–"

My phone's alarm went off before he could finish. The sunlight peeks through the blinds above my windowsill, a bright wave of yellowish white covering my lonely room. A ceiling fan whirs softly above me as the alarm blares in my left ear. I begrudgingly press snooze. As I fully open my eyes, the contents of my dream come flooding through my half-awake brain.

"You've gotta be kidding me," I mutter as I go back to sleep.

Chapter One

Charlotte

I have all of this love in my heart, and it's wasted on the nothing I have accompanying me. Every day, I wake up with a sense of dread, the loneliness creeping through my veins like an awful hangover. My heart aches as much as my knees, which are somehow both eighteen and eighty years old at the same time.

"Jeez, I'm disgusting," I accidentally say out loud as I roll onto the floor. I slowly pick myself up, throwing my blanket back onto the bed I fell out of.

I can feel my face start to heat up. This is indubitably embarrassing. The feeling of utter awfulness creates a hefty pit inside my stomach, making me feel full even though I haven't eaten since dinner last night. I feel...perpetually odd.

I slowly make my way to my bathroom. I turn the yellowish light on and wince at the awfully bright glow. Once my eyes adjust to the room, I glance at myself in the mirror. The mascara I didn't feel like washing off last night has trickled down my eyelids, almost reaching my cheeks. Using my thumb, I wipe away the drool that has accumulated near my mouth from last night's blissful sleep.

I stare at my horrid reflection. A ghastly figure appears behind me, its hands surrounding mine. A face covered in blond hair leans its chin on my shoulder. Our eyes lock, the figure's hazel eyes holding a sense of remembrance. I blink, and the figure is gone, as if it were a figment of my imagination. It definitely was.

Immediately after registering what the hell just happened, I step away from the counter, make my way to the bathroom wall, and slam my head into it as hard as I can. A loud thud echoes throughout the otherwise silent bathroom. After a brief splitting headache, I feel okay again– no more hallucinations in this brain of mine.

I turn on the water. I need to wash away whatever semi-mortal sin is encompassing me at the moment. I step in right before the water heats up, so I can feel the piercing frigidity of the morning. This step is entirely necessary and incredibly important, mainly so I don't forget that I exist. Sometimes I do. It's not fun.

In the shower, I keep thinking about the dream I just had. I've never had a dream so…surreal, so passionate before. I've had romantic fantasy dreams in the past, but they've never consisted of real people I knew. Dreams are supposed to be unrealistic fantasies with people who don't exist in settings that also don't exist in real life.

"It's always been you." That statement echoes in my head. Four words, technically five if you break apart the contraction, keep echoing in my head over and over as I scrub my shampoo into my hair. When is always? Why is always? Who is always? What is always? Where is always?

I let out a sharp cough as I wash the soap out of my hair. My shower routine is monotonous; I shower every morning before school, washing and conditioning my hair, double-cleansing my face, and washing my body with both an unscented bar soap and a gourmand, silky body wash. I pride myself on my ability to stay clean, despite literally everything else about my life. I *need* to be clean. I *need* to wash away the disgusting thoughts I'm having at the moment.

Once I feel adequately scrubbed, I turn off the shower and open the curtain. I grab a bright orange towel and do an initial dry-off. I walk to the bathroom counter and step on the scale. Gross. Disgusting. Vile.

I turn on my phone and open my note-taking app. I scroll through months, years of measurements, eventually reaching today's date:

"September 23rd: XXX"

I wrap my towel tightly around my body as I read the notifications that have appeared on my phone throughout the night. I've made a goal with myself to only check my phone after I've already fully woken up, because I don't want to risk saying something awful while I'm only half-awake. It's a habit that's good to have but incredibly hard to create, like most habits worth making.

I read through messages, group chats, and emails. I swipe through the typical junk mail and school notifications. Through the piles of emails from random brands advertising measly sales, I see a message from a sender I don't recognize. With my intuition and common sense currently in a daze, I tap on it.

"I hate you." is all the email said.

Without a second glance, I knew exactly who this was from and why it was sent to me. I immediately clicked on the sender and examined the twenty-character-long mashup of letters and numbers. It's a burner email from the exact person I knew it was going to be. With the way things have gone so far, I am starting to come to the belief that the universe doesn't even want me to try to have a good day today.

I take out my toothbrush, apply a concerning amount of toothpaste, and begin to meticulously brush my teeth. Every morning and night, I brush my teeth for five minutes straight, only stopping to spit out the toothpaste buildup. I had only found out recently that you're only supposed to brush for two minutes and thirty seconds at a time, but that seems way too little for the amount of stuff I consume daily. I couldn't imagine only brushing my teeth for that long; I'd feel disgusting and dirty.

After I finish brushing my teeth, it's time for skincare. My skincare routine in the morning is incredibly simple. I already washed my face in the shower, so I don't need to do it again. I apply a caffeine solution to my undereyes, attempting to hide the blatant dark circles I've accumulated over the years. After that, I lather on a water-based moisturizer to my face and neck. I check the weather app on my phone for the day's UV levels. Since the max UV for today is above four, I must apply sunscreen to my face and neck as well. I only use Korean sunscreens; they're much less oily and don't make my skin look like I applied butter to it. I want to look moisturized, not glossy.

After my skincare, I have a specific order that I apply clothes. First goes my underwear, then bra, then top, bottoms, and finally socks. Today, I put on a wine red hoodie and a pair of light-wash jean shorts. My socks are cuffed at the same exact length every time.

All of this just to barely feel normal.

I check the time on my phone. I finished getting ready about a minute earlier than I normally do. I go to my room, grab my backpack, and shove my laptop and phone charger in it. I swiftly jump down the stairs and walk toward the kitchen. I open the fridge and grab the closest Zero Sugar Red Bull. It has to be Zero Sugar or Sugar Free. I can't stand full-calorie drinks. They make me sick. All the sugar...all the calories...disgusting.

I crack open the Red Bull and take a giant swig as I fill up my water bottle. I shove my water bottle into its respective pocket as I reopen the fridge. I finish the last of my Red Bull before I grab a second Red Bull, placing it securely in my hoodie pocket for later.

The honk of a mid-sized sedan blares outside. I grab my house key and my backpack as I race out the door, met by a black Honda Accord. I swing open the passenger side door to see my best friend's pissed-off face.

"Hey, Vinny," I smile.

"You're late, Char," he sighs.

"When it's your turn to pick me up, you pick me up at 7:32. It's..." I glance at my watch. "Aw, shit, it's 7:33. How could I fumble so badly?"

"Oh, calm down and get in."

Vinny Martinez has been my best friend for nearly a decade. In that time, I've seen him grow from a stubby, snot-nosed kid to a functioning young adult. His hair is black, but if you looked at him in the sunlight, it would look blue from the insane amount of dye that he puts in it every month. He always looks nice, with his hair combed, his wired glasses straight, covering his beautiful brown eyes, and an outfit that *screams* performative. He's about four inches taller than me, standing at a solid 5'9.

I put my backpack down and sit in the passenger's seat. I put my seatbelt on as Vinny reverses out of my driveway. Once out of the driveway, he puts the car into drive and starts accelerating out of my neighborhood.

"This is the first time you've been late, Char. What happened this morning? Too much Red Bull?" he asks, half-joking. He's not too far off.

I think about everything that happened. My mind floods with the memory of last night. My face flushes with embarrassment. "I had a really weird dream last night."

"Tell me more."

I tell him everything. The passion, the dancing, the kiss, the four-word phrase. The figure in the mirror, the hand holding mine. The only thing I don't tell him is his name, and the fact that it's a "him" this time.

"This isn't about *her*, right?" he asks.

"Thankfully, no."

"Good. There's nothing wrong with having a dream like that. It's just a dream, it's not like it's real or anything. Just act normal, and those feelings will go away after a while. You're not the first person to have a wet dream, you know."

"It was not a wet dream! You're disgusting!"

He laughs. "If you say so."

The rest of the car ride is full of conversations about classes while we listen to Vinny's playlist. Every week, we alternate who drives whom to school, and this week is his, meaning it's his turn to play whatever music he wants. The funny thing about this is that we've mostly influenced each other's music tastes, so our playlists are mostly similar, so I don't mind listening to whatever he wants to.

I like to look at Vinny while he drives. He keeps the windows slightly cracked, so a small breeze flows through his obviously dyed hair. I would describe the color of his hair as an americano with a splash of navy blue creamer. His eyebrows, meanwhile, are the color of hot chocolate. Not sure why he doesn't dye them too; I've never asked.

After about fifteen minutes, Vinny pulls into the parking lot of our high school. Parking spaces are expensive here since there are so many students, so we share one, and whoever drives gets to park there. We always come to school together, so there hasn't been an issue yet. Our parking spot, #42, is right outside of the robotics classroom, where he and I tend to frequent. Nearly every day, we spend an extra hour or two after school with our team, working on various projects around shop.

I grab my stuff and hop out of the car. He locks it, and we walk inside. We have about fifteen minutes before class officially starts, but we like to get there early to get the best seats in the classroom, which is an *incredibly* nerdy thing to say, come to think of it.

While walking on the sidewalk to the front entrance, Vinny and I stay quiet. We talk so much during the car ride that there's usually never anything we need to discuss on the way to class. At least, nothing we ever want other people to hear. Some of our conversations get a little bit sillier than expected, and I have an image to keep. Not really, but I like to pretend I do. Not many people here care about me.

We finally make it to the front entrance of the school. Vinny opens the first door for me, and I thank him. I open the second door for him, and he thanks me. We have a mutualistic relationship when it comes to opening doors, among other things. When entering the main building, I usually don't pay much attention to what's in front of me. This morning, I decided to see what awaited me. It's a brand-new Monday, so I might as well try something new. I look up, and I see the same people I saw in the parking lot, with one exception.

About a dozen feet away stands a lanky blond boy leaning against a wall, talking with a taller boy. As Vinny and I enter, he turns to look at us, and all I can see are his blinding hazel eyes and soft smile. He waves as my mind turns to mush and my face immediately reddens.

Vinny looks at me and laughs. "Oh, shit."

There he is. Standing before me: the boy of my dreams.

Chapter Two

Charlotte

"I'm a mess, Vinny." I sigh as I shove my face into the math notebook on my desk.

"That's the sixteenth time you've said that in the past ten minutes. Are you sure you're trying not to think about it?"

"I need to distract myself," I say as I open the Red Bull I had hidden in my hoodie pocket.

"Char, if you're already this delirious, I don't think caffeine is going to help you. Is this your first?"

I shake my head. "I've told you so many times that Red Bulls make you anxious! That's what's causing this madness of yours."

He takes the can out of my hand and takes a swig for himself. I snatch it before he drinks the rest of it and chug it down. "I'll figure that out later in life."

More students shuffle into my multivariable calculus class. A tall, dark-eyed girl boasting frizzy pigtails skips into the classroom, a faint glow emanating from around her. Her orange blush matches her pristinely glossed lips. She's wearing a pink zip-up jacket and black jean shorts with matching pink sneakers and black, unevenly-cuffed knee-high socks. She's none other than Jade Brady, a close friend of ours since middle school. I haven't known her as long as I've known Vinny, but it's close, and she's someone I'd consider to be my best friend. Second to Vinny, of course; he's on another plane of existence in my eyes.

Upon seeing us, she excitedly jumps to our table and throws down her black backpack full of trinkets and colorful pins. "Good morning!" she exclaims.

"Mornin', Jade," says Vinny as she sits down at our table.

"How are you guys doing on this fine Monday morning?" she asks as she takes a glance at our stuff. "How many Red Bulls is that today, Charlotte?"

"Technically, only one-and-a-half, since Vinny drank half of this one. They're the short ones anyway."

Jade takes a quick look at my face, still warm from the previous interactions. She uses her hand to push my chin and our eyes meet. "You look peculiar. What's up with you?"

"Charlotte had a dream that gave her a crush on Sp–"

I smack Vinny's mouth shut before he says any other stupid things to the rest of the classroom. Somehow, even with a single syllable, she knew exactly who he was talking about. Jade is great at jumping to correct conclusions, especially when it comes to gossip. If something has happened with people in our school, Jade is somehow the first person to know about it.

"How peculiar," she says, "tell me more."

I retell the dream, ensuring I include the small details because she loves those. I told her about the phrase, the dancing, the ghost that appeared in the mirror before I went into the shower. She listened intently, tapping her finger on the table as she nodded in understanding.

"I see. So basically, you need to get rid of this crush before competition season starts."

"I know, but that's not until November. This shouldn't take more than a week. I can't focus on something like this when I have college apps to write and a robot to build."

"Unfortunately, hun, that's unlikely knowing you."

The bell rings, and my calculus teacher walks into the classroom, dropping a bunch of papers at his desk. "I have your exams graded. Mean was 73, high was 102, and low was 28. You guys know the drill; I'll call your name, and you come up here and pick it up."

He starts listing names. I'm about in the middle range of surnames, so I wait patiently for my turn. Vinny and Jade are ahead of me, so they get theirs first. I see good faces coming from the two of them, which is nice to see. Finally, I hear my name get called, so I stand up and grab my paper. *101.* Cool, but who did better?

I sit down and take a quick glance at Vinny's 102. "I knew it'd be you."

"Hey, I studied hard for this one, don't hate the player."

Jade shoves her paper into her bag. "A 97 is fine, right? It's still the beginning of the semester, I can bring it up pretty quickly, right?" she mutters to herself.

"Jade, chill out. A 97 is good."

"Whatever," she sighs, "anyway, Vinny, how's the funding proposal coming along? We need new drill batteries in the shop."

"I'm almost done with it, actually. I just need to edit it and send it over to the teachers, and we'll be all set."

"Perfect."

Class goes on as per usual. We introduced vector-valued functions today, which were a little hard to initially understand. I'll get it eventually. Pure math tends to come easier for me compared to other subjects like chemistry and physics. God, I *hate* physics. Nothing about physics makes sense to me; the entire premise of physics is that you have an equation with one variable that you need another equation to find, but then *that* equation has a variable that you need to solve elsewhere, so on and so forth. It's awful and I hate it so much. I'm glad I finished all of my physics classes last year, and I won't have to worry about it for a little while.

The bell rings again as I finish taking my last few notes. I scribble some nonsense down as everyone else starts to pack up their things. I throw my notebook into my backpack and walk out of the classroom with Vinny and Jade. The three of us make our way down the hallway to our next class, which is a poetry elective course. This was the only class that fit in all of our schedules, and we tried to make sure we had as many classes as possible together.

We sit in our respective unassigned-assigned seats, which are in the direct middle of the classroom. When the semester started, I made sure to pick the most optimal seating to minimize the number of cold calls while also ensuring we didn't look like slackers. I'd say it's worked pretty well so far.

I grabbed the giant poetry textbook off the desk and turned the page to Romeo and Juliet. I remember reading it in my eighth-grade English class, and for some reason, we have to analyze it again in my senior year.

"No need for textbooks today," my teacher, Mrs. M, announces as everyone sits down, "today we'll be watching clips from the 1996 Romeo and Juliet movie, or as many like to call it, the Leonardo DiCaprio version."

She turns on the projector and inserts a CD into the player. The movie starts, and Leonardo DiCaprio's face appears before us. Strikingly blond hair, reminds me of a certain someone–oh shit.

"This is the worst time to see this guy's face," I mutter as I bury myself in my hoodie sleeves.

"Oh, come on, he doesn't look like him at all, other than the hair." Vinny groans.

"That's the problem."

"Y'know, maybe you shouldn't go to the shop today, it might not be good for you," says Jade, "why don't you take a break and go home early?"

"I wouldn't mind skipping today if you want me to, you wouldn't be pulling my leg or anything," Vinny replies.

"I'll think about it, you know I hate skipping."

I try my best to pay attention to Claire Danes' rendition of Juliet instead of Leonardo DiCaprio's external features. This sorta works. I'm really hoping my next homework assignment has nothing to do with anything Romeo does; if so, I'm screwed. I can't even *think* about DiCaprio without thinking of him.

We don't get too far into the movie before the bell rings again, this time for our lunch period. I forgot to pack a lunch, so this is a great opportunity to go outside and bask in the sun for an hour. Vinny, Jade, and I try our best to get a good table outside during this time of the semester; being outside is incredibly therapeutic when classes get rough.

We make our way outside and spot an empty table. I immediately make a run for it and throw my backpack onto one of the benches. Successfully captured. I climb onto the table and lie down, my legs dangling on the sides while I stretch my arms out into a star-like position. I'm in my element.

My friends join me soon after. "You should eat something, Char," Vinny says as he tosses a bag of crackers on my stomach. I open the bag, pop a cracker in my mouth, and let out a large sigh. I begin to doze off, the blissful warmth of the sun hitting my face making me sleepy.

About ten minutes in, an unidentifiable hand picks up my arm and starts to softly shake it. I open my eyes, and it's Maggie Lin, one of the sophomore programmers. "What's up?"

"Spencer broke the robot again. Can you come take a look at it?"

I turn to Vinny and Jade, who are eating their lunches. "I can take a look if you don't want to, Charlotte," says Jade, "I'm sure I can figure out a CAN bus error."

I sit up. He breaks the robot every time he tries to push code to it. This happens nearly every other day. This is completely normal, but it feels abnormal now. I feel abnormal now. Stupid dreams.

"Nah, I've got it," I say as I roll off the table and grab my stuff.

"Take the crackers with you, please."

I nod, shove the bag of crackers into my hoodie pocket, and make my way to the robotics room with Maggie. She attempts to explain to me what happened and why the robot is broken again, but I don't think she completely understands what he's doing. No one ever does, really. He usually spends a few hours at the corner desk, typing away, and pushes something every so often.

She opens the door to the robotics room for me, and I thank her. We walk in together and see a blond boy hunched over a computer while our robot blinks red in the middle of the room. Tables are stacked on top of each other, and chairs are moved to the side to establish ample space for the robot. Hearing the door open, he looks up from his computer and smiles. I try to ignore his face so I don't embarrass myself again.

"Hey, Charlotte. Sorry to interrupt your lunch again," he says. It's the same way he always does, but this time it feels different. I'm probably overthinking it. If I don't look at him, maybe this feeling will go away.

I kneel next to the robot. We haven't progressed much with our mechanical building yet, so the robot is nothing but a chassis. I see a deep scratch on one of the table legs and a dent in the chassis' metal wall. "Jeez, what did you do this time?"

"I tried testing out color sensing on the robot, and I accidentally drove it into the wall. Now it won't move."

Maggie did such a horrible job explaining what happened that it's a lot less major than I thought it would be. I grab a multimeter from the electrical drawer. Battery voltage is good. I shake some wires around to see if there's a loose connection, and lo and behold, I see a flash of green when I push down on a sensor cable. I turn off the robot, unplug the wire, plug it back in, and turn the robot on again. Unfortunately, this is the majority of my work as the electrical lead of my team: Spencer Laine breaks something, I fumble around with the wires, and I eventually turn the robot off and on again. It's a constant cycle.

The robot blinks green, showing a stable connection. I walk over to Spencer, grab the controller from his hand, and drive the robot around to ensure that the connection is still stable. After I confirm everything looks fine, I hand it back to him.

"Thank you so much, I really don't know what I'd do without you," he says with the same grin he always has.

"No problem," I reply, "I'm gonna go back outside, don't break it again today."

"You're not gonna stay?"

Normally, if Spencer breaks something, I'll stay with him for the rest of lunch to chat with him while he works. Today, I'd rather do anything *but* that. I think if I spend any more time with him in the room right now, I'll want nothing more than to either crawl into the corner and sob or, instead, beg to recreate my dream.

"I have an argument to finish with Vinny. I'll see you later." I lie.

"Bye-bye."

I walk out.

Chapter Three

Spencer

I broke the robot on purpose.

I'm honestly surprised that she hasn't caught on yet. What idiot breaks a robot every other day? She should know by now that I'm not incompetent; I've been granted unlimited access to this robot for a reason. I know how basic wiring works, but it's much more fun when she comes in and I get to watch her work on it.

"Damnit, I wasted one of my chances," I mutter to myself as I hunch over my computer, playing a game of Tetris instead of actually working. Usually, I'm able to convince her to stay and hang out with me after one of these predicaments, but she was adamant about leaving this time. I wonder why. Did I do something wrong? She wouldn't even look at me.

I'm a mess of a human being. My troubled thoughts are swirling through my brain like mad. As my shaking hands press the arrow keys to continue playing this stupid Tetris game, my face begins to heat up with embarrassment. I lost my game. I lay my head on my keyboard and let out a large sigh. I feel empty.

I hear footsteps behind me. "Everything alright?" Maggie Lin, a sophomore on my team, asks.

I lift my head. "Yeah, just wallowing in self-pity."

She laughs. "Is this because of her?"

"Hush!"

"I agree that she was acting a little standoffish today, but you shouldn't beat yourself up over it."

"I guess so," I sigh, "I just don't know how to make these feelings go away. What are you supposed to do when the most beautiful girl you've ever seen in your life doesn't reciprocate?"

"Keep trying? Write her a poem or something."

"That sounds like a great idea until I have to actually give it to her."

"Remember, it hasn't been too long since everything happened with her last relationship. She may be taking a while to recover."

"I guess so. How would you handle something like this? These feelings that never seem to go away, even after all these years?"

She shrugs. "Girls just tend to flock to me. I've never been as helpless as you are."

"Great, thanks."

The bell rings. Usually, after one of my "mistakes," Charlotte and I would walk to our next class together, AP Government. We sit across from each other at the same table, and I have a hard time getting anything done because of it. It's the only class we have together this semester, and I only took it because I knew she was planning on it. I would've been just fine taking regular Honors Civics, but this was at the same time and was way too good an opportunity to miss.

Maggie grabs her stuff and leaves. I like having her around; she's good to talk to about girl stuff, especially since I'm not in the category of people she's interested in. She's also interested in taking my position as programming lead after I graduate, and I have to train *someone,* so it may as well be someone I can also benefit from. Mutualism.

The AP Gov classroom is unfortunately on the complete opposite side of campus. Usually, this is fine, since I have ample opportunity to talk to Charlotte on the way, but by myself, it's awfully monotonous. While making my way through the crowded hallway of students, I think about what I plan on doing after school. My options are incredibly slim: robotics, robotics, or robotics. I don't do much else during competition season, other than write an occasional poem.

I walk through the door of my classroom as soon as the second bell rings. Sitting at my table is none other than Charlotte Moretti. And Vincent Martinez, her best friend, of course. Those two are rarely apart from each other if they can help it. I've never seen a better friendship than theirs. I believe they've been friends since childhood, but I'm unsure.

Charlotte is, without a doubt in my mind, the prettiest woman I have ever seen. She's always put-together; her socks are always perfectly cuffed and her cute outfits always match. She looks best in red and navy; they compliment her dark eyes. Her hair is dark brown and curly, incredibly Italian, but her front-facing bangs are straight and voluminous, as if she blow-dries them in the morning. She smells like cotton candy perfume and Red Bull.

Vincent, on the other hand, is such an…interesting man. He's a very attractive man, way more attractive than I should consider him to be. His hair is sleek and his face is sharp and chiseled, like a meticulously designed statue. He's never seen without a pair of gold earrings, a necklace to match, and a light layer of clear mascara. He always smells good.

I sit down at my seat and pull out my computer for the notes I am definitely not going to take. "Hey Spence," says Vincent.

"Hey guys," I reply, glancing at Charlotte, who hasn't lifted her head from her notebook since I entered the room.

"You didn't break the robot again after I left, right?" she mutters, her voice projecting to the table.

"Of course not!" I smile.

The Gov classroom is cold, empty, and unwelcoming. The desks are uniform, the decorations on the wall are lackluster, and the thermostat in this classroom is probably half a century old. A sense of dread fills the room as the inevitable doom that is class starting. All joy and happiness comes to the Gov room to die.

Class begins, and I find myself staring once again. She's been covering her face with her left hand for the entire duration of class as she writes with her right. We're learning something about the three branches of the government; I don't really care at this point. My heart aches with both a sense of fondness and embarrassment; all I want to do is lift up her pretty face with my hand and ask what's wrong. Alas, I cannot do that, and all I can do is imagine what would happen if I did, in a scenario that could only be described as the most unrealistic dream ever.

I move my head to look at the slideshow my teacher was presenting and accidentally lock eyes with Vincent, who has been staring at me for who knows how long. He has a sort of look in his eye, one where he definitely knows something I don't. Maybe I do know. Vincent is such an interesting person; he'll know something about you before you even know yourself. He definitely knows *something*, who knows what it may be.

I shrug it off as I take a photo of the notes on the board. For the rest of class, about half an hour, I decide to be a good student and take notes on whatever we're learning about. The teacher mentions a test on Friday, which I never would've known about if I kept focusing my attention on a certain someone.

Lovesickness is a curse, and I am full of it. A wonderful woman has hexed me.

The bell rings once again, and I have one more class left before the school day officially ends and I get to go to robotics. My last class is multivariable calculus, which I tried to get at the beginning of the day, but that period was full when I submitted my forms. I pack up my stuff and leave as quickly as I possibly can, because staying would mean I'd have to make small talk with Vincent and Charlotte, and it seems like Charlotte would rather do anything else than talk to me at the moment. I wonder if I did something wrong. Is she pissed about the robot, or something else entirely?

Calculus goes as per usual. I actually have the opportunity to focus in this class because there's a significant lack of pretty girls named Charlotte Moretti in the room. I take my notes, help a classmate with a problem on the homework due Thursday, and leave as soon as the bell rings. I have important places to be and important people to see.

My calculus room was close to AP Gov, but on the opposite side of campus from the robotics room. It takes me nearly seven minutes to make my way over there through the troves of students trying to leave. Everyone is racing to get to their cars or buses, and I just want to survive this mess of students so I can get to robotics as quickly as possible. I have important testing to do.

Our first competition is thankfully not for another month, but that doesn't mean that tensions aren't high at the moment. Mechanical hasn't finished their work, meaning electrical can't even start most of their work, meaning I can only work with imaginary robots for the foreseeable future. It's not ideal, but thankfully, with the amount of simulations one can create nowadays, I still have a lot on my plate in the upcoming weeks.

Thankfully, the base code for the robot is pretty simple. I can recycle last year's code to make the robot move; the hardest part is making it so every other component on the robot moves correctly. It's grueling and time-consuming, but I love it so much and I wouldn't rather do anything else at this moment.

I finally make it to the robotics room as many others on my team are trickling in. I gravitate to the back of the room where the driver simulation table I built stays. Last summer, I decided to take a few weeks to create this simulator so the Driver would be able to train their driving and reaction skills even when there isn't a physical robot to practice with. It was a very long few weeks, but the smile I received from her when it was completed was so worth it.

Upon further inspection, I see Charlotte sitting at the simulation table, messing around with the controller. To be completely honest, I wouldn't have built the damn thing at all if anyone else were our team's Driver.

Charlotte has been our team's main Driver since her freshman year of high school. She's *really* good at navigating through game pieces and other robots, which is integral to avoiding damaging our previous robot during competitions. With all my time in robotics, I've never seen anyone better than her, even on other teams.

Simply driving the robot has a relatively low skill floor but an insanely high ceiling. All the Driver does is move the chassis part of the robot with an Xbox controller. The second driver, also known as the Controller, operates the extra functions of the robot, which could be lifting up elevators or revving up motors to shoot a ball. The Controller position is usually held by the person who knows the most about the robot's internal functions, aka the lead programmer, which has been me for the past three competition seasons.

Because of this, Charlotte and I work *really* well together. We essentially combine into one person when a Round starts, and combine our button movements to excel in competitions. We have this sort of synergy that really shines when we need it. During Rounds, she'll shout commands, and I follow with immense speed and precision, as if she pressed the buttons for me.

She's also so, *so* pretty when she drives. I, unfortunately, rarely get to see this happen in real time, since I'm mostly focused on doing my job, but if there's something wrong with the bot and all we can do is show off our driving, I get to put my controller down and watch her do her thing. It's bad for the robot, but great for me.

I decide to break the silence as I hear her Round ending. "How's everything going?" I ask, looking at her reflection through the computer screen.

She looks at me, her face pink. "It's going pretty good."

"May I sit here?" I motion to the chair right next to hers.

"Sure," she nods.

As I sit down, I notice the pinkness of her face is becoming darker and darker by the second. She looks...unwell. Is she coming down with something? That wouldn't be good. Hopefully she can get over it before competition season.

I listen to her fiddle around with the simulation as I pretend to do work on my computer. The teachers usually don't come in until about fifteen minutes after class, so I have time to kill until then. I turn my head to check on Charlotte's progress, but I have to turn back soon after, or else she'll notice my embarrassingly reddened cheeks. I blush easily, especially when I'm around her.

She's so pretty, like a poem you think about for years after you first read it. One you keep in the back of your mind every time you're feeling sentimental. She's as pulchritudinous as the longest, most convoluted word you could find in your local thesaurus.

I just wish she wasn't gay.

Chapter Four

Spencer

After what seems like forever, the teachers walk in, and all of the commotion present in the room recedes to a halt. "Happy Monday, everyone," says our lead coach, Mr. Davis. Everyone calls him Mr. D, but I call him my worst nightmare if I happen to break something. He's a yeller and will make the entire concrete classroom shake. Thankfully, he doesn't yell at me too often, and mechanical usually gets most of the yelling. Specifically Jade Brady, Charlotte's other best friend, but she's a professional instigator.

He makes his way to our table, completely disregards me, and turns his head toward Charlotte. "How many days until comp?"

She grabs her phone and does a quick Google search. "42."

"42 days until comp, everybody! We are *severely behind.* We already had game mechanisms on the robot at this point last year! We need to step it up or we're not making it to comp!"

Sometimes I think he cares more about competing than we do.

Mr. Davis finally notices I'm here, too. "How's your stuff going, Spencer?" he asks, his voice softening.

"It's alright," I reply, "I have some bugs I need to take a look at."

"Check your semicolons." It's *never* just a semicolon. Well, that's not true. Sometimes it is.

Mr. Davis has never been a programmer. He's tall and lanky, with white hair and a goofy pair of glasses. He worked as a mechanical engineer for some upscale defense contractors for about thirty years before he retired and decided to teach physics to high schoolers. He's a pretty good physics teacher, I'll give him that, but he knows essentially nothing about programming. Funnily enough, none of the teachers who help us manage this team do. I'm sorta stuck by myself.

He turns back to Charlotte. "Alright, Captain, what's on the agenda for today?"

"I'll put it on the whiteboard." She replies.

She turns off the simulation, pushes her chair in, and accidentally bumps her elbow into my shoulder. "Whoops, my bad," she says, wiping nonexistent dust off my shoulder. I don't understand why she did that; all she did was bump my shoulder. It didn't hurt or anything. I'm not going to complain. Jeez, why am I overthinking something as minuscule as a shoulder tap? I'm such a mess.

She walks up to the whiteboard, grabs a pink marker, and creates four equal-sized boxes. In each box, she writes a subteam: Mechanical, Electrical, Programming, and Business. Everyone sits at a table and watches her intently, waiting for their tasks.

"Today is going to be another mechanical-heavy day. Jade, I need a diagram of how much space I get to put my electronics in as soon as possible. We also need the elevator assembled by tonight. For electrical, there's not much for us to do until we get that diagram, so we'll just chill out until then. Business needs to keep working on that metal shop sponsorship. Vinny, I'd like to see some essay drafts completed by tonight, and I'll look over them later. For programming..."

She looks at me and smiles. "You know what to do."

I love that smile. She's so gorgeous.

I can't do much else other than give her a quick thumbs-up and a smile back. I stare back at my computer, where a game of Tetris awaits me. She sits back down next to me and opens her laptop; a game of Snake left open from the previous period appears. She closes the tab and opens a document titled "Romeo and Juliet Essay". The only words on the document are MLA formatting on top. She pulls a small book out of her backpack, presumably being the Shakespearean classic.

She turns to me, covering her lips with the book, so I can only see her dark brown eyes, nearly black in certain lighting, and a flash of pink dusting her tan cheeks. "You took this class last semester, right?" she asks.

"Yeah, why?"

"I have to write a paper about literally anything pertaining to Romeo and Juliet, and I can't decide on anything that feels right. What did you write about?"

"Oh jeez, I forgot about that paper," I reply, "I think I wrote about modern teenage romance in the lens of Romeo and Juliet. Their actions really weren't that extreme compared to what kids do now."

"I'm pretty sure killing yourself to be with your lover is extreme."

"Well, yeah, but before that, they were willing to go against everything their families and friends had believed in for generations because of love. I hear a lot about people pursuing love despite their parents or friends being against it. It's a cross-generational phenomenon, I think. Kids love to chase love, even if it hurts them."

Her expression darkens. "Good point," she puts the book down, her face still pink with some presumable illness. "I don't think she'll be a fan of me copying your essay, though. Maybe I'll take that and add a physiological twist. Our brains probably haven't evolved much since Shakespeare wrote Romeo and Juliet."

"You never know until you research."

"Jeez, I don't wanna look at this now," she groans. "How are college apps going for you?"

I've made it a rule for myself not to talk about any of the colleges I'm applying to with anyone. I think it just creates unnecessary stress and competition that I'm not really a fan of. It just doesn't benefit anybody.

Unfortunately, I'm really nosy about where *other* people are applying to. I have unconsciously kept track of where everyone important on the team is applying for early action. Jade, the mechanical lead, is applying to Stanford. Vincent, one of the lesser robot-brained, is applying to Brown for political science. Charlotte is dead-set about going to MIT. I'm almost finished with my early application to Harvard. I don't think I'm getting in, but Harvard has been my dream school for my entire life, and I would do myself a disservice by not applying.

Decisions for all of these schools come out the same day as playoffs for our district championships, if we do qualify. It'll either ruin my mood or make an already awful competition even worse. If I get in, it's a miracle sent from a higher power.

"They're definitely going," I reply, "I'm just waiting on some recommendation letters."

"I see."

The conversation dies there. After a few minutes of pretending to work while watching Charlotte create a few topic sentences for her essay, Jade comes up to the table and slams her computer on the desk. She looks terrified.

"I don't like that look, Jay." Charlotte laughs.

"With the way things are looking, electrical is going to be really tight this year."

Charlotte's smile quickly fades away. She looks at Jade's computer, displaying a CAD model of the robot. "Oh, dear."

"I'm sorry."

Charlotte slams her forehead into an empty spot on the table. Jade runs her fingers through Charlotte's curly hair and lifts her head with them. Charlotte's face is red. I assume it's partially from the blood rushing to her head from impact and partially from the anger. Her eyes begin to water.

"Is it worse than last year?" she mutters, already knowing the answer.

"We have slightly more space than last year, but we have a lot more electronic components to put in, so there's actually *less* room."

"Goddamnit. Let me go, please, and send me the CAD file so I can start mapping it out."

Jade slowly lets Charlotte's head down and removes her fingers from her hair. Charlotte picks up her head a few inches and immediately slams it down again. This happens a few more times.

"Quit doing that, it's not that serious." Mr. Davis chimes in.

She stops and raises her head all the way. "This is going to be the death of me."

"If it helps, Spencer is going to have an equally bad time when he has to start programming everything you want to put into the robot."

"You're really not helpful," she says as she checks her email, where Jade sent the CAD file. She opens it up and lets out a large groan.

"Hey, Benji, come here," she sighs.

Benjamin, a short junior with short mouse-brown hair and glasses, approaches the table. He's the only other student on the electrical team. Electrical isn't exactly the most fun subteam, according to literally anyone other than Charlotte. The only reason Benjamin helps her is out of pity, I think. I would help with electrical, but I'm too busy leading programming. Also, I electrocuted myself once in my freshman year. I swore off touching the electronics too much after that.

She starts telling him about potential placements of different electronic components. I sorta tuned out after a while, because none of it makes sense to me. I switched from my Tetris game to the codebase, a wall of red stinging my eyes. Jeez, there are a lot of issues here. Thankfully, I have until the end of shop day to fix them.

I listen to the mechanical team work with their drills and other heavy machinery while I look through different message board threads to see if anyone else is having my problem. I'm trying to work on an autonomous sequence without the robot, and while this has worked the entire time before just now, it's asking me to connect to a robot, which I simply cannot do at the moment.

I probably spent a good forty-five minutes scrolling through forums before I got my answer. I copied and pasted a piece of code posted by somebody from a team in Nebraska, compiled everything, and ran it with no errors. This usually never works, but I'm glad it did for once. Thank you, random user from Nebraska. A random programming lead in New Jersey thanks you for saving him an extra two hours of debugging and dreaming of throwing my computer out the window.

"What the actual *hell* are you doing?" I hear a loud adult voice boom. The entire room stops what they're doing and looks at Mr. Davis and Jade in their daily quarrel. She's broken her record of how long it would take from the start of the meeting until Mr. Davis yells at her. Her last record was 45 minutes, and she got to shop late that day.

"This is the best way to do it!" she rebuts.

"Your measurements are going to be off if you do that! Have I taught you *nothing* over these past four seasons? You're no better than a freshman!"

Since Mr. Davis was an actual engineer for nearly double her life, he truly cares about precision when it comes to machining. Jade, on the other hand, likes to take shortcuts. Sometimes I wonder if she actually believes in anything she argues about or if she just enjoys pissing him off. I believe it's an interesting combination of the two. I appreciate the show every meeting.

They continue to argue. I grab my headphones from my bag and connect them to my phone. I turn the noise cancellation setting to the max, turn on some music, and get back to work.

Soon enough, six o'clock arrives. Depending on what's going on right now, the end time for our meetings is just a suggestion. Since we're pretty early in the season, though, we tend to leave right on time. Late nights are for later on.

I begin to pack my things. I shut off my headphones, drop them in their respective case, and shove them into my bag. I save everything I've written over the past three hours, close the codebase, and shut down my laptop. I place it gently into its respective pocket and zip everything up. It may be a good idea to leave quickly before the sophomores get in their cars. Saves me a lot of sanity.

Though, waiting and walking out with Charlotte would be *much* better, so I do just that. I sit back down and pull out my phone, answering a text message from my mom that she sent this morning about taking out the trash when I get home.

Charlotte stands up and throws her backpack on one shoulder. As if I wasn't planning for this exact moment, I nonchalantly do the same, except I hold my backpack with both of my shoulders. I'm not a fan of the unevenness.

"Good progress?" I ask her.

"I'm seeing a lot of late nights coming soon."

"Don't worry, me too."

Vincent walks up to us. "Are you ready to go, Char?"

She nods, and the three of us walk out together. Jade usually walks out with them, but she's too busy machining to leave on time, so they leave her to work. Our parking spots are right next to the robotics room, theirs being much closer than mine. I'm about three spots away from their shared parking spot.

Charlotte throws her bag into the passenger seat of Vincent's car. I wave goodbye, and she does the same wave she always does when we leave together. It's similar to a princess wave, where she keeps her hand stationary and brings her fingers to her palm. Vincent waves goodbye too.

"See ya later, Spencer," she smiles.

"Bye-bye," I reply.

I step up the pace as I make it to my car. I open the passenger side door and drop my backpack on the seat, buckling it up. People say I overreact, but if something were to happen, my precious devices with our entire robot code would be safe. After securing my stuff, I close the door, walk to the other side of my car, and hop into the driver's seat. I turn my car on, turn on my music, and lean my head on the steering wheel, just above the horn so I don't scare the entire parking lot.

I'm a hopeless romantic.

Anyone would be if they were in my situation.

Hopeless

In love.

Love.

Her.

Chapter Five

Charlotte

The scene opens inside the front of a ten-year-old red Mazda CX–5. It's apparently a competition day based on the fact that the mysterious blond boy and I are driving together to the venue, me in the passenger's seat. He pulls up to the school, finds a secluded parking spot toward the back of the lot, and stops the car. The car turns off and I unbuckle my seatbelt.

"Wait, don't go yet," the mysterious boy says, "I don't want to go inside yet. We need to talk."

I turn to look at him, saying nothing. He grabs my hands, pulling me close.

"Darling, it's always been you. It always has been and always will be. Come with me and be my love. The Shepherds' Swains shall dance and sing for thy delight each May-morning: if these delights thy mind may move then live with me, and be my love."

He leans in and kisses my forehead. "It's always been you. I love–"

I wake up.

"God*damnit!*" I exclaim, throwing my pillow across the room. I need to stop paying attention in poetry class. How did he almost perfectly quote Marlowe? We *just* talked about The Passionate Shepherd in class. More importantly, how did *I* remember that?

Darling. Darling. Darling.

I always wanted her to call me darling.

She never did.

Maybe *he* would...

I dig my face into another pillow and let out a loud, high-pitched scream, kicking my feet in embarrassment. I thought I was finally over him. It's been nearly three weeks since the last dream. Why am I dreaming of him again? This is putrid of me.

These aren't dreams I should be having about someone, especially someone whom I've considered my friend for so many years. What would he think if he found out I'm experiencing these feelings? Would we even be friends anymore? How would we manage the team in such an awkward environment? Would everything crumble?

I check my phone. Nothing but the same emails I get every morning telling me to kill myself. She's made so many new email accounts at this point that I've given up on blocking all of them. At some point, I just became desensitized to it. I'm not saying it doesn't hurt. God, it hurts so much to see someone you used to love spew such hatred toward you. Someone you thought loved you.

Recently, I'd like to think the pain hasn't been as awful. These past few weeks haven't been unbearable, I guess. I've been able to think, eat, and exist without thinking about her, something I haven't been able to do in a very long time.

What if it's *his* fault? I wonder if it's because he's been forcing himself into my thoughts this whole time. Or, rather, *I'm* forcing *him* into my mind. As awful as thinking about him like this is, it's better than being in constant pain over her.

I don't like the thought of having a crush on him, but if it helps me get over her, it might be wise. A small crush won't hurt.

Screw it, let's embrace embarrassment. I'd rather be embarrassed than depressed. A crush probably won't ruin our friendship. He'll never need to know about it. If anything, I can utilize the crush now and make it go away later, right? That's it! I'll use these scary feelings to my advantage!

Doesn't make it any less shameful.

At least he's pretty.

Actually, come to think of it, he's *really* pretty.

"I'm so gross," I whisper, for no one to hear but myself.

I start preparing for my shower, which goes by quickly. I'm actually in a very good mood now, so everything feels like it's happening faster, as opposed to the usual slump I'm in this early in the morning. My shower was refreshing, all my soaps were restocked, and life feels good.

"It's always been you."

I'm gonna ignore that one.

I finish my nice, warm shower, and step outside into the bitterly cold refrigerator that is my bathroom. No matter what time of year, it's always freezing in my bathroom. My bathroom is the only one in the house that has this predicament. Every other bathroom gets disastrously hot during the summer, but never super cold.

After I initially dry off, I whip out the notetaking app on my phone and weigh myself.

"October 13th: XXX"

At this point, it's so ingrained in my routine that I have no reason to change it, even if I get better eating habits in the future. I like numbers, and the numbers are liking me at the moment.

I finish getting ready by putting on a dark grey long-sleeve shirt and black jeans. My socks are white and perfectly cuffed on both sides. I feel...normal today. Sorta.

I check my phone. It's almost time for Vinny to pick me up. I would normally drive today, but my car is in the shop getting its brakes replaced. Inconvenient, routine maintenance, that's all. I don't mind, though. I love being a passenger in Vinny's car.

I grab my laptop, throw it in my backpack, and run downstairs, where I swing the fridge open to grab a Sugar-Free Juneberry Red Bull. I crack it open and take a swig as I hear a horn honk outside.

I run out the door, locking it behind me, and make my way to the passenger side door. "You'll never guess what happened," I exclaim.

"You woke up late again? You got a new case of Red Bull? You... never mind, I ran out of realistic guesses."

"I had another dream about him."

"Oh dear. Get in the damn car."

I sit down, close the door, and buckle my seatbelt in. He starts to drive. "You don't seem as distressed about it."

"I'm going to use it to my advantage. Maybe this'll get *her* to leave me alone."

I explain everything. "Jeez, she's still messaging you? Isn't she busy with college classes or something?"

"Apparently not, but I've never felt freer from her since that dream."

"I guess that's fair. If you two start dating, though, I'm gonna make the entire team make fun of you for it."

"Oh, please, that's not gonna happen. In order for us to date, he'd have to like *me*, which is impossible."

"What makes you think that?"

"Well, we've been friends for years. You'd think he would've confessed to me already, right?"

He laughs. "He probably thinks you're gay."

"Why would he think that?" I ask.

"You've only dated girls since you met him. Your logic doesn't make sense; who confesses to someone they know they can't have?"

"I guess so, but I feel like I would've noticed if he was into me."

"You're right. The best-case scenario is that absolutely nothing happens, and everything becomes normal again after a while."

"God, I hope so."

After that heavy conversation, our chatter became light and impersonal, mostly about the classes we're in together. We have a test coming up in Multivariable Calculus, and an essay due in Poetry. All of this on top of college apps still being due, and a robotics competition in like twenty days. Being a senior in high school is hard.

He parks in our assigned spot. "Hey, look, there's your rebound now."

He points at Spencer, who just left his car and started walking toward the building. I sink into the passenger's seat out of embarrassment. "You don't have to call him that."

Once Spencer is far enough away that he won't notice us leaving, we hop out of the car and grab our stuff. Vinny locks his car, and we walk down the sidewalk we've walked down, every single day, for more than three years. I don't think the walk to class will ever get old to me; Vinny and I *always* walk and talk together, so there's never a dull moment. At least, never an awful moment.

Calculus was nothing to write home about. I took notes, tried my best to pay attention, and made a few jokes with Vinny about the teacher's handwriting. Today was mostly a review of yesterday, and tomorrow will be a review of the past couple of weeks in preparation for our test. I'm not worried about it more than I'm worried about everything else going on in my life. Once it all comes together, it kinda just turns into an agonizing mush in my brain. If I didn't have a planner showcasing all my assignments and their due dates, I'd be so lost. I already am, in a sense.

Before I even know it, the bell rings, and it's time to walk all the way to our poetry class. Today's class is a special one. Every single poem we're assigned to read and discuss has been posted on the syllabus since August, except this one, which is meant to be a surprise. I've been told that, in previous semesters, the teacher will go through students' final projects and select one to discuss next semester.

After a short walk consisting of menial conversation about the previous class, we enter the poetry room, where Jade is sitting at our table with a fatigued expression. "Mornin', guys," she mutters.

"Where were you in calc?" Vinny asks.

"I woke up, like, thirty minutes ago." Jade lives pretty close to the school, so this seems accurate.

"Late night at shop again?"

She nods. "Everything mechanical is on the robot now, so we won't delay your stuff anymore."

"Great, that means it's my turn to stay up late." I laugh.

"At least you won't have a bunch of freshmen trying to help you out. I swear, they didn't pay attention to training at all! I feel like Mr. D with how I yell at them all the time!"

"At least you *have* help. Benji's out for the entire week because of some illness, and he's the only kid I've got."

"It's both a blessing and a curse, Charlotte."

Mrs. M calms the class down. "Let's get started, we have a little bit of a downer today. This poem was recommended by a student who excelled in this class last semester. Has anyone heard of 'The More Loving One' by W. H. Auden?"

One person raises their hand. "That's more than I expected."

She passes out a piece of paper with the poem printed on it. It's quite short: four stanzas, four lines each. I skim it before she starts reading the poem out loud to the rest of the class.

"God, this poem is depressing," I whisper to Vinny.

"I know, right? Who would submit something like this to a high school poetry class?" he snickers.

"Probably the most lovesick loser in the universe."

Mrs. M finishes the poem and asks for class input. The same student who raised their hand earlier raises it again. "I find it interesting that this relationship is completely one-sided, and that the stars are completely indifferent about his deep love."

Another student chimes in. "It's weird that he also starts to become indifferent once the stars completely disappear. I think that may be a metaphor for the narrator's lover dying."

Students continue to discuss their overall analysis. I raise my hand once the commotion dies down, because participation is a grade in this class. "I believe it's sorta depressing that he wrote this when he was well into his fifties. It seems like something a teenage boy would write instead."

"Good point, Charlotte," Mrs. M replies, "speaking of teenagers, our next assignment includes a little bit of internal analysis. Re-read the poem and, on your paper, answer why you believe someone your age would relate to this poem enough to submit it to me for an exit ticket."

I write my name at the top of the paper, and at the bottom, I write:

"Seems like someone at this school is a hopeless romantic for someone they believe will never love them back."

The bell rings. I hand my paper to Mrs. M, who gives me a peculiar smirk, one she didn't give to the students who handed their papers in before me. I think nothing of it and leave the classroom with Vinny and Jade.

We speed-walk through the hallways to make it to an outside table. Thankfully, we found one quite close to the robotics room, just in case Spencer breaks something again. At this point, I wouldn't really put it past him. Sometimes, I think he breaks the robot just because he can.

It's sunny outside, but not agonizingly bright. I throw my backpack on the floor and sprawl on the table as Vinny and Jade sit down at opposite sides of the table. "I'm assuming you didn't bring anything for lunch, right?" Vinny asks.

"Incorrect," I reply as I reach for my backpack and grab a second Red Bull and a bag of pretzel sticks I forgot to take out last night.

"Did you bring anything of *sustenance* for lunch today?" Jade sighs.

"You're looking at it." I laugh.

"You're a hot mess." Vinny groans.

I lay back down, basking in the warm sun. October is a great month for lying outside; the weather isn't too cold yet in South Jersey, but it's cool enough that I won't break a sweat while wearing long sleeves.

"Do you want to tell Jade about the new advancement in your love life?" Vinny asks as he takes a bite of a sandwich.

"You've got it," I reply.

"If you say so," he laughs, "Char's accepting that she's got the hots for Spencer. Embracing it, even."

"Gosh, could you have said it any worse?" I exclaim, too loud for my own good.

"Charlotte, you do realize we compete in three weeks, right? Couldn't this wait until then?" chimes Jade.

"Isn't it better to get it over with than wait and make it worse? Plus, I am using this crush of mine to get over...you know who."

"I guess so. Oh, speak of the devil, look who's coming over."

My face heats up more than it already was from the sun. I close my eyes out of embarrassment. I hear footsteps through the grass that stop about a foot away from where my head is resting on the table. I open my eyes and see Spencer looming over me, casting a shadow over my body.

I never noticed this before, but he's pretty from this angle.

"What happened this time?" Jade laughs.

"I'm not sure, to be honest. I hope I'm not interrupting your nap. Would you mind taking a look at it, Charlotte?" he asks. Vinny snickers, and I kick his shoulder in response.

I sit up and swivel to face him. "Sure."

I hop off the table, grab my bag, and start heading toward the robotics room with him. "Where's Maggie? Usually she's the one to break the bad news."

"She said she was taking a makeup test for precalc or something," he replies.

He opens the door to the robotics room for me. I thank him. I walk up to the robot that's spewing red errors like it's no tomorrow. I kneel and signal for him to join me. Usually, I like working through these errors on my own, but it couldn't hurt to have him by my side.

Man, I feel like I'm playing a game. I feel childish. Crushes *are* childish, after all.

"You want me to help you?"

"I think it would be a good idea if you watched me work from time to time, just in case there's any chance I won't be around."

He smiles. "Makes sense!"

"Alrighty, let's get started then."

I dig my hands into the mess that currently is the wiring. I can't *stand* messy wiring. I asked Benji for help with it yesterday and he, unfortunately, did an absolutely awful job at wire management, to the point where I called off today's meeting just so I can be the only one in the room while I fix it. Something about making electronics and wires look pretty makes me feel like there's even a slight amount of order in my life. The wires need to be better managed than I am.

"What you wanna do is tug at things to see if anything is loose," I say to Spencer, "most of the time something like this happens, there usually is."

He picks up an open wire on his side of the robot. "Like this one?"

I sigh. It's a white signal wire, also known as one of the wires Benji was handling. "Yep, just like that one."

I turn the robot off, plug the wire in where it's supposed to go, and turn the robot back on. Seconds later, the signals flash green.

"Sometimes, if there's a lot of new electronics on the robot, I like to shake it back and forth and make sure there's nothing else loose. Wanna do it?"

"Sure!" he replies. He picks up the robot and violently shakes it, to the point where stuff that's not supposed to move bounces around the chassis.

"Woah, not that hard!"

He stops. Everything is still green. "Awesome. Thanks for fixing it again," he smiles.

"No problem, and it wasn't even your fault this time!"

The two of us stand up and he walks back to his chair. I grab my backpack and toss it by the chair next to him. Usually, after one of my routine fixes, I'll sit on the other side of the room and do homework, but I think it would be fun for my crushing brain to sit next to him this time.

I pull out my computer and open the document where my poetry essay sits. I'm halfway through it. Some analysis about a poem we read last week, nothing too special. Analyzing poems can be really tedious; there's always a hidden meaning under the thirty other hidden meanings you've found over the past three hours of analyzing. How am I supposed to figure out where the end is?

I glance at Spencer's laptop where he's playing a mildly intense game of Tetris. He notices me staring and immediately switches back to the codebase. I don't say anything. I feel like there's no need.

I continue typing and analyzing, and time speeds up. I have a very fast typing speed for everything except my poetry essays, where it slows to a snail's pace because I have no clue what to write. The words flow from my brain into my fingers. Nothing else matters but this random poem from the 1600's.

Soon enough, the bell rings. Time for AP Gov. The two of us pack up our stuff and I go turn the robot off and remove the battery. I don't yell a lot, but forgetting to take the battery out of the robot is one of those things that always pisses me off. The programmers usually are the culprits, because they need the robot to be on the most out of anyone else. I yell at Spencer about it a lot, but it's kinda been our thing for years. He doesn't take it personally, though he honestly should. I would *love* for the robot to be unplugged for *once*!

I plug in the battery to the wall charger and we walk out of the robotics room together. I open the door for the both of us. He thanks me. While we walk to Gov together, we have a pleasant but unimpressive conversation about the weather. It's getting colder and windier. Cold weather means competition season is coming soon, which is both exciting and excruciatingly stressful at the same exact time. It's both the best time of my life and the worst. Go figure.

"I like that I'm not sweating every time I go outside, but I'm *really* dreading having to wait for my car to heat up every morning." Spencer sighs.

"At least your car has good heat," I laugh, "my car likes to flip a coin on if the heat is going to work every morning."

"At least Vincent's heat works, right?"

"Yeah, Vinny's gonna have to get really comfortable with driving me around in a few months."

We laugh, but it feels different this time.

I look at him as we walk through a part of the hallway where there aren't that many students. I notice his hands in the pockets of his jeans, and his unwavering eye contact with the nothing in front of us. There's a soft, lingering smile on his face that never seems to go away. He seems happy, too bright for his own good. I envy him. How come his smile never fades?

We finally make it to the Gov classroom, where Vinny's already sat at his unassigned assigned seat. "Hello again," he smiles, "everything fixed?"

"Yep, and get this, it wasn't even his fault this time. Benji didn't wire the sensors correctly." I respond as I sit down.

"Doesn't that make it your fault then? It's your subteam." he asks.

"Probably. Sorry, Spencer."

"It's fine!" he exclaims, shaking his hands back and forth. "No biggie! No big deal at all!"

This class is godawfully boring. All the teacher does is go over slides, and we're expected to take notes for the entire class. It's such a bore. He has this mundane voice that could put a girl with four tall Red Bulls in her system to sleep. Trust me, I'm both the scientist and the test subject here.

I doze off for a few blissful minutes, but Vinny wakes me up by jabbing me in the arm with his elbow. I shoot up and continue copying down the slide on the whiteboard. I didn't actually miss anything; the teacher is really slow with his slide progression, as if it takes me five minutes to write down three bullet points.

The bell rings, meaning it's time for my last class of the day: AP Stats. My phone buzzes, and I read over an email from the Stats teacher:

"Hello students! Since it's the end of the quarter, I've decided to give those of y'all who finished all of their assignments a day off. If you didn't finish your assignments, I expect you to be here on time. Have a great Thursday!"

"Vinny, we don't have stats today!" I exclaim.

"Let's go! An extra hour and a half of free time!" he replies.

"Let's go to the robotics room!" I add.

His smile instantly fades. "Don't you wanna, like, relax or something?"

"No time for that! Let's go right now. Bye, Spencer!"

I hear Spencer say "bye-bye" as I grab Vinny's wrist and run out of the Gov room. I don't think he's ever said a single "bye" to me, it's always a double. It's interesting how cartoon-like he is, with his persistent smile and all.

Vinny tries to keep pace as we jog down the hallway, but eventually lets go. "I promise you, Char, the room isn't going anywhere."

"You don't know that!"

"I have to leave by five today for my brother's football game, so if you're not done by then you're walking home."

"I'll figure it out."

Vinny texts as he walks. "Who are *you* texting?" I ask with a grin.

"Jade is asking about the mechanical budget."

"I don't even know why we have a budget, she always goes over it anyway."

"If there was *no* budget, we'd go completely broke from her spending. No amount of tier-one sponsors would be enough for her."

"Gotcha." Power tools are expensive, especially when freshmen keep breaking them. Or Jade sometimes.

After a few minutes of swimming through student-filled hallways, we arrive at the robotics room. Vinny opens the door for me. I thank him. The automatic lights turn on, revealing that absolutely no one is here.

"Completely empty, just how I like it." I mutter to myself.

I dart to the electrical drawer where I grab all my tools and a box of wire spools, all different colors and gauges. I grab a square table from the supply closet and open it up in the middle of the room. Vinny and I pick up the robot and place it on the table. I grab a chair and place it right in front of the robot's rear. I usually don't sit down when I work, but for some specific work, it's nice to have a chair sometimes.

I get to work. I want this entire thing completely electronically connected by tonight, so Spencer has as much time as possible to break it before competition. Contrary to popular belief, his antics are essential for us to know if something is wrong with what we're doing. If he doesn't break it now, I'm going to end up breaking it later at a competition, where we have much less time to fix stuff.

Vinny pulls out a speaker from his bag and starts playing a shared playlist. We're usually not allowed to play music during meetings, specifically because the teachers think it's going to distract us, but I find that it helps me work more efficiently. Plus, there aren't any teachers to tell us we can't work now.

This year, a select few students were granted access to work in the shop without supervision. Spencer and other programmers were always allowed in since they weren't working with specific tools, but Jade and I were only allowed full reign once we turned eighteen. I became an adult over the summer, while Jade had her birthday last week. Vinny is a part of a special case where he won't touch the robot unless he has to, so there's no issue with him being here, even though he doesn't turn eighteen until March.

He queues a song I loved way too much back in middle school. "You better turn that off right now." I snap.

"Nah, live in your embarrassment," he says as he increases the volume.

I continue to work, as my thoughts move away from the stresses of the world and I focus on making this robot work.

It's been hell trying to figure out where things go and where wires fit, especially with mechanical's awful floorplan they provided me with. I wish I could just throw everything in and call it a day, but this would lead to *so* many problems in the future, especially with trying to debug if something goes wrong. Also, it just looks ugly. I won't let my robot be ugly.

An hour goes by. "Char, you should take a break." Vinny says, looking up from his laptop.

"I'm not at a point where I can stop yet." I reply. I can't stop. I physically can't. I don't think my hands would let me.

He sighs. "If you say so."

I keep working as the music flows through my ears and into my veins. I'm addicted. I can't stop.

Another half-hour passes, and I hear the bell ring. Doesn't matter. I'm not going home anytime soon.

I grab electrical tape and zip ties from their respective drawers. I'm probably about 50% done with what I wanted to do today. I am exhausted, but the adrenaline rushes through me like a drug laced with power wires. Everything is going to come together. This wiring needs to be more managed than I am.

The door opens, interrupting my flow. I turn my head and see Spencer walk in, his arm wrapped around his laptop. "Wait, I thought we weren't meeting today," he says.

"We're not, but Char wanted to work on wiring while nobody was here." Vinny replies.

"Gotcha. Vincent, you said you had some budget info to ask me about? After that, may I work here?"

"Sure, but you probably won't see a usable robot for a few hours at the least." I laugh.

"That's alright."

I keep working, now distracted at the thought of Spencer being here. I hadn't thought about him once throughout the entire time I've been working, but now that he's here, he's on my mind again. *Shut up, brain!*

I wonder if Spencer's appearance in the robotics room was a ploy by the universe to mess with my work, or just a coincidence. I guess he's here all the time, anyway. It's just a coincidence, right? He's always here, therefore he'll be here when I'm here. *God, I'm such a mess!*

I start working on the rear of the robot. I sit in the chair I conveniently placed here at the beginning, and a sudden wave of tiredness falls over me. I guess it would be okay if I took a cat-nap real quick, right?

I fall asleep.

Chapter Six

Spencer

My life is like a poem. I have all of these deep thoughts coursing through my brain at all times and can simply be articulated to say that I'm a hopeless romantic, and normal people would look at me and think I'm the most lovesick loser in the universe.

This morning, my mom asked me if there was anything I needed to tell her. I couldn't think of anything, so I shook my head. She said, *"you see…I just wanted to let you know that you can tell me anything, and you shouldn't be embarrassed to come out to your mother…"*

I almost spat out my cereal when I heard that. *"What are you talking about?" I exclaimed.*

"I'm just saying Spencer, you haven't brought a girl home to us yet…I wanted you to know that if you swing the other way, it's completely fine…"

"I'm not gay, Mom," I groaned, "I just…haven't found the right girl yet."

"If you say so, honey. Just know that it's totally okay."

I think my parents are embarrassed of me. My older siblings dated all throughout high school, yet I've been stuck on the same girl since my freshman year, with zero advancements. My mom is seriously convinced I'm into guys. No, Mom, I'm just obsessed with a girl who will never like me back. Ugh, I'm a mess. My life is *worse* than a poem. At least those end promptly, and the sadness ends soon after.

After Gov today, Vincent texted me asking if I could come to the robotics room today. He said he had something to ask me about the budget, but he hasn't said anything about it yet. He's sat in the chair next to mine ever since I got here, typing away at his laptop, sending emails and updating spreadsheets. I'm honestly impressed at his ability to not go insane from the amount of Excel he stares at every day. I swear he knows more commands and tricks than any teacher at this school.

Charlotte has been asleep for the past hour. Earlier, I heard her muttering to herself about a "quick cat-nap," but I feel like I'd be overstepping my welcome if I walked over to wake her up. I'm trying hard to not look at her while she sleeps, because that's gross, and I don't wanna look like a creep.

I've been spending my time waiting for Vincent to talk to me about whatever he needs to talk to me about by debugging this new implementation I've been working on. If I can get this to work, I'd be able to efficiently optimize Controller movements to where button presses are registered in mere milliseconds. Sounds impossible, but I'm so close. This would make me unstoppable if it works, and it's a great thing to include on my college apps as well, just in case I get deferred or rejected from my early action applications. I don't want to think about those possibilities but it's not impossible. Actually, it's *very* possible.

Vincent's phone rings. He answers. "Yeah, I'm leaving in a few minutes, don't worry about me." he says to the phone. He hangs up soon after.

He walks up to Charlotte and tries to wake her up, but she doesn't budge. She doesn't even move. He tries pushing her for about thirty seconds before he gives up.

"Hey, I've gotta go in a few minutes, would you mind taking her home today?" he asks me.

My face heats up. "Is she okay with that?"

"I told her she was going to have to walk home if she wasn't ready by five, and she was okay with that, so I'm sure she'll be more than okay with you taking her."

I've never driven Charlotte anywhere before. I'd believe myself to be a good driver, but I tend to get distracted if other people are in the car with me. If *she's* in my passenger's seat, I need to be on my best behavior. I can't take my eyes off the road.

"Yeah, I can do that."

"Thanks, man." he says as he throws his laptop in his backpack. He turns off the speaker playing music and puts it in its respective pocket.

"By the way, what did you want to tell me?" You said something about the programming budget?"

"Oh, yeah," he drops his backpack on the chair and walks up to me, "I didn't need to talk to you about that. I need to tell you something."

"What's up?"

He leans in to the point where his face is mere inches from mine. His dark brown eyes lock with mine. I've never been this close to Vincent before; his face is *so* clear, and it looks like he just plucked his eyebrows this morning. A fresh set of Aquaphor sits on his lips, and it kinda looks like he's wearing a light layer of mascara.

"I know your secret." he whispers to me, maintaining eye contact.

Oh no. How did he discover my secret? I haven't told a single person about this, ever! How did *he* find out, of all people? I get that it's been a while, but seriously, I tried so hard to hide it! Oh no oh no oh no oh no oh no. This is really bad. What if word gets out? My life is ruined. Everything I've built is completely ruined. What if *Charlotte* finds out? What would I do with myself then?

"How did you know I got a speeding ticket?" I exclaim, loud enough that I thought Charlotte would wake up. She didn't.

His serious expression disappears, and he bursts into laughter. "You got a *speeding* ticket? You drive like a grandpa!"

I'm confused. "You just said you knew..."

"I didn't know about *that!* How fast were you going?"

"Like 60 in a 55–" I pause. "Wait, if that's not the secret, what are you talking about?"

His smile fades as he grips my shoulders. "You like her, don't you?"

Oh no. I can feel my heart fall to the bottom of my chest as my eyes widen. If there wasn't a mess of intestines and stomach space, I'm sure it would've fell to my knees or something. My legs start to shake as I can feel my cheeks reddening to a deep shade of lobster.

"*...who?"* I whisper, as if it's not obvious.

His right hand lets go of my shoulder and he points to a sleeping Charlotte across the room. "Come on, you know exactly who I'm talking about. You're not stupid."

Vincent is smart. I don't think I can lie to his face. I feel like I'm about to faint. I can feel my eyes start to water. God, I feel disgusting. "Please don't tell her," is all I could muster up to say. *Please.*

"I would never, that's *your* job."

"Hell no, I'm *never* telling her."

"Why not? I know you've liked her for years. Why not just go for it?"

"You of all people should know why I can't do that."

"Why?" He thinks for a moment, and starts laughing again. "Wait, do you think she's a lesbian?"

My heart falls even lower. "Is she not?"

"Ha, I was right!" He exclaims. Recognizing how loud he is, he lowers his tone. "She's bi, dude. I thought she was out to everybody."

I can feel tears streaming down my cheeks. I'm not too sure what emotion they're trying to convey."I must have missed the memo."

"Apparently."

I finally register what he just said. "Wait, did you say you've known for *years?"*

He snickers. "I'm pretty good at seeing this stuff. I clocked you all the way back in freshman year. I have no clue how she hasn't noticed yet, especially with you 'breaking the robot' all the time."

"Oh come on, was that also obvious to you?" I sigh. All my tricks and secrets have been revealed to the world. Well, to Vincent.

"You're a smart guy, I know you wouldn't break it by accident *that* many times."

"If you've known for so long, why are you coming to me now?" I ask.

He pauses to think. "To be honest, I'm tired of watching you mope around, you damn poet. We're *seniors*, it's not like you have a whole lotta time."

"Are you sure this is a good idea? You know her better than anyone."

He shrugs. "It's your call. Look, dude, I've set it all up for you today. Drive her home, have a chat. I wouldn't do anything too crazy yet, but keep it in the back of your mind."

"I have to ask, has she said anything about me? You've got to have a reason to be doing this."

"I'm just trying to make your senior year a little bit less...poetically depressing," he laughs, "I can't say much else, but I don't think your chances are nonzero."

He walks to the door that leads to the parking lot. "You've got this, Spence. Let me know how it goes."

The door shuts behind him. Thankfully, Charlotte slept through the whole thing, even the loud door slam. I take a swig from my water bottle. It's hard to swallow with how flushed my face is and how teary-eyed I am. I try to calm down and face my computer.

Holy shit. Do I have a chance?

I stand, my knees shaking. I dart outside the robotics room and into the hallway. I lean against a wall and fall to a crouch, my hands cupping my face. I open my fingers so I can see in front of me and not much else. My palms burn from how hot my face is. I sit here for a few minutes, recollecting my thoughts.

This is one of the greatest days of my life, and nothing's really happened yet. Even though the embarrassment of the moment is killing me, I can't stop smiling. This is something I've been hoping for, something I've been dreaming about for years. I have a chance. It's slim, but it's nonzero. She's at least attracted to my gender. I want to ask her out. I want to hug her. I want to kiss her.

God, I really want to kiss her.

I hear quick pacing coming from the robotics room. I guess she's awake. I wipe my eyes, stand up, and brush myself off. I grab my phone and position the front camera to my face. I look normal enough to go back in.

"Oh shit, oh shit, oh *shit!*" a voice coming from inside exclaims.

I hear a loud scream and the sound of pushing furniture in the robotics room. What is she doing in there? Is she okay? I need to go there now.

I swing the door open and see Charlotte running around the room, sobbing, with her head in her hands. "Why did he leave? How am I getting home? God, why didn't he wake me up?"

She doesn't notice I'm there. She keeps running. This is bad. I think she's having a panic attack. I'm pretty sure she's mentioned in passing that she has them sorta often. I would have one too if I was a fifteen minute drive away from home and my ride seemingly abandoned me.

Without thinking, I run up to her and grab her by her shoulders, pulling her into a sorta-hug. I can feel her tense muscles start to relax, her head falling onto my chest.

"Charlotte, are you okay?" I ask.

She raises her head up and immediately tenses again. Her face is red with what I presume to be fear. "Spencer! What are you doing here?"

My brain starts to think coherently again and I immediately let go. "I'm so sorry about that, I don't know why I did that–"

"Did Vinny tell you to stay?" she interrupts.

What would be the best thing to say here? "He asked if I was okay with staying, but I was going to anyway. Is it okay if I drive you home?"

"Please."

She grabs me by my waist and pulls me back into a tight hug. "I feel like I'm about to collapse. Please don't let go."

I would never let go if you let me. "Okay."

I wrap my arms around her back, trying to ignore her bra band protruding through her shirt. That's *definitely* not something I should be thinking about while she's currently recovering from a panic attack. Unfortunately, I can't help but be happy that she wants to hug me, even if it's just for support. I mean, this is the closest I've ever been to a girl.

I hope I smell good, preferably like barely anything. Did I put cologne on today? I definitely applied deodorant, I never leave the house without it. There's nothing in my teeth from lunch today, right? Wait, she definitely can't see my teeth. Does my breath smell okay? I ate a mint before coming in and drank a bunch of water. Did I brush my hair enough today?

None of this is important. I just want her to feel better.

My chest suddenly feels damp. I look down and see Charlotte silently crying into my shirt. I rub my hand up and down across her back. "It's okay, you don't need to cry."

"I really don't know *why* I'm crying. It just feels like the right thing to do." she whispers, tightening her wrap around me.

"Let it all out then."

I rest my chin on the top of her head as I continue to rub her back. I don't really know what else to do here. I feel like I'd be overstepping my welcome if I kept talking, so it might be a good idea to just stand here.

After what felt like a few minutes but I wish was hours, she lets go. There's a large wet mark on my shirt. "Oh gosh, I'm so sorry about that," she says as she wipes her eyes.

"It's just water, it'll dry. Are you feeling better?" I ask.

"A little bit. I hope that wasn't weird."

"Not at all." I smile.

She grabs a paper towel from the sink area and finishes drying her eyes. "I really am so sorry for acting like that. The whole situation reminded me of something awful."

"What, if you don't mind me asking?"

She stares for a moment. "Last year, I fell asleep in shop after an argument with…y'know who…and she drove off in the middle of the meeting. Vinny was sick that day, so she was my ride. I had to hitch a ride with Mr. D. You never want him to drive you home. He talked my ear off about dynamics while I was fighting for my life over text."

"You know who" definitely refers to Charlotte's ex-girlfriend Sylvia. She's a year older than us and graduated last year, and she and Charlotte were together from the summer before our sophomore year to the end of our junior year. They split at the end of the school year.

Sylvia is an awful person. She's toxic and always had a problem with anything Charlotte did. She was our Captain last year, and an awful one at that. She made sure to make a point of it every single time the two of them had an argument.

It always hurt to see them together. I wanted to tell Charlotte that she should break up with Sylvia and be with me instead, but I didn't have the guts to. I wish I did, because that girl broke her beyond repair. Charlotte finally ended things with Sylvia at her high school graduation, which did *not* go over well. She cursed her out in front of their parents and the entire school. Sylvia trashed the build room and left letters everywhere talking about how disgusted she was with her. I tried being there for her, but I was terrified of going too far. The last thing she needed at that time was support from someone who was also in love with her.

I'm glad she's gone, but it still hurts knowing that her actions still negatively impact Charlotte.

"Vincent made sure that I was staying before he left. He tried waking you up for a few minutes, but you were out cold."

"Yeah, Vinny would never be like her," she lets out a small laugh, "thank you so much for staying with me."

"Of course, anytime. Think of this as payment for fixing the robot all the time."

"Oh yeah, I should start charging you for that! I'd be rich!"

We laugh. "Are you going to keep working on the robot, or do you want me to take you home?"

"I don't think I'm in the right mental state to keep working, is that okay?"

"Yep, I also hit a stopping point for today."

Charlotte puts her electrical tools away and packs up her backpack. I toss my laptop in my bag and swing it over my shoulder. The two of us walk out of the robotics room and make our way towards my car sitting alone in the parking lot. Seems like everyone else left. I don't know too much about sports schedules, but they've presumably finished practice as well.

I unlock my car and toss my backpack in the backseat. Charlotte opens the passenger side door and places her backpack on the mat as she sits down. I open my driver side door, sit down, and buckle up.

I open my GPS on my phone and hand it to her. "I don't know where you live, can you please put it in?"

She grabs my phone, taps for a few seconds, and hands it back to me. I have her address. *Ew, don't be a creep.*

I turn on my car, turn on the radio, and back out of my parking spot. "You can connect your phone if you'd like."

Sometimes, I love listening to classical music while I drive. If I'm not listening to it, I'll either listen to the radio or a rock playlist of songs my dad introduced me to. It's incredibly calming, which is necessary to mentally prepare myself for the day ahead and wind me down after a long day of school. Charlotte likes to listen to alternative or punk rock, mostly from the 90's and 2000's. Music doesn't really affect my driving, and I think her playing her own music will help her feel better.

I shift my car into drive and exit the school parking lot. "Vinny says you drive like a grandpa. Is this true?" Charlotte asks.

"I used to drive really sporadically, but I had a really terrifying experience driving home from a competition, and ever since then, I try to follow the speed limit as strictly as possible."

"Gotcha. So, basically, yes you do."

I laugh. "Maybe."

The drive is silent until I am about a mile from school. "Hey, did you enjoy the poetry class when you took it?" she asks.

"One-hundred percent, yes. It's a little embarrassing, but I've always loved poetry, ever since we learned about poems in elementary school. It's my favorite type of literature."

I must sound like a major nerd.

"Who's your favorite poet?"

"Wow, that's a good question." I think for a moment. "I really like depressing poems, so probably W. H. Auden or A. E. Housman. Both of them have really interesting poems about love, loss, and acceptance."

"Oh, we just did an Auden poem today, what's your favorite from him?"

"Jeez, another great question. If I had to pick one, I really like 'The More Loving One'. It's a beautiful but awfully tragic poem with amazing metaphors. I love the idea of stars representing love, and how he can accept being without his mystical lover."

"What a coincidence, that's the one we went over in class today!"

We keep talking about classwork and exams. We both have a pretty big test coming up in calculus that I really need to start studying for. I've been putting robotics first these past few weeks and my grades have become worrisome because of it. I still can make straight A's, but it might take slightly more effort than usual.

I pull into her driveway and put my car in park. She unbuckles her seatbelt and lunges over the middle console to give me a hug. "Thanks again for helping me today and driving me home."

"Of course, anytime." I smile.

"We should study for calculus together soon. Or talk about more poems, whichever comes first."

"I'd love that!"

She grabs her stuff, hops out of the car, and slams the door behind her. I watch her walk up to her door before I reverse out of her driveway.

On my way home, I think about the whirlwind of a day I just had. Everything started completely normal, lunch was great, the rest of my classes were normal, but robotics was everything *but* normal. I hugged Charlotte; I got to hug her for a *long* time. Vincent called me out and I accidentally revealed that I had gotten a speeding ticket. I might have a chance with the girl of my dreams. There's just one thing that I can't place my finger on:

What poem did I submit to Mrs. M last semester again?

Chapter Seven
Charlotte

I must cite the irreconcilable differences with myself. I'm *tired* of playing these impossible games. I want peace within myself. I crave happiness. I crave relief. I *need* all this to stop before things get worse. My world spins just as fast as everyone else's, but I have this lingering, potent feeling that mine spins *differently*. Not in any particular way, just in the sense that I feel different than everyone else and I don't know why. I spend hours every day to feel as human as I think I'm supposed to be, but to no avail. I am myself, and that feels like the worst thing I can possibly be. I feel like a poet, but who the hell would wanna be one of those?

I didn't have a dream about Spencer last night. I wish I did, because the person I *did* dream about was so, so much worse. I saw *her* again.

"Why aren't you responding to my messages, darling*!*" a voice booms in my head. The "darling" was enunciated and full of hatred; it's the exact opposite that you'd expect from a term that's supposed to be endearing. It makes my skin crawl just thinking of it.

Darling. Darling. Darling. Darling. Darling. Her voice plagues my head to where it's all I can think about. She never called me darling. I never deserved to be called darling. Nothing else is allowed to matter at this moment. I am shackled by my stupid thoughts that won't go away. I can't, I can't, I can't–

"GET OUT OF MY HEAD!" I scream.

"What the hell? I just asked about the calc homework." says Vinny, sitting in my passenger's seat.

"I'm sorry, I was preoccupied."

"I can tell. Are you at least focusing on the road?" he asks.

I nod. "I'm so sorry, Vinny. I was thinking about the dream I had last night."

"Ooooooh, did you have a dream about Spencer again? Go on, tell me the deets."

I don't respond, and his smile fades. "You would've reacted if it was about him."

"It wasn't."

"You dreamt about Sylvia, didn't you?"

I nod again. "If you're comfortable, tell me about it."

"It was just...a combination of everything she's sent me these past few months, both physical and digital."

"Jeez, she doesn't know when to stop, and did you say *physical?*"

"Yeah, at the beginning she sent physical letters. I think she stopped because my mom posted in our community Facebook that she was going to the police if more showed up."

"God, she's horrible. Do you want me to take over and drive?"

I shake my head. "No, driving is easy. It's the rest of my life that's excruciatingly hard."

"I'm gonna be honest, Char, that was really cheesy."

"I know." I sigh.

I pull into parking spot #42, slightly crooked but still in the lines. Thankfully, I have a small enough car to where this isn't a problem. The parking lot is also almost completely empty. "Wow, you suck at parking." Vinny laughs.

"I'm not great at being completely straight." I reply with a snide grin.

"Neither am I, and I park a lot better than you do."

Today is a teacher-work day at our high school, but Vinny and I, along with a few of our teammates, decided to come in because our first competition is tomorrow. Vinny thinks we're ready, but I'm personally terrified. I haven't been able to get enough driver practice this season because I've been way too busy making sure the entire team doesn't go up in flames. It's a lot of work; I hope it'll actually be worth all of the time and effort we've put in this past semester.

Spencer pulls into his parking spot as we exit my car. Him and I have a lot of driving practice to do today once we know everything is working right.

"Vinny, you didn't forget anything at home, right?" I ask.

"Hopefully not, but I'll check before we leave for the hotel."

The competition is about two hours away at some random high school, so my entire team booked hotel rooms so we didn't have to drive too much over the weekend. Personally, I'm not a fan of driving two hours one-way to a venue that opens at 9am. I packed two four-packs of sugar free Red Bulls for the trip. Hopefully, that lasts me long enough.

The school pays for our rooms, Jade and I split the extra cost of a nicer room so we didn't have to room with a bunch of underclassmen. It's fine for the first couple of years, but I actually need sleep over the weekend without dealing with a bunch of girls gossiping about who knows what. It's fun when I am allowed to have fun, but I don't have time to have fun this season.

The responsibility of winning falls entirely on me. I am both the Driver *and* Captain of this team. If we lose, it's all my fault. *All* my fault.

All my fault...

"When's your meeting, by the way?" Vinny asks.

I check my phone. "Shit, it starts in three minutes!"

I book it to the front door of the school and race down the hallway to the nurse's office. I swing the door open and walk right past the receptionist's desk to the hallway where all the rooms are. I knock on the second door to the left with a nameplate that says "Mr. S: Mental Health and Wellness Specialist".

"Come in, Charlotte." a voice mutters from inside.

I open the door. "I appreciate you being able to meet with me on such short notice, sir."

"Of course, dear, anytime. Now, sit down and tell me what's going on."

I sit down. Mr. S is the school's therapist, and his office is where all of the students with issues visit. That's exactly why I'm here, though in my case, I submitted a petition to have biweekly meetings on my own accord; most of the time, students are only sent to him if they did something heinous.

I had never considered getting therapy before, even though I should have. Jade and Vinny recommended it to me a while back, saying that it might be "good for me" if I have an adult to talk to who isn't my parents. Well, I'm also an adult, but he's an adultier adult.

Because I'm of age, nothing I say can be brought back to my family, which is much appreciated. I don't want to concern them with my sorrows and meaningless grief over something I once had or my immense stress about the future. It's easier if they don't know, and I figure it out myself. And my friends, of course.

"I have a competition this weekend and I'm awfully stressed out."

"Why?"

"I'm not really worried about the driving part, but this is my first performance as Captain. I'm gonna have to talk to so many judges and explain all of the nitty gritty details that I don't really understand, and I'm so scared.

"Y'know what, I *am* worried about the driving part. I always am. It's terrifying and stress inducing and I feel like I'm going to pass out after every Round. It's so hard to not stare at the audience and feel disgusting."

"Who's going to be there?"

"My team, the other teams, parents and friends," I think for a moment, "typical crowd for a competition like this. I'm just worried that a certain person will be there, but it's unlikely."

"Why are you thinking about it then?" In our first meeting, I spilled about my previous relationship about thirty minutes into the meeting. I feel very safe around this man; I know he won't hurt me.

"Her college is really close to the venue we'll be at, so it's not super unlikely. I just hope that she doesn't, it'll make *everything* worse."

"Your friends will be there for you, though. You have your entire team with you. Can you point out two or three people that would help you?"

I nod and hold up three fingers, for Vinny, Jade, and maybe Spencer. "Then I believe you'll be alright. Stay close to those three and everything will go smoothly."

"If you say so."

We continue to chat for another thirty minutes or so, about school, robotics, and anything else. I was a little bit embarrassed by the idea of seeing a therapist at first, but after the first few meetings, I realized that this is actually so useful. I firmly believe everyone should try therapy at least once, even if they don't think there's something wrong with them. Most of the time, there is.

A phone alarm goes off. "Are you alright with stopping here?"

I nod. "I think we've reached a good conclusion. Thank you so much for taking the time out of your day to meet with me."

"Again, don't mention it. Let me know how your competition goes, alright? I'll root for you."

I sit up and exit his office, softly closing the door behind me. I make my way back to the robotics room and think about what Mr. S said about this weekend. What would I do if I saw her? What can I do to make her go away and stop harassing me forever?

I'll think of something, probably. Or, more likely, something will come to me on the spot.

I open the robotics room and see Vinny, Spencer, and Jade sprawled across a table. "Welcome back," says Vinny. "Did your meeting go well?"

"I'd say so."

"Are you ready to practice, Charlotte?" Spencer asks.

"Yup. Is the robot ready?"

"As ready as it'll ever be."

I take a look at it. We've been working on this robot since school started in the middle of August. November just started a few days ago. As the days have become shorter and colder, our robot has become stronger and more optimized. We should be able to finish a Round in under three minutes.

The game's components change every year, but the structure is always the same. About thirty-five to forty teams attend each competition and compete one at a time. We're not really competing against each other, rather using the same space to show our robots off. I like this competition structure because it eliminates robot-to-robot violence and significantly reduces collateral damage.

A Round usually consists of a robot driving around an obstacle course while completing various tasks. This year, we're essentially playing a game of relay but with ourselves. The baton gets shoved into our robot at the beginning and we have to use it to complete various puzzles. The robot shoves the baton into a chute where it flies across the field into a container where we have to shoot a pre-loaded ball at a moving target to knock it down. After that, the robot has to climb a set of monkey bars about six feet up in the air, followed by a few similar game mechanics until we finally reach the finish line.

There's a reason we prioritize optimization, and it's that any small mistake could cost us time, which costs us rankings. Thankfully, each team gets five tries, and the best one gets counted, but that still means we need to make every moment count. Every second is a useful one. This means I need to be the best driver the entirety of New Jersey has ever seen. Doing well here means we advance to the Mid-Atlantic District Championships. If we perform well *there*, we go to *World Champs,* where my team has never been before. I have a huge responsibility on my hands. My shoulders hurt from the weight of my team.

"We're looking *really* good!" I exclaim.

"Thank goodness." Jade sighs with relief.

I sit next to Spencer as I open the driving simulator. Spencer taking the time out of his day to build this for me has been *so* useful, especially for when the robot isn't functioning enough to drive it. I remember him saying it took him a really long time to finish, and it's basically perfect. I couldn't ask for anything better.

Man, he sure does a lot for me.

I turn to look at him. He's happily typing away at his computer, a goofy grin plastered across his face. I'm starting to appreciate that he's always happy around me. It's something to look forward to.

He turns around, and I realize I've been staring at him for about a minute now. I immediately turn back to my computer. I hope he didn't notice.

"Are you ready?" I ask.

“Absolutely.”

He connects his laptop, which is already connected to the robot via a long blue wire, to the laptop with the driver simulator on it. The computers sync and start analyzing our robot's dimensions and components. A pop-up appears on both of our screens, displaying our team number, 904208, and an empty text box that says “Robot Name:”.

“What do you wanna name the robot?” Spencer asks.

I ponder for a moment. “We should name it after Mr. D. How about Ross?”

“He’s gonna kill us if we do that.”

“It’s fine, we’re seniors.”

I go ahead and type it in. The simulator finishes its analysis of the robot and loads in the game zone. Once it’s fully loaded in, we grab our respective controllers, both older X-Box ones. Mine’s black, his is white. They’re the same controllers we’ll use to control the *real* robot this weekend. Despite all the fear in my heart, I am excited. Competitions can be fun if I make them fun.

“Ready, partner?” Spencer asks. Ever since we’ve started competing together, he’s always called me partner. It feels…different this time. I never really cared about it before, but the phrase is making me feel warm and tingly inside.

“Ready as I’ll ever be.”

“Let’s go!” he exclaims as we begin practicing.

Our first Round ended in about four minutes, but if you don’t include the slight lag during the monkey bars, it was about three minutes and thirty seconds. We will *never* reach district champs with these times. I need to do better.

We try again, and again, and again. We practice for nearly an hour and a half before Spencer decides he needs a break. I should probably take one too. I grab a Zero Sugar Red Bull from my backpack, crack it open, and take a swig. I then grab my water bottle and guzzle down some of it. It's balanced.

Throughout the past ninety minutes, we've slowly been improving, and our latest attempt was three minutes and one second. I think if we spend a couple more hours doing this, we could even reach 2:50. The simulator is a bit more optimized than the field can be sometimes, so a 2:50 here would be a 3:00 there. A 3:00 should qualify us for district champs.

While we've been practicing, Jade has been helping Vinny write our proposal we're supposed to provide to judges on Sunday. Along with the various questions they'll ask us, we also have to give a lengthy presentation followed by an engineering notebook describing our thought processes for every single component of the robot. It's tedious but can get us insane points if we mess up a bit.

I get up, stretch and walk to their table. "How're things?" I ask.

"I hate my life." Vinny groans.

"I hate his life too." replies Jade.

"I fear I'm going to be working on this until *really* late tonight."

"Just sleep in. You don't have to actually be at the school until ten."

"I could never do something like that."

"Well that's your own problem."

"Piss off," he retorts.

“With love.” I wink, flipping him off.

I sit next to Spencer. I reach over to grab my controller and accidentally brush against his hand. I can instantly feel my face heat up again. *Jeez, what am I, twelve? I haven't had a crush like this since middle school.*

He grabs his controller without saying anything. Hopefully, he didn't even notice. If he did, hopefully he doesn't mind. If he does mind, I'm just screwed, and I'll drop out of high school immediately. I'll become a bum and live in my mom's basement forever.

Wow, my mentality hasn't changed since middle school either.

More practicing ensues. We keep getting closer and closer to that sub-2:50 mark, until we finally hit it at around 4pm. 2:49.84.

“Let's go!” I exclaim. “We did it!”

Spencer drops his controller and gives me a high five. We lock eyes for a moment as our hands touch. His smile is so big, it looks like it's about to escape his face. Our hands stay pressed together as we stare at each other for a moment. For a second, it seems like nothing else matters at the moment–

Seemingly noticing what's going on, he blushes as he swings his hand toward him. I bring mine down and look away from him. God, that was embarrassing. I'm a sick freak.

“We should...pack up.” he mutters, his face still bright pink.

“Yeah, I need to set up the electrical toolbox.” I respond, standing up again.

We don't bring all of our tools to competition, just the important ones. Two years ago, after we overpacked and couldn't find a single multimeter, I printed out an extensive electrical packing list that I follow every single time we're going somewhere. I won't let *packing* be the reason we fail.

I drag a small bright green tote labeled "electrical" from the storage cabinet. I open it and toss the essentials: a multimeter, spools of wires of varying colors and gauges, and the tools necessary to make a quick wire change, in case something frays or rips off. It's unlikely but not impossible.

I close the tote, lock it, and drag it to the middle of the room. The teachers and all of the underclassmen will come in a couple hours to pack everything in Mr. D's truck. As upperclassmen, we've thankfully graduated from needing to get screamed at by him for an hour as we pack. We're going to start driving to the hotel as soon as we've finished packing the basics, and everyone else will handle it later. If we leave before Mr. D gets here, we essentially eliminate useless yelling. Wonderful.

"Vinny, are you ready to go?" I ask.

"Yeah, lemme just finish this paragraph I just started." he replies.

"You can do that in the car. Come on, it's getting dark out already."

Jade, Vinny, Spencer, and I walk out of the robotics room together to our cars. Jade wasn't so lucky with parking passes, and she's a little bit further out than we are. We wave goodbye as she goes in the opposite direction toward her Honda Civic.

"See ya soon, Spencer." I smile. Vinny says nothing, but waves goodbye to him.

"Same to you guys." He matches my expression.

Vinny and I hop into my car and I buckle myself in. "Vinny, what do I do if *she* shows up this weekend? How do I get her to stay away from me for good?"

"If you pay me $20 and drive me to school all of next week, we can pretend to date for the weekend. I'll even let you kiss me." he snickers.

"I feel honored about your oh-so-generous deal, but she's well aware about where *you* swing. I need to do something else. Something so outrageous, so *outlandish* that she'll stop tormenting me."

I sit for a moment, and a plan pops into my mind. "Y'know, I might have an even better idea."

Chapter Eight
Spencer

I love you with a focus and resolve that will never slip. I feel content when I'm around you; when you look in my direction, I melt into the ground I stand on. I long for your embrace, for your gaze to snatch me away from the terrors of the outside world. My heart beats for you in a way that matches the rhythm of the songs you blast in the car. I'm dying for you to press your lips against mine, I yearn to sing the song of love to you and contently fill my heart with enough joy to survive millennia. My love is hopeless, but my heart is an awfully strong weapon.

I close my journal and lean my head back against the hotel bed headboard. I let out a large sigh as the book slips down my thigh and onto the bed. "What're you writing?" Vincent asks from across the room.

"I like to journal first thing in the morning. It helps me adjust to the day." I reply.

"Why is it in your math notebook then?" He points at my journal, a spiral notebook identical to the notebook I use for calculus notes. It even has "multi calc" written in Sharpie on the cover.

"So my mom doesn't read it."

"Damn, are you confessing to crimes in there or something?" he laughs.

"Nah, it's just embarrassing…" I begin to mumble.

"I'm just kidding, dude."

I like to jot down my mopey teenage boy thoughts so they can escape my brain before I have to deal with the rest of the day. If I spill my poetic displays of affection now, I won't accidentally blurt my feelings out loud. God, I'm an embarrassment.

I reopen my journal and read some of the lines I wrote over again. "*I'm dying for you to press your lips against mine–*" what the hell? What was I thinking when I wrote that? I haven't even *had* my first kiss yet; I don't know if it's actually worth the hype. I mean, I'm sure it is, but how am I supposed to know? I'd rather just hug her. I'd love to wrap my arms around her again.

Benjamin walks out of the bathroom, shirtless with a towel wrapped around his shoulders, wearing a pair of blue jeans and no socks. "Bathroom's ready." he mutters as he kneels down next to his suitcase, rummaging through it. He grabs our team t-shirt, throws the towel on his bed, and puts it on.

Benjamin, Vincent, and I are sharing a hotel room for this weekend's competition. With the odd number of guys, I volunteered to share a bed with Vincent, since I've known him longer. Benjamin is, from what I've heard, also a major kicker, which is a big no-no for me. Vincent, on the other hand, is a lesser-known sleep demon called a grabber. I woke up a few hours ago to use the bathroom and found that I couldn't move because he had grabbed my arm with his left hand and pulled my t-shirt down with his right. I feel a little violated.

"You can go," I tell Vincent.

"I got ready while you were fast asleep," he snorts. In all actuality, I wasn't asleep; I was catching up on the sleep I lost while stuck in his arms. I was just resting my eyes, I swear.

I get out of bed and grab my shower materials from my suitcase, along with the clothes I want to wear today. Well, I have to wear my team shirt, but I chose a pair of light blue jeans to contrast the dark grey we have to wear on top. Vincent designed the t-shirts this year, so I can't really complain.

I walk into the bathroom and become bombarded with the heat emanating from the room. I turn on the fan, which apparently wasn't turned on for the last shower. I wipe down the counter that is somehow fully drenched with sink water. Jeez, did Benjamin shower in the sink? Either that, or they built a pool in here while I was sleeping.

After drying the counter, I dropped my stuff off and turned on the shower. I like my showers hot and steamy to wash away my morning thoughts. I undress while thinking about the day ahead. I'm beyond excited; it's my first competition as a senior. I'm entering my final season. I never really thought this day would come. Today's the beginning of the end, huh.

I hop in the shower, the scalding water piercing my back with a tingle that feels so bad but so good at the same exact time. I wash my hair, like I do every day. I know you're not really supposed to wash it every day, but my hair gets super greasy really quickly, especially over competition weekends, and I'm not going to take any chances. I need to look good. For the judges, for my family, for *her*.

I grab my wash cloth and take my bar of soap out of its container. I lather the wash cloth in soap under the water for about ten seconds and complete an initial scrub of my body. After I wash the first layer off, I squirt a generous helping of liquid body wash into the wash cloth and do another cleaning. I really prioritize smelling good, so I wash the parts of my body that tend to collect more sweat with antibacterial soap before washing my entire body with a fun-scented body wash. The one I packed for the weekend is Coconut Vanilla Crush–not exactly the manliest scent, but I think it's cool. My mom isn't a fan.

I finish my shower and turn the water off. The entire bathroom now smells like coconut. I grab my towel, do an initial pat-down, and wrap the towel around my waist, tying it in the middle. I grab my toothbrush, run it under the sink, squeeze some toothpaste on the bristles, and wet it again. This is the only correct way to brush your teeth, in my opinion. Anything else is way too dry and feels like I'm brushing my teeth with chalk after a while.

After brushing my teeth, I swish mouthwash around for about thirty seconds while I put my contacts in. My vision is only slightly bad; it's bad enough to where I need glasses to drive, but I can function in everyday life without them. I tell people I prefer contacts so I can wear sunglasses when I drive. In all actuality, I think I look hideous with my glasses on. I chose a pair of glasses I thought looked cool in my freshman year, and my prescription hasn't changed much since then, so I've never had a reason to buy a new pair. I look like a huge nerd when I wear them.

I moisturize my face, apply sunscreen, and lather my underarms with vanilla Old Spice deodorant. Then, I take off my towel and slowly put on my clothes, in the order of:

underwear, tshirt, socks, and finally my jeans. Every day, this is the exact order that I put on my clothes. There's no real rhyme and reason to it; I started doing it at some point and have stuck with it ever since. I like a routine.

I search for a blow dryer. I find one underneath a few towels in one of the cabinets. I plug it in and flip my hair forward. I don't have that much hair, so drying my hair doesn't take too long, but it's enough to where it'll get all frizzy if I air-dry it. I quickly rub my hand back and forth across my head to evenly distribute the drying power. Once my hair is sufficiently dry, which takes about a minute, I turn it off and flip my hair back. I think I look okay. Hopefully.

I push my toiletries to one section of the bathroom sink, grab my toiletries, and walk out of the bathroom, keeping the fan on just in case someone else needs to go in there before we leave. Benjamin is sprawled across his bed while Vincent is applying mascara in the mirror. He turns to me. "Come here for a sec."

I listen. He puts the mascara on the table, grabs the biggest tub of Aquaphor I've ever seen, opens it, and scoops some out with his pointer finger. He presses his finger to my face and spreads the Aquaphor across my lips.

"I could sense your chapped lips from the bathroom." he sighs.

"Thanks," I awkwardly laugh.

He sniffs dramatically. "You smell good. Is that Coconut Vanilla Crush?"

I nod. "I have, like, three tubs of that back home," he laughs.

I turn to Benjamin. "Are you ready to go?"

He rolls out of bed and grabs his backpack. Vincent and I grab our stuff as we leave the hotel room and lock the door behind us. I place one of the hotel keys in my wallet and place it in my pocket. For simplicity's sake, I'm driving Vincent and Benjamin to the school. We take the elevator down four floors and walk to the continental breakfast station. I grab a cup of strawberry yogurt, a banana, and a plastic spoon. I sit down, open the yogurt cup, and unwrap the spoon. I don't like eating anything super heavy in the morning or else I won't feel good for the rest of the day. This is just to get me going.

The other two sit down. I hear a distinct voice walking past my table. I look up from my yogurt and see Jade and Charlotte walking toward the exit. Charlotte has her hair in a pair of pigtail braids, her bangs voluminous and hanging on her forehead without any separation. Her safety glasses hang from the collar of her team shirt, pulling it down enough to see her collarbones and not much else.

Every time I see her, I think *"wow, I don't think she could get any prettier"*, and every single time, I'm proven wrong. I don't think there's ever been a time where I haven't found her pretty, but she looks especially beautiful in her robotics outfit. Maybe I find her so pretty in this outfit specifically because she always looks happy when she's wearing it. Her big smile shines so bright that this dim hotel lobby becomes vibrant.

Vinny calls her and Jade over. "Aren't you guys going to eat something?" he asks.

"I had a protein bar this morning." Jade replies.

Charlotte chimes in. "I had a Red Bull. We're going to the school early to scope out our competition."

Vincent lets out a deep sigh. "I have a few granola bars in my backpack."

"You're the best, Vinny!" She gives him a quick hug from behind. When she lets go, she walks up to my side of the table and leans over me, her braids two inches from my face.

"You ready for today, Spencer?" she asks, sustaining her gorgeous smile.

I nod, covering my blushing face with the hand not holding the yogurt spoon. "Ready as I'll ever be."

"Awesome. See ya soon."

"Bye-bye."

Her and Jade exit the hotel. As soon as the sliding doors close behind them, Vincent bursts into laughter. "What's your problem?" I ask as I open my banana.

"I'm so sorry, but you're so funny. I think Charlotte is the most oblivious person in the entire world."

"Hey, what do you mean by that?" I exclaim.

"You're soooo obvious. How do you even compete next to her?"

"I focus on performing and I don't look at her until after the Round is over."

"Wait," Benjamin interrupts, "I'm going to be so honest Spencer, I did *not* know you were into girls."

Vinny starts laughing again, this time holding his stomach with one hand and his face with the other. His eyes start to water from all the laughter. I lower my head and sigh. "Jeez, it seems like *everyone* thinks I'm gay."

"People are just weird like that, Spence," Vinny says after gaining his composure, "you have good hygiene, good music taste, and are emotionally stable. A lot of people mix up being a mentally sound dude with playing for the other team. I, personally, never thought you were gay."

Coming from a gay man, that makes me feel better. Kinda.

We finish eating about ten minutes after, throw our trash out, and make our way to my car. I unlock it and Vincent tosses his bag into the passenger's seat without calling shotgun. I guess it's a combination of seniority and that I would've given the passenger seat to him anyway. Benjamin sits in the back behind Vincent.

I turn my car on and exit the parking lot as Vincent gives me directions from his phone. The school is about a ten minute drive away from the hotel, and in the meantime, I play music from my dad's rock playlist. In my car, the driver gets to pick the music, with occasional songs queued by my passengers. Since the drive was so short, only three songs played, all of them being mine.

I pull into the school parking lot and park in the front, right next to Charlotte's Toyota Camry. It's 8:53, and the event begins at 8. The venue opened at 8:30 for two students per team; Charlotte and Jade snatched that opportunity immediately. The parking lot is practically empty; everyone unloaded their robot and parts last night, and competition doesn't start until 9:30, so there's not much of a reason to be there so early. I want to be in the Team Zone, the area where robots sit in between Rounds, early in the morning so I can check the codebase about a hundred times and test various components to make sure everything is perfect. I know it is, but I have to check a million more times or else something bad may happen.

I turn my car off and we all sit in silence for a moment. Benjamin somehow fell asleep again in my passenger's seat. Vinny turns to me and smiles. "Good luck today, dude."

"Thanks. We've been practicing a lot, so I think we'll do really well."

"Oh yeah, good luck competing too. I meant good luck with your predicament."

I freeze. "I wasn't planning on doing anything with that today."

"If the opportunity comes, take it."

I sigh. "Vincent, I don't think this is a good idea. She's only been single for, like, six months at this point, and that last relationship didn't exactly end great. Don't you think I'd be rushing it?"

"Honestly, Spence, I think this would be exactly what she needs. She wants to move on, and you might be able to help her with that. You're a pretty cute guy, after all. Help her get her mind off of that whole fiasco."

That's a new one. I've never been called cute before. "I wouldn't want to be seen as a rebound."

"Don't call it that, they've been done for half a *year* already. Think of it as a...redirection. You're better at wordplay than I am, I'm sure you could come up with a better term."

I ponder for a moment. "I guess that makes sense."

"I'm pretty good at this stuff. I'm not saying you have to make an opportunity, but if you see one, take it before there are no longer any opportunities."

He's right. I wish he wasn't, but he's so right. We're almost halfway through our senior year, and I've done nothing. If we go to different universities, and we most likely will, I will lose my chance entirely. I don't think I'll ever be able to love someone else like I love her. I'm in too deep, and I need to do something about it before I can't.

The thing is, I have no clue how the hell I'm supposed to do it.

"Benjamin, wake up, it's 7:59." Vincent leans over the center console and shakes Benjamin awake. He wakes up and we all exit my car. I press the car lock button on my keys three times for good measure as we make our way toward the school. I watch as high school-aged kids get out of various other cars in the parking lot, all in matching shirts. My heart beats fast with excitement. Even though it's my fourth season competing, walking into the venue for the first time is always so exhilarating. I feel alive. I'm in my element.

We walk into the Team Zone, which is just this high school's gym with tarps over it. I walk over to where our team's specific Zone is located. I find our robot with a sign above it that says "904208: Smith High School Devils". We're either named after the hockey team or the actual Jersey Devil. I toss my backpack in the corner of our 11'x11' section designated to our team and grab my laptop out of it. I plug my laptop into the robot and open the codebase. I turn the robot on and start my meticulous investigation.

I have routine checks that I do every competition. First and foremost, I ensure that the robot chassis can move, which is arguably the most trivial and necessary component. Then, I go through every single operation the robot is supposed to do and ensure it can still do them. This involves a lot of pressed buttons and quick movements to catch game pieces before they get tossed across the gym. After that, I check the code itself to make sure it's pristine. We're judged based on the way the code operates and how it looks to a person who knows absolutely nothing about coding. A judge should be able to look at the code and know exactly what's going on and when it's supposed to happen, or else it's not commented well enough. We use Java, which is pretty straightforward in my opinion, but the judges have to pretend like they know absolutely *nothing* about coding at all. It's tedious but I'm sure being scrutineered like this is important for future college and career opportunities. At least, that's what I think they're preparing us for.

A pink-haired woman, seemingly in her mid thirties, walks up to our Zone and hands me a piece of paper. "Here's the schedule for today," she says.

I take a look and point out when we're competing. We compete at 10:30, 12:30, 1:45, 3:15, 4:30, and 5:45 respectively. The 10:30 Round is our practice round, and the other five actually count. It seems like a long time between Rounds, but when you have forty other teams that need to take turns, competitions can take a *long* time, especially with lunch breaks. If there are delays, you could see competitions running from 9am to 10pm, with only a break for lunch. In this competition, we got lucky, and our last Round of the day is earlier than normal. In one of my sophomore year competitions, our fifth Round was the last one of the day, and there were multiple delays throughout the day. We didn't end up leaving the venue until after 11pm, and we had to be back by 10am the next day for playoffs.

I highlight our Rounds with a highlighter I didn't know I had in my backpack until I searched through it right now. The paper goes on the table, and I continue to check through our code for the next hour or so.

At 9:35, I feel a tap on my shoulder. I look up from my computer and see Charlotte smiling in front of me. "Hey, wanna come watch some Rounds with us?" she asks.

I close my laptop. "Sure, where's everybody else?"

"They're already in the stands. Is everything looking good?"

"As good as it'll ever be."

"Then let's go!"

She grabs my arm and pulls me out of the Zone. I jog to keep up with her pace, and we make our way to the stands, which are just bleachers facing the basketball court they turned into a competition field. She sits next to Vincent, who's sitting next to Jade. I reluctantly sit next to her.

The first Round started before we sat down. The first team up, The Unicorns, shakily drives around the track, missing a few of the targets. I heard online that most of their team members last year were seniors, and they're still trying to build up to the same skill level they previously had. They were a powerhouse last year, so I'm curious to see what their decline looks like.

They finished their first Round in five minutes and ten seconds. Not great by any standards, but the Driver and Controller high-fived and hugged after it was over. It's a practice round, anyway. They, along with their Transporter, the student who takes the robot to and from the field, pick up their robot and take it off as the next team brings their robot on.

We watch Rounds for about forty-five minutes or so. I've seen all these teams every season, and I'm starting to recognize all the key members of each team. For example, the Controller on Team Shell-Shocked has been controlling ever since I started. He's gotta be a senior at this point as well. It's been cool watching him improve as I've improved. I've had a couple conversations with him; he seems like a cool guy. I've never seen him break a sweat while competing.

Charlotte stands up. "Maggie, Spencer, let's get going. We need to start getting ready for our first Round."

Maggie was assigned to be our Transporter this season, mainly because of the amount of effort she's put in to learn programming. Since the Transporter role isn't skill-heavy, we normally give it to a younger student who puts in a noticeable amount of effort so they can feel like their efforts paid off.

The three of us exit the stands and walk back to The Zone, with Charlotte and I in the front and Maggie trailing behind us. Charlotte looks back at Maggie. "First competition on the field, how are you feeling?" she asks her.

"Amazing. I'm so excited to watch you guys up close."

"Are we really that fun to watch?" Charlotte snickers.

"I'd say so." I reply.

"Oh, hush." She bumps my shoulder.

We enter The Zone and Charlotte goes through her own pre-round checklist, this one being more hardware-heavy. She turns on the robot and starts violently shaking it, presumably to make sure that none of the wires are loose. After she feels satisfied, she turns the robot off and checks bolts, screws, and other mechanical fasteners to ensure that everything is tightened securely. Once she's done, she turns the robot off, takes the battery out, plugs it into the charger, and places a new battery in.

We're supposed to queue ten minutes before the Round starts, and it's about 10:20 at this point. Maggie takes the handle of the robot cart and starts pulling it toward the hallway that teams use to bring their robots onto the field, which is in the opposite direction of where audience members go to the stands.

Charlotte and I follow Maggie and the robot. She turns to me and smiles. "How are you feeling?"

"I feel alright. This is the Round we can make the most mistakes in. How about you?"

"I feel so sick to my stomach, it hurts," she replies, her smile unwavering.

"It'll be okay. No one out there is going to care if we mess up the practice round. You *saw* the Rounds before ours."

"I know, I know. I just have this steady, awful feeling in the pit of my stomach that won't go away."

"I get it. I promise, everything is going to be okay. Make sure to drink water after the Round, alright?"

"Gotcha." She softly smiles, and we continue our walk to the field.

We line up in the queue. Another team, Shell-Shocked, is ahead of us, waiting to load. Their Controller notices me and walks up to me, giving me a fist-bump. "What's up, Spencer?"

I don't remember his name. "Hey man, how's it going?"

"I'm ecstatic. You?"

"All is well. How's the robot this year?"

"Absolutely amazing. You've gotta watch us!"

"Of course. Make sure to watch us too!"

His team begins to take their robot onto the field. I try to sneak a bit closer to the field to watch him and his Driver, a younger girl. The match begins, and they're a bit tipsy. She seems new; she definitely wasn't their Driver last year. He's absolutely perfect, but her driving brings them down a little bit, and they finish in three minutes and thirty-two seconds. As soon as the match ends, he slams his controller down onto the Driver Table and yells at her.

"What the *hell* was that! That's nothing like we practiced!" he exclaims.

"I'm sorry! I was nervous!" she retorts.

"Nervous isn't going to cut it! When we get back to The Zone, you're bringing the robot to the practice field. Got it?"

I watch her nod as her eyes start to tear up. I turn over to Charlotte, who also watched the whole interaction. "Wow, I don't like him." she says.

"I thought I did, but that was rough."

Maggie starts hauling the robot to the field as Shell-Shocked takes theirs off. I look at the stands absolutely packed with people. Usually they're not that packed on Saturdays, since it's just qualification Rounds today, but it's almost full for some reason. Oh well, more reason for me to win.

I see my parents sitting next to Jade's family. They wave to me, and I smile. I've always found it corny to wave like crazy while on the field. It makes me feel better at this game than I actually am.

I walk over to the Driver Table, place my laptop down, and plug in our controllers. I grab my white controller and make sure it's calibrated correctly for the hundredth time. I then do the same with Charlotte's controller.

Maggie and Charlotte pick up the robot and place it at the starting line. They turn it on and leave. Maggie brings the robot cart to the finish line and Charlotte walks up to the Driver Table, grabbing her controller.

"Ready, partner?" I ask, as I always do. I've asked this one little question before every match. It's tradition at this point.

"Of course." she smiles.

"Our next team is team 904208, The Devils from Smith High School!" the announcer's voice booms through the speakers. Charlotte and I make devil horns out of our fingers and put them on the sides of our heads. It's our school's thing, and I think it makes us look cool.

"Ready, set, go!"

The timer starts, and we begin. The robot speeds to the first checkpoint, a target we have to hit with a pre-loaded ball. Charlotte adjusts herself real quick, and screams "GO!". I listen, and shoot the ball at the target. It hits. A small container is released from the top and we race to it as I lift the robot's elevator. The top of the elevator, holding a baton, rotates at a 45-degree angle and drops the baton in the container. I lower the elevator as Charlotte races to the monkey bars and rotates the robot 180 degrees. I lift the elevator again, and the same component that was holding the baton grabs the first monkey bar and lifts the robot up. Then, a second arm grabs the bar and the first arm lets go. The robot is now six feet in the air. The first arm grabs the third bar, which is slightly shorter than the first bar, and the second arm lets go to grab the fourth bar which leads us to the floor again. I send both arms back into the robot as we race to the final challenge, a balancing act. Charlotte slowly but efficiently drives onto the seesaw and locks it in a position where both sides are completely even. Once the green light flashes, the timer stops. Charlotte and I look at the timer.

"The Devils finish in three minutes and twenty-one seconds, setting a new record to beat for the day!" The announcer exclaims.

I turn to Charlotte and we high-five. "That was awesome!" I smiled.

"It was pretty good, but we'll do better next time!" she replies with a similar level of enthusiasm.

In the corner of my eye, I see the figure of a lanky young woman, with jet-black box-dyed hair and piercing blue eyes, standing by the divider between the field and the audience. She is seemingly pissed. I focus on her to try to see who she is and why she's mad at us. When I finally understand who it is, my heart drops to the floor. *Her.*

What the hell is Sylvia doing here?

"What's wrong? Your smile faded–" Charlotte turns around to see what I was looking at and instantly stops talking as soon as she notices Sylvia in the stands. She turns to me, her face pale and expressionless.

"Oh god, no." she mutters.

I can't say anything. Charlotte starts rambling. "Oh my god, what is she doing here? Why is she here? She just wants to torment me? Why is she mad? Why did she have to be here? How do I get her to leave? What am I going to do? I need her gone! How do I get her to leave me alone?"

I grab Charlotte by the shoulders. I need to help her. "It's going to be okay, she can't hurt you from here. She won't hurt you while I'm here."

God, that sounded weird.

"Spencer, I have a really big favor to ask. Can you help me get rid of her?" she asks me.

"Of course. You want me to talk to her? Ask her to leave?"

"I don't think that's going to work. I need to do something you're gonna have to get real comfortable with real quick."

"What do you mean–" My question is interrupted by Charlotte grabbing me by the collar of my shirt and bringing me down to her level, leaning in.

She kisses me.

Chapter Nine
Spencer

The kiss doesn't last for more than three seconds. It was short and sweet, not much about it but it was the greatest thing I've ever experienced. My face is so red that I feel like I'm about to begin a nosebleed.

When she lets go, my lips feel cold. Charlotte stares at me, mouth agape, her face tomato red. I look up and see Vincent sitting in the stands, his jaw dropped down to the floor. Sylvia, seemingly even angrier than before, storms off in a rage.

I realize the gravity of the situation. "Charlotte, what was that for? The stands are full of people. My *parents* just saw you kiss me!"

"I'll explain when we get back to The Zone," she stammers, "I'm so sorry. Please know it was for a good cause."

She runs off to pick up the robot with Maggie. I grab my laptop and the controllers off the Driver Table and make my way back to The Zone alone. Usually, I wait for Charlotte and the Transporter, but I need to be on my own.

My mom is going to kill me.

I make my way back to our Zone, drop my stuff off, and sit in the corner of our square. I pull out my phone, and a text from my mom appears.

"You should've told us you had a girlfriend! Congrats!"

I toss the phone and drop my head into my hands. I can't articulate a single thought other than the memory of being kissed. It's all that plays through my head. I can't focus on anything other than the feeling of her lips pressed against mine.

"I'm dying for you to press your lips against mine" – I wrote that this morning. I wasn't expecting it to *actually* happen today. What the hell is my life? I'm supposed to be thinking about robots!

I hear the robot cart drive past me. Charlotte hauls the cart around and brings the robot into our Zone. "Where did Maggie go?" I ask.

"I told her to go back to the stands. I need to talk to you."

"I need to talk to you as well."

"Presumably about the same thing?"

I nod. "You go first then."

I lift my head up. "Charlotte, you just took my first kiss from me."

Her eyes widened, her face reddening again. "You haven't had your first kiss yet?"

"Not until right now."

"Oh my god, I'm so sorry," she says, sitting down next to me, "I didn't know about that."

"Why did you kiss me?" I ask.

"That's what I wanted to talk about. Sylvia's been crazy ever since I broke up with her. I mean, she's been sending letters every day since it happened. I've gotten texts, emails from burner accounts, and even messages on my school accounts. I figured the only way to get her to stay away from me was to prove to her that I moved on.

"I'm so sorry, Spencer, it was the first thing I had thought of. It was a spur-of-the-moment kind of thing, I wasn't really thinking. Please forgive me for taking such a special moment from you."

I guess I can't really complain too much that she took my first kiss here. I had always wanted it to be her, just not in this public of a situation. If this helps Sylvia stay away from her, I'm alright with being a part of it. We both benefit in the end. She gets closure, I got a kiss from the prettiest girl I've ever seen.

"Of course I forgive you. I probably would've done something much worse if I was in your situation. What do you think the best course of action is now?"

She thinks for a moment. "Hopefully that scared her off, but if it didn't, could you pretend to be my boyfriend, just for this competition? Again, I'm so sorry that this has to happen, but I won't be able to do my best with her around."

Boyfriend. I like that word. The word I don't like is *pretend*, but I can handle it. I want to help her. I *need* to help her.

"Of course I will." I smile.

She pulls me into a big hug. "Thank you so much!"

She lets go and cools down. She stands up. "So wait, you've really never kissed anyone before?"

"Nope, I've never had a girlfriend or anything."

Her jaw drops. "*Seriously?*"

I nod. "Is that surprising to you?"

"Entirely! I mean, you're a really cute guy. You're telling me you've never had a girlfriend before?"

"Cute?" I repeat.

She covers her mouth in embarrassment. "Whoops, that kinda slipped out, but yeah, I think so."

She thinks I'm cute. Holy shit. Is she just saying that to make me feel better for embarrassing me in front of the crowd, or does she actually believe it? I'm not too sure, but I'd like to hang on to the fact that she's telling the truth. Holy shit, she thinks I'm cute. I want to reciprocate and say she's the prettiest girl I've ever seen, but that might not be the best idea. She has a lot going on at the moment.

I let out a quiet laugh. "But yeah, I've just never had the opportunity to have a girlfriend."

"What a shock," she smiles, "let's go back to the stands. You go first, so it doesn't look weird. I'll come out in a minute."

I leave The Zone and head to the stands. Vincent immediately spots me and gives me a childish glare, covering his mouth with his hand. I sit next to him as he bursts into laughter.

"I told you to take any chances you got, but I didn't mean like *that!"* he laughs.

"I didn't do anything! She did that!"

His smile fades. "Did she at least *ask* first?"

"Not really? She asked if I could help her, but never specified how."

He sighs. "Jeez, she's a mess."

He turns to me and places his hand on my shoulder. "Are you okay? I know I'd be freaking out right now if someone did that to me out of nowhere. How are you feeling?"

"I think I'm alright. It was a shock, sure, but I guess I can't really complain, right? If I could have my first kiss with anyone, even though it was in a weird situation, I'd rather it be with her."

His eyes widen. "You haven't had your first kiss yet?"

"Well, I did just now."

"Wow, that was awful of her. Are you sure you're alright?"

"I mean, I'm feeling good. Can't really complain."

He laughs and pats me on the back. "Whatever helps you sleep at night, dude."

Charlotte enters the stands soon after and sits between the two of us. I notice her puffy eyes, as if she was just crying earlier. "Are you alright?" Vincent and I ask at the same time.

She nods. "Yeah, just tired."

I try to pay attention to the Rounds happening in front of me instead of snooping on the texts Vincent and Charlotte are sending each other. They're sitting *right* next to each other, can't they just talk? Maybe it's because I'm here. Maybe they're talking about me.

The next team finishes, and I look up from the field and lock eyes with Sylvia, whose piercing blue eyes are shooting daggers right in my direction. Charlotte looks up with her phone, sees her, and immediately grabs my arm. "Is this okay?" she asks.

"I mean, you're already doing it, so yeah." I reply. Of course it's okay.

This is all fake. I'm trying to be normal about the whole situation, but unfortunately I am nothing but a hormonal teenage boy who hasn't experienced physical touch from a girl he loves before. This is all new to me. Even if it isn't real, can't a guy just pretend like it is? Let me lie here in the company of none but desperation.

Soon enough, it's time to queue for our first official match. Charlotte, Maggie and I exit the stands, grab the robot cart, and bring it to the field. "How are you feeling?" Charlotte asks.

"Decent. You?"

"As okay as I can feel with the impending doom looming above me."

"It'll be okay, she can't come down here."

She laughs. "Don't worry, I won't kiss you in front of all these people again."

Unfortunate. "Sounds good."

Charlotte and Maggie take the robot to the field again as I set up the computer at the Driver Table. This Round is actually important. I have something I need to prove, and I will prove it right here, right now. I need to show everyone that I am the best, that all my excruciatingly hard work has led me to this point. Countless hours and late nights staring at my laptop screen will soon pay off.

Charlotte comes back to the Table and grabs her controller. "Ready, partner?" I ask.

"As always."

Our team name gets called once again as we raise our hands to make the devil horns. We grab our controllers as the Round begins. Everything goes entirely as planned; I'm faster with our movements than last time. Charlotte's driving is sharper. We're in the zone for the entire duration of the Round. I feel alive. This is where I am meant to be. Nothing else matters at this moment.

The Round ends. I look at the timer. Three minutes and eight seconds, thirteen less than our last round. That's a significant improvement. I toss my controller on the Table and lift my hand up to give Charlotte a high-five. Instead, she pulls me into a tight hug.

"We're doing great!" she exclaims.

* * *

The rest of the competition continues as normal. Our next four Rounds gave us times of 3:06, 3:07, 3:03, and finally 2:59. Our last and best round ended around 6pm because of a post-lunch delay. The team that went right after lunch was late, and I overheard that their drive team was stuck in line at a fast-food joint.

After our last match, Charlotte and I make our way back to our Zone. I pack up my stuff as Charlotte does her nighttime checks on the robot. She plugs in the battery from the last match, writes some charging data down, and checks the wiring for any frays. We haven't had any issues yet, but it's good to make sure that none will happen tomorrow.

Tomorrow is playoff day. The sixteen teams with the lowest times face off tomorrow in an elimination-bracket. Teams pair up with one other team, so there's eight different "groups" of teams. Each Group "goes against" another Group, and whoever has the fastest Round average advances. During Group Pairings, the highest ranked team chooses first, then second, then third, and it goes on from there. First place can choose second, but this is usually frowned upon because it doesn't make it fair for the rest of the teams. Of course, upsets can happen, but it's not super common. If first picks second, that Group usually wins the competition, which sucks for everyone else but happens very often.

Based on times, we're ranked second, only behind Shell-Shocked. I guess their Controller really scared the

Driver into performing better. Their best time was their third Round, which finished at two minutes and fifty-seven seconds. I'm a little peeved that someone who's such a dick to their own teammate is beating us, but that's alright. We'll beat them later.

The team in third place is ten seconds behind, and they hit that score in their second Round. Their third, fourth, and fifth rounds were all pretty bad in comparison, so I wonder what's going to happen there. All Rounds are uploaded online about an hour after they happen, and everything is livestreamed. Charlotte and I will have to sit through a lot of footage, but that's a tomorrow thing. Tonight, I need to relax.

Charlotte and I walk together to the parking lot where Benjamin, Vincent, and Jade are waiting for us. I unlock my car and Vincent slumps into the passenger seat yet again.

"See ya later, Spencer," Charlotte says as she opens the door to her car.

"Bye-bye."

I hop into my car, turn it on, and wait for Charlotte to back out of her spot before I do the same. A car rushes behind me and I lose track of where Charlotte's car went. Oh well, I'd rather not drive behind her anyway. Might not be best for my focus.

"Did you see Sylvia again after our 12:30 Round?" I ask Vincent as we pull out to the main road.

"Nah, I think you scared her off. Hopefully she doesn't come back tomorrow."

"Yeah, I hope so. This whole pretend-dating thing is kinda weird."

"She filled me in at the bleachers. I guess this is your first taste of what a relationship is, right?"

I blush. "I guess so, it's just...weird. It's not *really* a relationship, but I wish it was."

"Fair. At least youse can go back to being friends after this weekend."

"The thing is, I don't *want* to do that. I'm too greedy. I feel like I'm taking advantage of this awful situation."

"I mean, if it's not a problem for her, why not? I want nothing more than my friend to be happy, and if this is making her happy, so be it. Think of it as a mutualistic relationship."

"Jeez, don't remind me about sophomore year bio."

"Whoops, I forgot about that class."

The conversation dies down for the rest of the drive. I park next to Charlotte's car, but her and Jade are already gone. We got stopped at a few more red lights than they did, so they got a pretty significant lead.

I turn off my car and we exit, hauling our backpacks over our shoulders. We make our way into the hotel, up the elevator, and to our room. I pull my wallet out of my pocket and unlock the door for us. As soon as we walk in, I toss my backpack next to my bed and grab a pair of black sweatpants, my contacts case, and my glasses from my suitcase. I'm tired of wearing jeans and contacts; I feel like they're stuck to my body, and I need them off as soon as possible.

I enter the bathroom, locking the door behind me. As I'm changing, I go over everything that's happened today, just as I've done half a million times already. This entire day feels like a dream. Is there any way today could get weirder?

I pinch myself. Nope, today is real.

I exit the bathroom, freshly changed, and I notice my phone buzzing on the nightstand. I flip it over and see that Charlotte is calling me. I pick up the call. "Hello?"

"I saw her in the hallway. She's staying at this hotel."

My heart falls to the floor. What is this woman's problem? Can't she just let poor Charlotte be? Booking a room at the same hotel we're at is a new low. How did she even find out? There's a bunch of hotels teams are staying at in this area. How did she know we were here?

"Jade left to have dinner with her parents. Can you come here? I don't want to be alone."

"Of course," I say, entirely without thinking, "what room are you in?"

"421. Thank you, I hope I'm not being too much trouble."

"Absolutely not. I'll be there in a minute, alright?"

"Alrighty, bye-bye." She used my line.

"Bye-bye," I reply as the call ends.

Vincent gives me a strange look. "Who called?"

"Charlotte did. Apparently Sylvia is staying at this same hotel, and she asked me to sit with her in the room."

"Well go on, then, what are you waiting for?"

"I don't know, isn't this something that you're supposed to do as her best friend?"

"I mean, probably, but if she asked you, there's a reason behind it." He smirks. "Good luck."

I exit the room, tapping my pocket to make sure I have my wallet with me. The door slams behind me as I walk down the hallway to room 421. We're in room 402, on the complete opposite side of the hallway, so it's about a hundred feet away. I knock three times on her door and she immediately opens it as if she knew I was there. Of course she did; she was expecting me.

"Hi again," she smiles, her voice noticeably shaky. She changed into a pajama shirt and pants, but her hair is still in the same braids from this morning. I really shouldn't be thinking this right now, but she is so pretty. I wish I could tell her that.

She kicks off her slippers and lays down on the bed furthest to the door and closest to the air conditioning. She pats down the other side of the bed, signaling me to join her.

"Are you sure?" I ask.

She nods. I take off my shoes, place them in the corner of the room near the door, and sit on the corner of her bed. She snorts.

"Come on, don't act like a stranger. Make yourself comfortable."

She moves to the left side of the bed and I rotate myself so my body is parallel with the long side of the bed. I lean back on the headboard, my knees bent.

"Thank you for coming on such short notice." she says.

"It's really no problem at all. How are you feeling?" I ask.

"Awful, but much better now that you're here."

"I see."

"Your glasses look nice. I haven't seen them in a while."

I blush. "Thanks. Contacts have been much more convenient lately."

We sit in silence for a while after that. She's laying on her side, and to maintain peace with myself, I'm trying my hardest to not look at her too much. I lean back and stare at the popcorn ceiling, thinking about the calculus test I have next week. That's next week's problem.

After about ten minutes of lonesome thought, I pick up my phone and scan through my messages. I finally respond to my mom's text from this morning, with a simple "Thanks." I'm not too sure about how I'm supposed to explain the whole pretend situation to my family. It might be easier to just not mention it, but I don't think Charlotte would like it if I lied to my parents about us dating. That's tomorrow night's problem, I guess. Hopefully, my mom is so glad I'm not gay that she doesn't say anything about it.

I turn to Charlotte and see that she fell asleep. She's so pretty, definitely the prettiest girl I've ever seen, and right now, I'm basically sharing a bed with her. If I told myself a few weeks ago that this is where I'd be now, he would call me crazy and schizophrenic. Despite that, everything that's happened is completely real.

"God, I wish you would kiss me again." I whisper to the void. At least, I thought it was the void.

Her eyes immediately open, and our eyes interlock. "What did you just say?" she exclaims, her face flooding red.

"Oh shit!" I yelp as I jolt up, falling off of the bed.

"Oh my goodness, I didn't mean to scare you! Are you okay?" she asks.

"Yeah, I'm alright. I'm so sorry about that."

"About what?"

"What I just said."

"Sit back down," she commands, and I listen. She sits up and leans her head toward mine.

"Do you want me to kiss you again?" she asks.

I don't say anything. I can't say anything. "I mean, I need *some* way to repay you, right?"

I don't answer. I physically cannot answer. "It also might be nice to let off a bit of steam, right? Both of us are stressed from today. Is this something you want?"

I nod. "I need a verbal agreement, Spencer."

"Y-yes, this is something I want."

Her right hand grabs my left, her fingers intertwining with mine. Using this hand, she pulls me closer as she leans in, slowly closing her eyes. She kisses me again, this time longer and more passionate than the first one. I want to look at her, but something about this makes me want to close my eyes and truly live in the moment.

After about seven seconds, she breaks free, and my eyes open again to see her smiling from ear to ear. Our faces are about five inches from each other. Her cheeks are pink. "Alright, your turn," she says.

"My turn? I don't know how to kiss someone." I stammer.

"Oh come on, it's not that hard. Just go for it."

I can do this. This is the moment I've been waiting for since my freshman year of high school. All of the lonely, yearning nights have led to this moment right here. I can't ruin this chance. Don't mess up.

I lean in and, with as much focus as I can muster, I give her a quick peck on the lips. It lasted less than a second, but I feel like my heart is about to explode. She lets out a cackle.

"Wow, you *really* don't know what you're doing."

"I wasn't lying." I chuckle.

"Want me to take over?" she asks.

I nod. "Yes, please."

"Alrighty, try to keep up then."

She wraps her arms around my shoulders and pulls me back in. She runs her fingers through my hair as she keeps kissing me over and over. I try to kiss her back, and when I do, she pulls on my hair and brings me closer. I sit like a statue, my arms hanging by my side. She breaks free, and I open my eyes to her grabbing my arms and placing them over her shoulders. Her eyes glazed, she looks at me with an expression I've never seen from her before.

"Touch me," she whispers.

"Where?" I ask.

"Anywhere you want," she mutters, "I'll double-tap you if I want you to stop. You do the same for me, alright?"

"Gotcha," I say as I pull her back in.

Kissing is kinda like a video game. You get better at the different mechanics of a video game as you progress. This is a game I feel like I'm picking up pretty easily. At least, she hasn't specifically stated that I'm doing an awful job.

She's stolen all of the thoughts I have about anything other than what I want to do with her next. All I can think about is her and her lips pressed against mine. My focus of life and the moment at hand begins and ends on her lips.

I'm scared to touch her somewhere she doesn't want me to. Her command was completely vague, so I don't really know where the boundaries lie. I think the best course of action is to copy what she does, because she wouldn't do something to me that she wouldn't want me to do to her. She rubs her hand across my back, and I do the same to her. I can feel her bra band.

She uses her other hand to grab my shirt collar and pull me closer as the hand on my back makes its way down to my legs. I reciprocate, using one hand to keep myself positioned on the bed and the other to grab her thigh. All I can think about is how much I want this; all thoughts of how wrong this is are completely thrown out the window. I want this so bad. Nothing else matters in this moment.

I open my mouth to breathe a bit and I feel something warm, wet, and tasteless enter. As soon as I process what it is, I immediately break free. She sticks her tongue out, a devilish smile plastered across her face.

"Sorry, force of habit," she says, "are you okay with it?"

"Yeah, but I don't know what I'm doing." I reply.

"Follow my lead."

I lean back in and kiss her again, leaving my mouth slightly open. I feel that warm sensation once again, and a tingle travels through my entire body. I instinctively push my tongue forward, and she lets out a muted moan as she pulls on my shirt so tight that it feels like she wants to rip it off. I would let her if she asked.

After a few minutes, she lets go of the kiss and digs her face into my neck. I feel a tingling, almost burning sensation as she kisses me. It feels so bad, but so good at the same exact time. She grabs my hand and places it on the back of her head, and I softly push her head forward. After kissing my neck a few times, she comes back to eye level, and I kiss her lips again. I'm in heaven.

She turns her body, lies on her back, and pulls me down with her. I'm now leaning over her, my hands pressed onto the mattress next to her head and my knees surrounding her thighs. I glance over her entire body. Her braids are frizzy and messed up, about to fall out. Her necklace hangs lopsided around her neck and I can see bullets of sweat dripping down her face. She's panting, her eyes widened and locked with mine. Her face is tomato red, and mine probably is as well. I'm sweating like crazy, what's the temperature in here?

"You are *so* beautiful..." I blurt out. I, unfortunately, only notice what I said immediately after it comes out. I usually think before I speak, but I can't think about anything other than the fact that I'm in a position I could've only dreamed of.

She smiles. "You think so?"

I can't help but nod. "Yeah, you're the prettiest girl I've ever seen."

"I'm flattered. Now come down here."

I listen. I lower my body and press my face against her neck. I begin to kiss her, but she double-taps my shoulder. I look up. "What's wrong?"

"Something's poking me. Is your phone still in your pocket?"

Oh shit. I didn't even notice. "Oh my god, I'm so sorry–"

She laughs. "Whoops, I've never been like this with a man before. I completely forgot. Keep going."

She thinks I'm a man? I feel like a boy. Although, these aren't exactly boyish acts. Boys play in the dirt and do math homework. Men kiss women and other men.

I continue to kiss her neck as my hands travel around her shoulders, torso, and thighs. I avoid specific parts so she doesn't get uncomfortable. I can tell I'm doing something right when her sounds get louder and she pulls me even closer. I can't stop myself from matching the sounds she makes. My heart is beating so fast that I'm shocked that I can still breathe. She makes even the dirtiest noises sound pretty.

I break free from her neck and pull myself up to eye level again. "Am I doing a good job?" I ask, panting.

"More than a good job," she smirks, her stare matching mine, "you're a really fast learner."

"Is there anything else you'd like me to do?"

"Keep going, pretty-boy."

"Pretty...boy?" I stammer.

She winks. "Yep. Now come kiss me again."

I feel my lips press against hers once again. Our mouths automatically open; it's obvious that we both want what's about to happen. With our bodies pressed together, I feel warm and fuzzy inside, as if my entire body is coming down with a fever I can't sweat out. Her muffled moans are music to my ears, filling my mouth with enough motivation to keep going. I am unstoppable. Nothing else matters.

Her arms wrap around my back, pulling me even closer to her. She lifts the back of my shirt, her sweaty hands pressed against my bare back. I can feel the piercing cold air emanating around the rest of the room. I don't care; all I want to think about is the fact that she's touching my back. I am on top of the world. She is my world.

Charlotte's phone buzzes as if someone's calling her. I break free from our kiss, a thin trail of mixed saliva connecting our mouths together. "Why'd you stop?"

"You should probably answer that."

She sighs. "Yeah, I guess so."

I slyly kiss her one more time before I lift myself off of her and lay down on my back on the right side of the bed. I check my phone to see that it's been nearly an hour-and-a-half since I left my room. What just happened felt like both a million years and a few minutes.

My entire body is throbbing. My heart beats with the speed of a thousand airplanes, and my mind is racing as if it's gearing up for a Grand Prix. I stare at the ceiling as Charlotte sits up and chats on the phone for a few minutes.

She hangs up and puts her phone back on the nightstand. "Jade's gonna be back in about an hour. Wanna stay until then?" she asks.

"Sure. How are you feeling now?" I reply.

"Really good, completely stress-free. You?"

"I feel amazing."

"I can tell," she snickers, glancing at the lower half of my body. I look down and immediately sink back into the bed, covering my hands with my face.

"That's my wallet!" I exclaim, my voice muffled by my hands.

She laughs and grabs my wallet from my right pocket. "I wasn't born yesterday."

She puts my wallet back and hops off the bed, grabbing a pair of black shorts and something else out of her suitcase. "I'll be right back, I need to…go change."

I hear the bathroom door close. My ability to think slowly starts to come back, and I can finally form a coherent thought. Wait, why does she need to change, wasn't she already in her pajamas–

Oh.

I pick up my phone again and open my email, deleting a bunch of spam emails I've accumulated over the past week or so. I swear, some companies never stop emailing me even after I've unsubscribed. It's really starting to annoy me.

Memories of the past hour and a half begin to flood through my mind. Holy shit, everything that just happened…just happened. I not only kissed the girl of my dreams, I did so much more in such little time. This isn't a dream, right?

I pinch myself. It hurts.

How did I get here? It just started as a "thank you for saving me from her" kiss, and led to ninety minutes of passionate everything. At least, it was passionate from my end. I don't really know women that well, but it seemed like she was enjoying it. She told me I was doing a good job. She wouldn't make noises like that if she wasn't into it, right? What the hell do I know? This is my first time!

She steps out of the bathroom in a pair of shorts that go about a third of the way down her thighs. She took her braids out and threw her hair up into a bun. She looks tired, and so, *so* pretty.

"That was exhausting! I feel ready to go to bed. We should do that again sometime. It's really nice to take your mind off of things for once."

My face flushes once more. *Again sometime?* She wants to do it again?

"I'd like that," is all I can say, way more than what I'd be able to say if my fear receptors weren't completely overwhelmed by teenage hormones.

She throws herself on the bed and curls up next to me, one arm wrapped around my stomach and one under my arm. She lays her head on my chest and lets out a big sigh.

"Can we stay like this for a bit?" she asks.

I could never say no to that. "Of course."

I run my fingers through her hair as I feel her body losing its tension. Minutes later, I look down and notice she's asleep. I can confirm it's true this time, because her breathing is slow and deep. I can't believe I'm in this situation.

How is this going to affect our friendship? Is this a thing friends do? She's still going to want to be friends with me after this, right? I don't think friends usually moan each other's names while kissing each other, but what do I know? This must be how the people at the crucifixion must have felt: satisfied but desperate and somehow unaware of what they had just created. Maybe this is completely normal and we'll go back to being normal friends tomorrow.

I can feel myself dozing off.

Welcome to two ruined lives.

What the hell has mine come to?

Chapter Ten
Charlotte

I wake up holding onto a long pillow. I feel gone, like virginity on prom night. My body feels stiff, warm, and sweaty. What the hell did I do last night?

I had an incredible dream last night. I brought Spencer back to my hotel room and I kissed him again. I kissed him so many times. I taught him how to kiss me and we made out for more than an hour. He touched me like a gentleman. While this was a huge step from my previous dreams, it was amazing. It felt so real.

"You're the prettiest girl I've ever seen." That one thing he said in the dream plays in my head a dozen times over. I can't get over it; even thinking about it now makes me blush. I think he's one of the prettiest boys I've ever seen, but I couldn't possibly tell him that. I also don't really find many boys pretty; he's one of the special ones I never really noticed until now.

I feel someone grab my arm. "Charlotte, wake up, you two have to get ready soon," says a feminine voice above me.

I open my eyes to see Jade shaking my arm back and forth. "Good morning, what do you mean 'you two?'"

"Are you blind? Look at who you slept on."

I turn my head and see that the pillow I had woken up on was actually Spencer's body. The memories of last night flood into me like a vaccine filled with passion and angst.

Oh god, that *was* real.

"You're the prettiest girl I've ever seen."

He actually said that. He actually said that to me. Maybe it was a spur-of-the-moment statement, but those words came out of his mouth. He thinks I'm pretty. I'm pretty. He's pretty.

I instantly come to the realization that I made out with Spencer Laine last night, and it was actually real. We kissed more times than I can count. I pulled him, grabbed him, kissed his neck, I did everything. The craziest part is, I loved it.

My mind travels to last night when I pulled him on top of me, how he stared at me with eyes that told me he wanted me– no, that he *needed* me– and he called me beautiful, the prettiest girl he's ever seen. I can feel where his hands touched me last night. I loved when he grabbed me. I really liked it.

I remember saying "We should do that again sometime". Why the hell would I say that? Now he either knows that I like him or he thinks that I regularly make out with my friends. I don't do that on the regular. Other than that one time with Vinny, but that was a practice round. Nothing important.

"God, I wish you would kiss me again" is what he said right before everything began. He *wanted* to. It was totally mutual and something friends can do sometimes, right? Jeez, now I want him again.

"I'm going to shower, but you need to wake him up. I'll need an explanation in the car." Jade says as she walks away.

"Gotcha."

I get up, the world suddenly becoming very cold. I lean over to Spencer. It would be fun to wake him with a good morning kiss, but I don't think we're at that point yet. Jeez, you make out with someone once and now you start daydreaming about your future relationship. I'm such a disgusting whore.

I shake his arm to wake him. "Spencer, wake up, we have to get ready for comp."

He opens his pretty hazel eyes and sits up. "What time is it?" he asks.

"It's 7:50. We slept all night."

He checks his phone and sighs. "Well, shit. The guys are gonna think I'm dead."

"I'm sure Jade told 'em where you were."

I look at him, with his disheveled hair and barely open eyes. He's really pretty. Gorgeous, even, but that might be the morningtime horniness talking.

"Charlotte, was everything that happened last night real?"

I laugh. "If you're thinking what I'm thinking, yeah."

He blushes. "Oh, jeez."

I look down and notice a prominently reddish-pink mark on the right side of his neck. Oh shit. I forgot I did that.

"You might wanna ask Vinny if he can touch this up for you, I don't know if the team t-shirt is going to cover it up."

I press down on the hickey I gave him and he winces. "How bad is it?"

I grab my phone, take a picture, and show it to him. His eyes widen, shocked. "Dang, why'd you bite me for so long?" *Bite?*

I wanna flirt with him for a little bit longer. "Because you sounded really good when I was doing it."

His face reddens again. "I-I could say the same thing about you."

I look outside. We have time. "Y'know, you don't have to leave just yet."

"Are you saying you want to kiss me again?" he asks. How bold of him

"Do *you* want me to kiss you again?" I smile.

He thinks for a moment. "As friends?"

"As friends."

"Then yeah."

I lean in, wrap my arms around his shoulders, and kiss him. He brings his arms around my back as he leans into the kiss. Neither of us have brushed our teeth, but I don't really care. This feels so wrong but so right at the exact same time.

I sit on his right thigh and redirect one of his hands to my left thigh. Without a moment of hesitation, he grabs it, using it to pull me even closer.

I break free from the kiss, whispering "you really *are* a fast learner".

"I've been told that a lot," he replies, and we continue.

After about a minute, I notice a flash of light and a quiet giggle coming from behind me. I turn around and see Jade taking a video of the two of us. "You have a *lot* of explaining to do later, Charlotte Moretti."

I immediately jump off of Spencer, almost falling to the floor. I look at Jade, who hadn't started her shower yet. "Whoops." I smile.

I turn to Spencer, who's completely frozen in fear. "You should go back."

He hops out of bed, throws his shoes on, and yells a quick "bye-bye" before running out the door and into the fourth-floor hallway. As soon as the door closes, Jade turns to me with an evil smirk.

"Now that he's gone, why the hell did I come back to the room last night to see you two on top of each other?"

"I wasn't feeling great after you left, so I asked him to come over. One thing led to another, and we accidentally fell asleep."

"What do you mean 'one thing led to another'? What did you *do*!" she exclaimed.

"Nothing!" I retorted.

"It had to be something since I just caught you sitting on his lap! Tell me, did youse do it or not?"

"Ack, no, of course not! We just kissed a few times, that's all! Just a friendly thing! No clothes came off!"

"'Kissing' and 'friend' do not go together. You need to confess to that poor boy before he thinks you're using him."

"I will, I just need the right time."

"I'm sure making out with him would've been the perfect time–hey!" I interrupt her comment by throwing a pillow at her.

"I'll figure it out, okay?"

"I'm sure you will. Now, I'm sending these to the groupchat."

"Oh god, Vinny's gonna kill me."

"That's the whole point, hun."

Jade walks back into the bathroom and I check my phone. I see a notification from the groupchat between me, Vinny, and Jade. I open it to see a photo of me and Spencer sleeping together, with me in his arms. Vinny reacted to it with a skull emoji.

Knock. Knock. Knockknockknockknockknock. Someone's about to blow the door down, and I know exactly who. I open it to see Vinny rush in and grab my shoulders, shaking me back and forth.

"You saw the photo." I mutter.

"And the video that Jade *just* sent as I was calmly walking over here."

"I know damn well it wasn't a calm walk."

"Who are you to dictate my life?" he snorts. "Now, sit down and tell me *everything* that happened. Don't leave out any details."

"Isn't this a car-ride conversation?"

"I'm riding with your boytoy, remember? The best time is now. Go on, spill the beans."

I tell him everything that happened last night. The tension, the passion, everything. I don't leave anything out, going into all the nitty-gritty details I'm sure he didn't actually want to hear.

"So yeah, then we woke up, and now you're here."

"You left out the part where you kissed him again while Jade was in the bathroom."

He pulls out his phone to show me the video that Jade just took of us. My eyes widen as I see the incriminating proof.

"You need to do something about this. The poor boy is probably confused out of his mind. You need to talk to him about this whole thing."

"What whole thing? We just kissed a few times, no big deal. I was just paying him back for helping me yesterday."

"No, you just wanted to kiss him. This seems like a pretty big deal to me, Char. This isn't something that friends casually do."

"Except for that one time–"

"You know that doesn't count. Anyway, you need to decide whether you're actually going to pursue him further. Do you like him?"

I nod. "I need verbal confirmation."

"I think I really do like him." *Damn, I really just admitted to it.*

"Then you need to do something about this. The boy's never even had a girlfriend before. You're going to hurt him if you don't tell him the truth."

He grabs my shoulders. "Look, Char, I love you, but you and I both know that you're playing with his heart. This can't continue."

"Come on, you know he doesn't like me like that."

"How can you be so sure?" he asks.

"We've been friends for years. Wouldn't he say something by now?"

"I mean, you'd think so, but *look* at him. He's not exactly the kind of guy to put himself out there like that."

"I guess so." I think about how he acted when I asked him if he wanted me to kiss him. He could barely speak. It was so cute.

Jade walks out of the bathroom, freshly showered. A towel is wrapped around her shoulders, separating her wet hair from her team shirt. "Hey, Vinny. Did you see the video?"

"Why do you think I'm here?" he laughs.

I groan as I throw my body back into the bed. I really shouldn't have done that to him. I was too blinded by the desire to kiss him again. I couldn't stop myself, and he didn't want to stop me– what else was supposed to? I used his moment of weakness to do what I wanted to do: kiss him. I'm so disgusting. I'm a sinner.

"Vinny, did you bring anything that could cover a hickey?" I ask.

"He gave *you* one?" Jade exclaims. "I didn't think he knew how to do that."

"No, the opposite."

"I didn't bring any coverup makeup," Vinny sighs, "this is a learning opportunity for the both of you."

"I'm tired of learning opportunities." I say as I push my face into my pillow. Jade grabs my waist, pulls me off the bed, and leaves me standing up.

"You need to get ready, we have a competition to win."

"Ugh, you guys *hate* me."

"Actually," she says, "we love you, and that's why we're being so harsh. You're the experienced one in this relationship of yours, and you need to act like it."

Vinny walks out to finish getting ready, and I grab my stuff and walk into the bathroom to shower. I put on my shower shoes and turn on the shower water, turning the knob to the middle setting. I like my showers warm, not scalding. I'm not the biggest fan of boiling alive in the shower.

I go through my shower routine, replaying everything that happened last night again and again and again until I can't see straight. I'm so unfocused on the task at hand that shampoo falls in my eyes. It burns. Bad. I think I deserve it, though. This feels like something that should happen to me, given the current state of my life.

I quickly finish my shower and dry myself off with a hotel towel, trying not to think about the other hundred people who have probably used this towel in the past month. Out of sight, out of mind, right?

I apply my caffeine solution, moisturizer, and sunscreen, in that particular order. I'm not really going to be outside too much today, and the UV index barely hits five today, but it's better to be safe than sorry. I'm terrified of aging like milk, and based on my familial line, it's not unlikely. I want to be what I deem as pretty, which is way out of budget for my genetics. Yuck, I'm so weird.

I throw on my team shirt, a pair of jeans, and everything else I need, blow-dry my bangs, and throw the rest of my hair into the same pigtail braids I wore yesterday. I'm too lazy to blow-dry the rest of my hair. I have a *lot* of hair, so it would be a huge waste of my time to dry everything manually. My hair will mostly dry throughout the day in the braids. An added bonus is that my hair tends to get really frizzy when I dry all of it, so braiding while wet makes them look sleek and tameable.

I walk out of the bathroom and see Jade scrolling through her phone on her bed. "Are you ready to go?" I ask.

She stands up, throws her phone in her pocket, and grabs her backpack. "Yeah, let's get outta here."

I grab my stuff and shove my room key in my right pocket. I swing my car keys around my pointer finger as the two of us exit the room, the door slamming behind us. "We've gotta stop doing that, I'm sure the people around us are sleeping." I remark.

"They're probably sleeping in after getting kept awake from whatever you two were doing last night," she snickers.

"Oh, screw you."

"See how you're not denying a thing?"

"I'm surprised Vinny wasn't recording me when I told him about it."

"That wouldn't be right. I need the beans spilled straight from the source."

"Of course you do."

After exiting the elevator, Jade grabs two granola bars from the breakfast line. We leave the hotel and walk to my car. Spencer parked to my right, and there's a blue Ford Focus on my left. I swear I've seen that exact car before.

As we come closer to the car, I examine the exterior to identify any features that would help sooth my deja-vu. My heart drops as I see an all-too-familiar dent on the center of the front bumper. Only then do I see the license plate. The awful memory of how that dent appeared arises from the back of my mind and drops itself into the very front and center.

"God, why do you have to ruin everything! My parents are going to kill me when I get home! Do you know what you just caused? I'm dead!" a shrill voice screams from the driver's seat.

"Why is this my fault? It wasn't my idea to sneak out!" a voice that sounds exactly like mine retorts.

"Yes it was! Why are you lying to me!"

I remember fumbling with my phone to find the text messages between us that showed that she texted me at 1am the night before, asking to hang out. I point the phone in her direction.

"I don't want to see that! Stop lying to me! I can't stand you!"

Bang.

We both get sent forward. While trying to park, she drove a little too close to the wall in front of us and hit it. She wasn't going too fast, so it didn't do a lot of damage, from what I noticed later on.

"Look what you did! I swear to God, what is wrong with you!" she shrieked.

"I didn't–"

I'm interrupted. "Shut up. I don't want to hear it. Get out of my car, now! *Get out!"*

We were in an empty, abandoned parking lot, nearly fifteen miles from my house. My car was still at my house. "How am I supposed to get home–"

"I don't care. Figure it out. Get the hell out of my car."

She unlocked the door. I grabbed my stuff and hopped out faster than I should've.

"I love you," is all I could muster.

"Shut up," she scoffed as I closed the door. She immediately reversed out of the spot and sped away before I could process what exactly happened. I sat on the curb, sobbing for about five minutes. It was a cold January evening, the ground still damp from the rain that morning. My shirt was soaked from my tears and my pants wet from whatever dirt water the curb collected. After collecting myself, I grabbed my phone and called Vinny.

"Where are you?" he asked. He knew.

I shudder. "Are you okay?" Jade asks.

I nod. "I'm alive."

I unlock my car and make my way to the driver side door. A piece of paper is lodged into my mirror. I grab it as I open the door. Once I'm inside and the horrors of the outside world can't catch me, I open it up and read it aloud for Jade to hear.

"You are a liar, a cheater, and a slut. Don't rope that boy into your filthy plans."

My hands tremble as the piece of paper falls from my hands and into my lap. Jade picks it up and reads it again.

"Char, are you okay?" she asks.

Tears fall from my eyes to my thighs. The pit in my stomach just drilled a hole into my intestines, signing an extended lease. "I thought I was over her..." was all I could muster.

"I'm so sorry, Char. She's just trying to get in your head."

"It felt like I was over her last night, but now I feel like I've gone right back to square one."

"I won't make fun of you for that comment this time. Can you tell me more about what you were feeling last night? I don't need the details, I just want to know how you feel."

"I had just seen her in the hallway last night, but when Spencer came over, it was as if she never existed. It was the first time she completely escaped my mind for an extended period of time. I know it's gross, but all I could think about was him in the moment. When I was with him, I felt happy, like I was my own person and not held back by memories of her. He made me feel *human*, rather than a bottomless pit of vain.

"I'll admit, it definitely went way too far last night, but I was so happy, and it seemed like he was too. He's so gentle and kind. I asked him to touch me, and he was so polite about it. He didn't do anything wrong, he didn't even try. I felt spoiled, and in the moment, I didn't want to be anywhere other than with him. I feel disgusting to admit it, but it's the truth. He made me feel at peace."

I turn on my car and start driving. "Let's get going. We're gonna be late if I keep whining."

"Y'know, Char, I'm surprised." Jade says.

"About what?"

"I should apologize about my judgement earlier. I thought this whole fiasco could be described as raging teenage hormones, but it's clear that there's a much stronger connection. While I'm still gonna make fun of you for it, I'm really glad that you're happy and you found a way to get her out of your head.

"Just promise me that you'll confess to Spencer soon, okay? Don't wait too long. That's my only ask. I don't think you want to lead him on."

"It's gonna take me a while to muster up the courage to do that. What happens if I get rejected?"

"I doubt it. I saw the way he looked at you this morning. His eyes were practically glued to you."

"What if that was just 'raging teenage hormones' as you said?" I ask.

"If *you* have an excuse, maybe *he* does too."

The rest of the short drive is filled with silence, but not the bad kind. It's the kind of silence that feels natural, calm, and relaxing. Everything we needed to say has been said; conversing further wouldn't add anything new to the conversation except for more fuel to make fun of me with, which Jade does love doing.

I park in the venue parking lot, near where I parked yesterday. Upon parking, I turned my car off and reclined my seat as far back as I physically could. I let out the largest sigh I believe has ever escaped my mind. I can't really describe how I feel at the moment; too many mind-boggling thoughts are conflicting with each other in a bloody fistfight. I hope the Spencer thoughts beat the Sylvia thoughts. Good versus evil, if I may.

"We still have a few minutes before the venue officially opens, do you wanna stay in here until then?" I ask Jade.

"Sure."

We sit in silence. I close my eyes, thinking about sweet nothings and dreams I've had and want to have. I think about the past twenty-four hours and how the next twelve or so are going to go. I ponder over what I'm gonna eat for lunch. Usually, on Sundays, we use a portion of our team budget to buy pizza for everybody. It's nothing special, and the grease on the pizza always makes me sweat, but it's something I always look forward to. Sometimes the most insignificant moments with your friends are the most treasured. I love my friends so much. They bring out the best of me and force me to improve and mature as a person.

I begin to doze off, but I'm startled awake by the sound of a car pulling into the parking spot to the left of me. I expect the worst, but Jade smiles and waves in the car's direction, so it can't be anyone that bad.

I lean forward as I shift the knob that brings my chair up with me. I turn to my left and see Vinny's face plastered on the passenger side window of Spencer's red Mazda. Vinny finally moves his big fat head and I see Spencer smiling at us. I smile and wave in response.

"Is it time for us to go in?" I ask Jade.

She glances at her watch. "Might as well."

We hop out of my car and I grab my bag from the passenger's seat. The boys exit Spencer's car in a similar fashion. As soon as everything's all locked up, we make our way toward the school.

Spencer shuffles through the large group to walk next to me. "How do you feel about playoffs today?" he asks.

I look in his direction, but all I can see when I look at him is the face he made last night as I kissed his neck. I remember how he leaned his head back, the noises he made, and the way he pushed me closer after I showed him where to push. This intense imagery isn't helped by the very obviously purple bruise on his neck, open for the entire world to see.

"Decent, I'd say. You?" I reply as if I wasn't thinking about what I was just thinking about.

"Pretty good! I'm excited."

"You're not worried?"

"Nah, I feel pretty stress-free."

He copied what I said last night. What a goofball.

"Good to hear." I smile.

Jade, Spencer and I enter The Zone while Vinny and Benji make their way to the stands. Spencer and I have a lot of strategy to talk about, and Jade is along for the ride. Jade likes to sit in on our strategy talks so, depending on who we pick for playoffs, she knows which teams to go to and help. My team likes to prioritize helping others if nothing's wrong with our robot, and Jade leads it all, providing mechanical fixes to any team that asks. She'll even help our opponents, despite Vinny's vocal complaints.

The three of us sit down in the empty space of our Zone. "Jade, how many matches did you watch yesterday?" I ask

"Well, no one's robot exploded, so I got the pleasure of watching all of them. If we're ranked 2nd, I think we should pick–"

"Hey, we need to talk to y'all."

Our conversation is instantly interrupted by a guy wearing a shell necklace that matches the one on his t-shirt. It's the Controller from Shell-Shocked, the current first-place team. I don't like him. I think his name is Shawn. At least, that's what it says on his badge, which has his first name and team number in big letters. We all have to wear them to even be allowed in The Zone.

"What's up?" I reply.

He turns to Spencer. "I need to talk to you about strategy."

Spencer points to me. "She's the one who deals with all that. You should know this by now, we've been competing against each other for three years now."

He sighs and turns back to me. "What about strategy?" I ask.

"You guys are barely behind us. I know it's looked down upon at this level, but we automatically win if we pair up. I'm just saying, we want to pick you guys."

"Good to know. We'll have to think about it." I reply.

"Why?" he asks.

"We have to discuss with our team a little bit, but thank you for considering us."

"Yeah," he says, walking away.

As soon as Shawn's too far away to hear, Spencer leans in and whispers "we're gonna reject them, right?"

"Duh," Jade and I reply in unison.

"Anyways," I begin, "I think we should pick..."

The conversation continues without more interruption. Our conversation is civil yet interesting. It feels so serene; I flash back to my sophomore year of high school when we discussed strategy together for the first time. God, ever since I've become a senior I've felt so nostalgic about everything, even though I'm well aware that competitions were some of the most agonizingly stressful times of my life. Despite this, I still look back at the memories quite fondly. Something something rose-tinted glasses blah blah.

"It's almost ten," Spencer says, "we should head down to the field for Group Pairings."

The Group Pairing ceremony is where teams select which teams they want in their Group for playoffs. It's an exciting time, especially when teams reject each other. The audience loves it when things don't go as planned, and they'll love what's about to happen today.

This is our first time being in second place going into playoffs. Our previous seasons have been...bleak, to say the least. We've performed well, sure, but not as well as we're doing right now. A sub-3-minute time seemed impossible. We spent so long this spring and summer making sure we had the most competition-ready team we possibly could, and I'm so proud of how far we've come. Even if we don't do well in playoffs, our improvement from previous seasons speaks for itself.

I'm especially proud of how far Spencer has come throughout the years I've known him. When we first joined the team, he had a big pair of shoes to fill. Our previous lead and Controller, Kamal, was regarded as one of the greatest programmers of his time. He's currently studying computer science at Carnegie Mellon. Since Kamal graduated two years ago, though, I believe Spencer hasn't just filled in his shoes; his feet are way too big for them now. He's improved so much over the years, I can't be anything but proud, as his friend, teammate, and Captain. He's an amazing programmer, and a heavily skilled Controller.

For the Ceremony, the drive teams of each team come to the field, so it gets pretty full. When we get there, about half the teams have arrived already. We check in, and stand in a line. Looking up at the stands, I see Spencer's parents yet again, but I don't see mine. Typical.

Spencer leans his head toward my ear. "I forgot to mention, but we may have a little problem," he whispers.

"What's up?"

"So..." he stammers, "I'm not exactly sure how to say this without it sounding really awful, but my parents saw what you did yesterday and now think I have a girlfriend."

My heart drops. *Girlfriend.* "This is a rough ask, but can we just pretend for a little longer? I'm sorry about how awkward this is, but they're just gonna be even more confused."

I guess he can't tell them that he was just helping me out because this isn't what friends usually do. Friends help each other out by finding other people to kiss.

I decide to make light of the situation. "You're not just saying this because you want me to kiss you again, right?"

He blushes. "No, I wouldn't want to make you uncomfortable. Just...if they come up to you, would you mind going along with it? I'll figure it out soon."

I have a lot of things I need to get figured out too. "Yeah, sure. I need to pay you back somehow."

"You said that last night." he remarks.

I'm going to go out on a whim and test the waters. "Yeah, but I think the whole event ended up being pretty mutual, so I still owe you one."

"What do you mean by that?" he asks.

I'm in too deep. Full send. "Well, you weren't the only one who wanted to kiss again last night. Paying you back wasn't my only intention."

I grab his arm. I glance in his direction, but he's not looking at me. Rather, he's staring into space as if he's trying to ignore me while his face is beet-red.

"Oh," is all he could muster. I hope this doesn't make me seem whorish.

I can't tell him the full truth. Not yet. I need a lot more time.

A loud shriek from the intercom startles the audience. "It's 10am on the dot, so let's get started with the Group Pairing Ceremony! All of our top sixteen teams are on the field, so let's see who'll be paired with who! Starting off with our fastest team, number 511317, Team Shell-Shocked!"

Shawn and his Driver, who I don't really know the name of, walk up to the announcer holding the microphone. "We're Team Shell-Shocked from Point Pleasant, and we'd like to select Team 904208 to Pair with us today."

"That's The Devils, the second-place seed from Smithville." the announcer booms.

Spencer and I make our way to the microphone. Shawn gives us an exasperated glare alongside a devilish smirk. Spencer leans in and whispers "you've got it, right?"

I nod as I grip the microphone. "We are The Devils from Smithville, and we'd like to respectfully decline this Pairing."

The crowd erupts in a roar. I immediately feel my phone buzzing from my pocket. I walk back to the group of other drive teams and pick up the call from Mr. D.

"What the hell is wrong with you two?" he screams from the stands. He's scaring the students who have the unfortunate fate of sitting next to him. "Are you *trying* to lose the best shot we've had of winning a competition in *years?*"

"We talked it over and decided they weren't the best fit for us."

"Best fit? The best fit is winning! If you sell this competition, I swear to *God–*"

"Sir, you've trusted my decisions in the past. Just trust me, okay?"

"You better have a mastermind plan in that inflated head of yours, Charlotte."

"I always do, sir." I hang up the phone. Spencer turns to me, terrified. I guess he could hear Mr. D through the phone. Or, rather, he could hear him from the stands.

"I'm so lucky Mr. Davis doesn't bother me as much as he bothers the rest of you guys." he says.

I chuckle. "He does it out of love…I think."

Shell-Shocked ends up picking the fourth-place team, ranked ten seconds below third but is way more consistent. "Damn, I wanted them." I mutter to myself.

"No you didn't," Spencer interjects.

"Hush, I'm trying to throw them off."

"Our second Group Captain is team 904208, The Devils!" the announcer booms as Spencer and I walk up to him yet again. I grab the microphone for the second time.

"We're The Devils from Smithville, and we'd like to ask team 905870 to work with us today."

The thirteenth-ranked seed, The Unicorns, runs up to the mic and accepts our Pairing without a second thought. I glance up at the stands and see Mr. D visibly fuming, his hands covering his face. My teammates' faces are full of shock. I feel my phone vibrating once again, and it's Vinny this time.

"I know you have something planned, but can we at least be filled in a little bit on what's going on? The Unicorns broke in their last Round! I think Mr. D is going to pop a blood vessel."

I smile. "Where's Jade?"

I watch him search through the stands. A grin forms on his face. "Char, you're a slick bastard, and I love you for it."

"Love you too." I reply as he ends the call. I blow a kiss to him and he reciprocates.

"When you guys offered help fix our robot, I didn't think *this* was why. Why'd you pick us, knowing we were broken?" asks their Driver, a young girl.

"Because we can fix it." I smile. "Our mechanical lead is working on it right now."

"What's our strategy then?"

"Keep doing what you've been doing. We took note on your constant improvement, and once Jade's done, your robot will be perfect. I mean, going from five minutes and ten seconds to three minutes and twenty-three seconds is no easy feat."

"Much appreciated. We haven't had much time to practice; our programmer finished the code three days ago."

"Believe me, I know how that feels," I laugh, elbowing Spencer.

The other six Groups have officially been paired. As an eight-team tournament usually goes, we will go against the seventh-ranked Group, in the fourth Round. This means we have a lot of time to make sure the Unicorns' robot is mechanically perfect. I'll check their electronics, too; I didn't see anything wrong earlier, but Jade's best work usually includes her breaking electrical my precious components.

Spencer and I, along with the Unicorns' drivers, make our way back to our Zones immediately after they say it's okay to do so. I surprisingly feel great, despite knowing my teammates are beyond pissed at me at the moment. Taking risks like these are necessary to make our team look great. I'm trying to build a legacy that we've never seen before.

"How are you feeling?" Spencer asks.

"Somehow, great." I reply.

"Wow, really? That's great to hear!" he smiles.

"Damn, is me being happy really that surprising?" I laugh.

"You tend to get stressed during times like these. I'm really glad you're keeping your composure right now. If this mood changes, please let me know, okay?"

I can't help but goofily smile at him. "Of course."

Jade's happily working away on the Unicorns' robot. "How are things looking?" I ask her.

"Give me five more minutes, and we'll be perfect." she replies, her head still stuck inside their bot.

"Great to hear." I can always count on Jade to do a great job, even on a robot she's never worked with before. Jade is the most competent mechanical lead I've ever worked with. Actually, she's the most competent mechanical lead I've ever *seen*. I've come across so many teams with mechanical leads that either don't know how to lead a team or don't actually know enough about hardware, to the point where they probably shouldn't have been considered lead in the first place. She's someone I can depend on, and she can depend on me for fixing the electronics she's broken.

"How did Mr. D take the news?" Jade inquires.

"About as bad as you'd expect." Spencer laughs.

"You guys should head to the stands and watch Shell-Shocked for me," she says, "I'll come out when we've tested this."

"Alrighty, let me know if there are any electrical issues." I reply.

Spencer and I walk out of The Zone and into the stands. I immediately lock eyes with his parents, who are sitting right next to our entire team. They wave, and signal for him to come up and sit with them. I keep walking in the other direction, but Spencer grabs my arm and I skid to a halt.

"I think they want you to come with me." he winces.

Everytime something awkward or embarrassing happens in my life, it comes to blow up in my face once again immediately after. I was hoping I'd have at least an hour before I had to stand in front of his parents. I feel like I'm representing myself in court for a murder charge I joked about.

His mom, Andrea Laine, stands up to hug him and give him a quick peck on the cheek. He quickly breaks free from the hug, sitting down on the bleacher in front of them. She takes a look at the bruise on his neck but doesn't say anything of it. Mrs. Laine's arms remain wide open, this time in my direction. I reluctantly accept the hug and wrap my arms around her astonishingly slim waist for a few seconds before breaking off and sitting next to Spencer. I can just *feel* Vinny taking photos of me right now.

"How are you doing, Charlotte?" his dad, Kean Laine, asks.

"Pretty alright, excited for the game today. How are you?"

"Still pretty shocked. You two surprised us yesterday."

"My bad," I nervously chuckle.

"Don't feel sorry, hun!" his mom exclaims. "I'm glad that my son has finally found someone, especially someone as smart as you are! I was getting a little worried that he didn't actually like girls."

Spencer's head falls into his hands out of sheer embarrassment. How odd. Nothing about Spencer's demeanor made me think he was gay. Maybe I'm just around Vinny too much, but I never would've thought anyone could've perceived him as such.

"Well, Mr. and Mrs. Laine, you've raised a very kind boy." I smile. I didn't have to lie about that one.

"Thank you. How come your parents aren't here, Charlotte? I'd love to have a chat with them." says his mom.

"Oh, they were busy this weekend," I lie. My parents have the mentality that once you've seen one competition, you've seen them all; they don't really understand that the game changes every year. As soon as I started being able to drive myself to competitions– no, as soon as I found a ride to competitions, they stopped attending, mostly because they didn't feel the need to. I'm okay with it, I guess. I feel like I perform worse when I have their eyes on me.

"Unfortunate. Maybe we'll catch them at the next one."

"Maybe." I turn my head to watch the first Round. In playoffs, the second member of the higher-seeded Group goes first, then the second member of the lower-seed, then the Captain of the lower-seed, and finally the Captain of the higher-seed. I've always found it to be a weird way to set it up, but it could be nailed down to simply saving the best for last.

As Shell-Shocked's pick, Team Rattlebones, finishes up their Round, Spencer leans in to whisper "hey, can I hold your hand? Y'know, to make this look a little more convincing."

My face flushes. Be normal, he just wants to make our relationship look more real to his parents. "Sure," I reply, my right hand slowly traveling to his left. Our fingers interlock, and I instantly forget about anything strategy related. I just want to grab his shirt, pull him closer, and kiss him until I forget how to breathe–

Oh my God, can you shut up and be normal!

I quickly turn away from his pretty face and focus on the important matters at hand. The second member of the eighth-seed, the sixteenth-place team, fumbled really hard. Their robot fell off of the monkey bars, and I saw bolts fly everywhere. They pressed the "Give Up" button, which allows them to end the match early, but adds extra time depending on how far you got through the Round. Since the monkey bars were toward the middle of the course, an extra two minutes were added to their time, giving them a measly time of five minutes and two seconds. Unfortunately, I doubt this first part of the bracket will be an underdog story.

The eighth Group's Captain, Firecracker Robotics, didn't perform very well either. Their Driver doesn't look like they're doing too well. I can see it in their eyes; the sense of dread that being in the eighth Group entails. I know they wanted to get picked. I know exactly how it feels to be good enough to be a Captain, but not good enough to be the Captain of a high-ranked Group. It's a very familiar feeling; making it to playoffs and only being able to perform once before your title is completely stripped away by a powerhouse of a team.

It's finally Shell-Shocked's turn. I watch as Shawn brings their stuff to the Driver's Table as his Driver and Transporter bring the robot to the field. I see his smug face, an expression that can only be held by someone who's completely convinced they have this competition in the bag. Maybe they do. I hope not.

They end up completely crushing their Round, finishing in three minutes flat. While it's not their best, it's just enough to eliminate the eighth Group without a second thought. I always felt bad about the eighth Group, especially as someone who has been a member many times.

Round two of the bracket is always the most fun to watch: Four against Five. Watching the two Groups with the most even stats compete against each other is always so fun. This was the closest playoff bracket I have ever seen this early; Four beats Five with an average two seconds lower. I know that had to have hurt the Captain of Five. Based on personal experience, I'd rather lose by thirty seconds than one second.

The next part of the bracket is a *huge* upset. The Captain of the third Group broke down during their run time, and Group six ends up clutching the win. My team is sitting next to theirs in the stands, and I saw who I assume is their Captain sobbing. Playoffs are an awful time. If you let the tribulations of competing get to you, the downward spiral is inevitable. It's insane how many students let a silly robot competition dictate their mental state for months. I'm one of them.

"We need to head out," Spencer says, stand up. He lifts me up with him, entirely on accident. We've been holding hands for about an hour at this point. I've been a big fan. I wonder if my hands are too sweaty.

He doesn't let go of my hand as we make our way down the bleachers. I notice Maggie running down as soon as she notices us. As the last team to perform, we have time before we need to get there, but I'd like to go through my checklist first. No matter what, it needs to be gone through. I will *never* let us go on without going through it.

We quickly make it to The Zone and I dart to our robot, letting go of Spencer's hand in the process. I grab a test battery, turn it on, shake it around, and press critical components. Everything's good from what I can see. I look up at the Unicorns wheeling their robot out. "How's everything?" I ask.

"Your mechanical lead did an amazing job! We're working perfectly now. Thank you so much!" the driver exclaims.

"Of course, don't mention it. Do great out there, okay?"

"Yep!"

I turn to Spencer. "It's nice to see fresh faces on these drive teams. It's not something you see all too often."

"I think you've just been a Driver for a while." he replies.

"Yeah, yeah, I'm old."

"No, you're experienced."

"What you're saying is I'm *geriatric!*"

"I'd never say that!" he turns away. I can tell he's smiling with that goofy smile I've grown so fond of. Too fond.

Maggie begins to wheel the robot cart toward the field. Spencer and I trail behind, our hands gravitating toward each others. "You know, my parents aren't here." he says calmly, a light pink dusting his cheeks.

"Gotta practice before you perform, right?" I grin.

His hand squeezes mine tighter after I say that. Wow, I'm really being obvious here. I'm leaving nothing to interpretation. I'm shocked at my confidence with this whole situation. Maybe everything that happened last night actually *helped* me. Maybe it wasn't an excuse and I really needed to let off some steam.

We make it to the field, still hand-in-hand. I watch as Vinny takes another opportunity to take a picture, as if I wouldn't notice. My groupchat with him and Jade is probably full of pictures of us sitting with his parents. I'll deal with them when I drive him and Jade home later.

The second team of Group seven did…okay. Not great, but not as awful as some of the teams I've seen. On the contrary, The Unicorns, who went before them, did absolutely *amazing*.

The announcer takes no time to comment on their performance. "In a change of direction, The Unicorns' robot 'Pegasus' completely surpassed yesterday's records! With an outstanding time of three minutes and twenty seconds, they've outperformed many teams ranked above them!"

I turn to look at Jade, whose smile is going to turn the entire stadium blind. I'm so proud of her. She's worked so hard to become our mechanical lead, and everything's paid off so far. I want us to be known as the team that other teams immediately go to when they need help.

Group Seven's Captain goes next, and they also perform very well, also breaking their record from yesterday. Unfortunately, with how their pick and our pick performed, it's going to be particularly easy for us to win.

"How are you feeling?" Spencer asks, finally letting go of my hand as he grabs the laptop and controllers from the robot cart. I suddenly feel cold.

"The pit in my stomach is smaller than usual. You?"

"I feel amazing."

"Seems like you always do."

"With you by my side, how else am I supposed to feel?" he blurts out. After noticing what he said, he runs away to the Driver's Table, visibly embarrassed.

Maggie and I pick up the robot and slowly lower it to the exact position we've had it this entire competition. There's a few different orientations, but we prefer the simple way, placing the robot straight and in the middle of the line.

I walk back and greet Spencer at the Driver's Table. "Ready, partner?" he asks.

"As always." I smile.

"Here comes our second-placed team, The Devils, with their robot 'Ross!' I'm not sure where that name originates from, but it's an interesting one! Three, two, one, GO!"

We begin. Driving is very simple, with the hardest part being focusing. My mind is always ten steps ahead from my hands on my controller. I always know what I'm doing next, what Spencer's doing next, and what's coming next at us. It's an art that I've been practicing ever since my freshman year of high school. I wouldn't say I've mastered it or anything, but I've come quite close.

We balance. Round ends. I look up at the clock: two minutes and fifty-eight seconds. We beat our record. We're advancing to the next round.

"Great job, Charlotte!" Spencer exclaims as he gives me a high-five.

"Same to you! You did amazing!" I smile.

"Group Two will be facing off against Group Six in Round six of our playoff tournament!" the announcer booms.

"We've got this," he whispers.

"Of course we do."

My team leaves the stands, meaning that pizza is here. Man, I've been looking forward to this lunch the entire weekend. Pizza and competitions go as well as Spencer and I do…as Driver and Controller, of course. We make one hell of a team. Just a team, nothing more.

While making our way to the cafeteria, I see Mr. Davis standing by the door, looking at his phone. We catch his eye, and he puts his phone away. "See how you should trust me?" I ask.

"Don't get too cocky yet," he replies coldly, "your average was a second off of Group One's. You can still lose."

"We'll do better next time, I promise."

"I hope so."

Spencer and I dart to the cafeteria where Jade and Vinny left us two seats. I grab two slices of pepperoni pizza and sit down next to Vinny. Spencer sits with Jade.

"How did the presentation go?" I ask Vinny.

"It went really well, the judges really liked what I had to say. You guys should definitely try to make it at district champs."

"I don't think I would've said anything useful with how stressful today has been." says Spencer.

"Did you guys like our first Round?" I ask.

"Yeah, you guys did really good." Vinny muffles, his mouth full.

"I agree. I was impressed the entire time. The Unicorns did really well too."

"Great pick on your part, Charlotte." says Spencer.

"It was a group decision." I reply.

"Yeah, but you were adamant about them. I didn't see it at first, but once I looked at their robot, I saw that they had a lot of potential locked behind a wall of inexperience."

That's one way to put it, Jade. Talk about being unprofessional.

"Well, how's Group six looking, in your opinion?" Vinny asks.

"They only won because Group three broke down," I point out, "they didn't actually do *that* good."

"Then we should have it in the bag, right?"

"Totally."

The lunchtime conversation transitions from playoffs to school, which we unfortunately have tomorrow. We have a calc quiz as soon as school starts, and believe me, I'm not excited. I haven't studied a bit; I'll study when I get home and can wash the competition excitement off of me.

Benji runs through the cafeteria, right toward our table. As a devout vegan, he never joins us for pizza, and instead sits in the stands and continues watching. Upon reaching our table, he grabs my shoulders and immediately starts shaking me back and forth, causing me to fall to the ground.

"What the hell is up with you?" Vinny asks.

"Group One just lost to Group Four," he pants.

I immediately stand up. "Holy shit, are you serious?" I exclaim.

"Go see for yourself. Shell's pick had to hit the buzzer a minute in. There's no way they come back from that."

I take one last glance at my half-eaten pizza crust. I've had enough of my lunch. I grab Spencer, whose plate is completely clean, by his arm. "We need to go now."

He agrees. Hand in hand, alongside Benji, we sprint to the stands to see Shell-Shocked performing their Round. I look at the times on the screen:

Group Four AVG 3:28, Group One AVG 6:12.

Holy shit. Shell-Shocked would have to finish their Round in mere seconds if they wanted to beat Group four. They're going to be eliminated, and our chances of winning skyrocketed.

They finished with a record-breaking 2:56, but it wasn't nearly enough for them to win. Group One has officially been eliminated.

As soon as their Round ends, Spencer and I book it to The Zone to prepare our robot for our next Round. Maggie is already there, reading a webcomic on her phone. Upon seeing us, she stands up and prepares the robot cart. I go through my little checklist, and everything looks pretty good.

The three of us make it to the field, just in time for The Unicorns to appear. They completed their round in three minutes and seventeen seconds, a three-second improvement from their last Round. I'm so happy. All of our collective hard work is paying off just like I planned.

Group Four ends with a 3:28 average. As long as we are under that, we are going to win. We haven't been that slow this entire competition.

We pull this next round off with a 2:57, which is better than we did previously, but not as good as Shell-Shocked. Wait, who cares about Shell-Shocked? They're eliminated!

I'm sure Shawn is *pissed* right now. I wouldn't want to be his Pair.

"Do you see that, Charlotte? We're going to *finals!*" Spencer exclaims as we follow Maggie with the robot.

"I can't believe it!" I reply, mimicking his enthusiasm.

Thankfully, we have a fifteen-minute break before finals, which Spencer and I spend sitting in our Zone, watching the teams around us pack up. While chatting about who knows what, Shawn barges into our Zone.

"Congrats on making it to finals. I wish we were the ones going against you," he says.

"Thanks," I reply, "you guys did really good. It's a shame we didn't face off in the end."

"Yeah, because we definitely would've won." he says with a snarkiness to his tone.

"We'll see about that in two weeks," Spencer chimes, referencing our next competition.

Shawn walks away, scoffing. I turn to Spencer and smile. "I'm glad you're not like that."

"Yeah, me too." he chuckles.

We're left to stare at nothing but each other. The outside world slows down and hums at a beat similar to the one in my heart. Short, fast, and loud. We're sitting a few inches away from each other, our eyes locked. There's a million reasons why this is completely wrong, but none of them matter to me at this point. I want to do it. I *need* to do it.

I kiss him again. Quickly, less than three seconds, but it satisfied my craving. As I break free, he stares bewildered, his face a light shade of pink.

I come to my senses. "Shit, I'm so sorry, I don't know why I did that–"

I'm interrupted by him kissing me back. His hand grazes mine as he pushes closer to me. After about five seconds, he lets go and smiles, his face a darker shade than before.

"Sometimes it's easier to not think about it now and deal with the embarrassment later." he whispers.

I laugh. "I like the way you think."

"Alright, you freaks, time for finals." Vinny interrupts. It's probably for the better, because I don't know if I would've been able to control myself, even around all of these people. I would've kissed him again, and again, and again...

We immediately stand up from the floor of our Zone. Maggie enters and grabs the robot cart as I do my checks yet again. Everything's good. We've got this. We can do this. I can do this.

It's a group effort if we win, but it's my fault if we lose.

"How are you feeling?" Spencer asks, as he always does.

"Better than I was a few minutes ago." I wink.

"You're welcome, I guess," he mutters, "if that's what you were referring to, I mean..."

We make our way to the field for the last time today. We need to make this next Round our best Round ever. It's what we need.

Since we are technically the lower-ranked seed in the finals, we go third instead of last, which is completely fine. I don't really like the idea of having to wait for the other team's results, but what can I really do about it?

Group Four's pick finishes their Round in three minutes and fifteen seconds, faster than the Unicorns have ever done. I can feel the pit in my stomach return and grow quickly. It's okay, we can make up for any time they lose us. We've got this. I can't let the pick of our opponent affect me too much.

Much to my surprise, The Unicorns finish their Round in three minutes and sixteen seconds. Enough for us to break the margin. Once it's over, I run to their Driver and give them a huge hug.

"You guys did great!" I exclaim.

"Thank you, we couldn't have done it without you!" she responds.

Music to my ears.

Maggie and I drop the robot off on the field, the same way we have so many times over this weekend. I walk over to Spencer, whose smile could blind anyone in a three-mile radius.

"Ready, partner?" he asks.

"As always."

We're off. I am in my element. We need to win this. Every movement is calculated, every command to Spencer is fluid. As we've done for years, we have merged into one person, the ultimate robot operator. Months of constant practice, late nights, and missed assignments lead up to this one very moment. We made it this far; we can't back out now.

We clear the monkey bars like it's nobody's business and balance almost immediately. As soon as the buzzer goes off, I throw my controller at the Driver's Table and look at the timer. Two minutes and fifty-four seconds. *Holy shit.*

I turn to Spencer. "We did it," he whispers.

"Not yet, but we're close."

We say nothing else while loading Ross back onto the robot cart. We walk in silence, and as soon as the cart is dropped off at our Zone, we book it to the stands to watch Group Four's Captain, The Purple Dragons, perform.

Vinny greets me with a hug. "Char, that was amazing!" he exclaims.

He looks up at Spencer. "You did great too, but I'm sure you don't want a hug."

"I wouldn't mind." Spencer replies, adding onto our hug.

As the starting buzzer begins, we rush to sit down and watch. I can tell the stress is getting to their drive team; I can see it in their eyes. They mess up. They almost crash. Balancing takes a lot longer than it has.

The timer stops after three minutes and one second. Their Controller falls to the floor. They've lost.

More importantly, we've won.

We've won.

We.

Have.

Won.

I instantly stand up, jumping up and down uncontrollably. Spencer tags along, and I hug him so tight we almost fall over and down the bleachers. Imaginary confetti falls from the sky. I can't believe it. We won our first competition in over a decade.

I turn to Mr. D, who's trying to hide his excitement. I give him a devilish grin. "Do you have anything left to say?" I ask.

"Nope, guess you proved me wrong," he mutters. What an old geezer. I've never heard him admit he was wrong before.

The game announcer grabs medals and a giant trophy from a box. "The winner of this event is Group Two, Captained by Team 904208, The Devils!" he booms as we run down the steps to grab our rewards, Spencer and I first in line.

The crew hangs our medals on our necks, and Spencer grabs the trophy. We wait for the rest of our team to get their medals before we pose for a photo that'll definitely go in our yearbook this year. Spencer and I kneel down in the very front, holding the trophy together. Vinny is standing to my right, and Jade stands like a statue to Spencer's left. The camera flashes, and everything is over, until I see a lanky figure out of the corner of my eye.

God, does she have to ruin every moment?

Spencer pokes my shoulder and points in Sylvia's direction. "Do you want me to do anything?" he asks.

"Come with me." I mutter, as we take the trophy over to the other side of the bleachers, where she stands.

I can see she's pissed as I come closer. She wanted this trophy more than anyone else, and we won it just as she graduated. I feel empathetic for her, but not overly empathetic. We worked hard for this.

"Why the hell are you bringing that stupid trophy over here?" she snarls. "Are you just trying to rub it in that you're better than me? This is low, even for you, *Charlotte.*"

I take a deep breath. I've been thinking about what I would say if I saw her again today. Any waking moment I wasn't thinking about Spencer or robotics, I was thinking about her and all of the heartwrenching statements I could spit out. I've been waiting for this; it's the perfect combination of cringey and meaningful. Here goes.

"I will soon forget the color of your eyes, Sylvia." I turn and walk away.

Later on, in the car with Vinny and Jade, I tell them about the whole interaction. "That probably hurt her like hell," Jade says.

"Good, she deserves it after all she put Char through. How do you feel, Char?" Vinny asks.

"A lot better, honestly, like something has been mostly lifted off my shoulders. It's still there, but less pressure is placed on me."

"Great. Now, you can focus about the issue at hand. Rather, the boy at hand." Jade snickers.

"Oh, dear." I sigh.

"Now that she's kinda out of your mind, you should use this extra time to figure out how you're going to ask Spencer out."

"Shouldn't I wait until robotics season is over?"

"Definitely not! This is the best time."

"Ugh," I groan, "It feels like there's a divorce in my heart, and half of my love is going to robotics, the other half to him."

"Damn, none for us?" Vinny asks.

"You two are on a completely different plane of my love."

Chapter Eleven
Charlotte

Laid down in the backseat of a Ford Focus. Empty highway. No one in the driver's seat, but we're cruising down the highway. Nobody in sight. Unknown highway, nothing around for miles. Straightaway. Nobody is driving, but we rapidly accelerate through the night.

I open my eyes to see the bottom of the seatbelt is holding me in place. A shadow of a woman rests over me, her lanky figure pressed above mine. She's yelling, been yelling for a while it seems. I couldn't make out what she was saying until now. I look down. Where the hell is my shirt?

"You bitch! How could you do this to me?" she screams, shaking my eardrums with every note. This feels all too familiar.

"What did I do?" I ask, leaving out the almost necessary "this time".

*"You know what you did! You're using that…*man…*to get in my head! You're using him! You just want to see me suffer! You're with him so I suffer!*

"What is he that I'm not? I loved you. I loved you for two long, grueling years, and this is how you repay me? I did so much for you. I drove you places. I listened to you when you bitched and moaned for hours. This is the thanks I get? You getting with a man six months after we broke up? What does he have that I don't, other than a dick!"

I ponder over what I'm going to say in response. I need to be an asshole. I need to be cruel. I need to say something that I would have never said to her while we were together. A line stuck out to me from a movie I saw last night with Vinny. I'm going to slightly paraphrase it.

"He tastes like you, but sweeter."

She screams again, raises her hand, and smacks the everloving shit out of me, waking me up in the process.

My face stings, even though no one really hit me. As I lie here in the company of none but desperation, I ponder over the decisions I've made to leave me in this melancholy state of mind. Most people don't have dreams about their exes that force them into a slump for the rest of the morning. This isn't normal. I'm not normal. I just want to be normal.

I roll out of bed and onto the floor. My alarm doesn't go off for another hour, but I went to bed at 9pm last night for the first time in years, so I feel fine. I'll just sit in Vinny's house while I wait for him to get ready. His parents love me. At least, they seem like they do.

I slowly get up and make my way to my bathroom, where I quickly strip down and turn on the shower to medium heat, preparing to wash the dream I just had down the drain. Sometimes I wish I was an alcoholic; it seems like it's a lot easier to forget about certain people when there's an insurmountable amount of booze in your system. Too bad drinking is also awful for your brain, and it's kinda all I have. I'll probably try it at some point though.

After my warm shower, I quickly dry off and prepare for my daily weigh-in. I used to do this because I forced myself to lose weight in my junior year of high school, and now it's one of the only routines I have left. It's toxic to continue, but I can't stop because of how connected I am with it. It's who I am at this point.

"November 11th: XXX"

I throw on my clothes for the day. Today is a Wednesday, which has nothing to do with my outfit, but I'd like to pretend it does. I checked the weather this morning, and it's pretty warm for a mid-November day, with highs around 63 degrees, so my outfit consists of a pair of dark blue low-rise jeans, a white tank-top, and an oversized navy blue zip-up jacket. I add my white socks, perfectly cuffed. A simple outfit, nothing special, but I like it.

I grab my backpack and run downstairs, grabbing a Sugar-Free Red Bull from the fridge and a lunch bag my mom packed from the counter. She hasn't packed lunch for me in years, but she's worried about me not eating due to competition stress. I don't mind, I've secretly missed her lunches.

Our next competition is this weekend, and I'm beyond excited for it. This is the Mid-Atlantic District Championships, essentially a crucially important competition. Any team that qualifies for playoffs at the district event automatically qualifies for District Champs, but because of our shocking win two weeks ago, we've caught the eyes of teams in Delaware and Pennsylvania. I've even seen people online, from all parts of the country, discussing our robot and performance. I'm loving all of the attention, but it also stings for some reason.

I grab my keys, toss my Converse on, and walk out the door to my car. It's a lot colder than my weather app insinuated, but I'll be fine for the day. I throw my stuff in the backseat and leave for Vinny's house, which is about a ten-minute drive away. While driving, I listen to loud music to distract me from my awful pre-morning. I crack open my Red Bull at a stoplight and take a swig. I should've drank water beforehand; the Red Bull hurts going down. It tastes like anger.

I pull into Vinny's driveway nearly an hour before I'm supposed to. I turn off my car, lock everything up, and knock on his front door. His mom opens it and smiles at the sight of me. "Good morning, Charlotte. Always lovely to see you. Early start today?"

"Yeah, woke up early. Is it okay if I come in?" I ask.

"Sure. He's upstairs if you want to go up there."

Vinny's parents are well aware of his orientation, so they've never been worried about me hanging out with him at any time of day. They know we're not getting up to anything sinister up there. I could never think of Vinny in that way.

I take my shoes off and jog up the stairs to Vinny's room. His is the first room on the left, while his brother's is on the right. I knock on his door six times, each one louder than the last. The bathroom door opens, and Vinny pops out with a toothbrush in his mouth and a towel around his waist. "What are you doing here so early?" he asks, completely unfazed.

"Woke up early. Nightmare." I reply.

"You can go in, I'll be done in here in a few," he says, closing the bathroom door behind him. I open the door to his pristinely clean room and sit in his fancy desk chair, checking my phone for any emails or texts. Nothing other than spam emails and messages from our robotics team's chat app, talking about which parent is picking up the pizza for this Sunday. I don't care who picks it up as long as we get pizza.

Vinny walks into his room, the towel still stuck to him. "Close your eyes for, like, a minute." he says. I swivel his chair around to face the wall and close my eyes.

I sit like this for five minutes until he turns me around and laughs. "I've been done for a while now, but I wanted to see how long it would take for you to check."

"Dude, remember last time I checked before you said you were ready? I saw a lot of you I definitely shouldn't have."

"Oh yeah." Vinny and I have seen a lot more of each other than we'd like to admit. I guess that's just how best friends are, though. Probably.

He pushes me off of his chair and continues to get ready, throwing all of his expensive creams and serums onto his face. I'm honestly jealous of how perfect his skin is; I mean, I definitely don't do as much as he does, but I'm jealous of the amount of effort that he is willing to put in for healthy skin.

"So, tell me about the dream you had," he says in between applications.

"Well," I sigh, "I was in the back of her car, she was screaming at me, I essentially said that Spencer was better than her, and she smacked me so hard I woke up from it."

"Jeez. How are you and Spencer, by the way?"

"Pretty alright. I think a majority of the tension from comp has died down, and we've gone back to normal. I've been trying to flirt with him a bit more, though, and I think it's going well."

"Does he notice?"

"Half the time, yeah. I can tell when he notices because he gets visibly flustered. Sometimes it seems like he doesn't register it."

"Guys are just like that sometimes," he groans.

"Yeah, unfortunately."

He finishes getting ready, and the two of us go back to my car and drive to school.

The ride is silent for the first few minutes. "You're playing the playlist you play when you're not feeling well. What's up?" Vinny says.

"I don't feel too great, really," I reply, "I feel kinda empty."

"Is it because of the dream you had?"

"Maybe. It's definitely a part of it, but who's to say."

"I see." He pulls out his phone and sends a text.

"Who are you texting?" I ask.

"Jade is asking for the slides that we're going to use for judge interviews this weekend."

"Gotcha."

I park in our parking spot and we enter the building, chatting about who knows what. Probably the weather. It feels even colder before; maybe it's the actual temperature, maybe it's my mindset.

My first two classes of the day aren't really special; multivariable calculus was just full of lectures and notes, and we had a workshop day in our poetry class, which was essentially an entire period of working on writing poems for our next project. I find it hard to write poems, because every single idea I come up with is an idea that has previously existed. The poem is required to be sonnet-length or so, and it's due next week. I'll probably work on it at the hotel this weekend.

While Vinny, Jade and I walk down the hallway to our lunch table outside, my phone buzzes from my pocket. I pull it out and see that Spencer is calling me for some reason. "Hello?"

"Hey, the robot's acting weird, can you come and take a look at it?"

Typical Spencer nonsense. "Sure, give me a few minutes to get there."

"Thanks!"

I hang up. "Spencer broke the robot again. I might not be joining you guys for lunch today."

"That's fine," Jade says, "we'll sit in my car for lunch today. It's too cold to sit outside."

"Alrighty, I might join you later."

"Yeah, right," Vinny snickers.

We part ways as Vinny and Jade exit the building and I keep going forward to the robotics room. I enter the room and see Spencer hunched over his laptop. He's wearing a dark purple hoodie and light-wash jeans. I look at the robot, and everything is green. No issues at all.

"I thought you said there was something wrong." I say.

He closes his laptop and stands up, facing me. "There is something wrong, but it's not on the robot."

"What are you talking about?"

"Vinny said you weren't feeling well and asked me to talk to you. Is everything okay?"

That sly bastard. I knew he wasn't texting Jade about the slides. She never cares about the slides. "I'm fine."

"Are you sure? You look like you haven't slept well in days. I've noticed for a while, but I didn't think it was my place to ask."

"I think I'm okay."

"Promise?"

"Yeah."

"I want to believe you. Would you still like a hug?" He extends his arms. This is one of the few times I've seen him without a smile on his face. He looks concerned.

"Sure," I say, accepting his hug. He's warm and soft to the touch. As he wraps his arms around me, I melt into him. I can feel my eyes start to water. I accept my fate.

"I'm not okay, I promise," I mutter into his chest.

"That's what I thought. Care to tell me about it?"

I want to hug him for the rest of lunch. "If I tell you, do you promise to not let me go?"

"Absolutely. Would you like to sit down on the bench?" he asks, referring to the bench we have in the corner of the room, right next to the desk. I've slept on it before a few times during late meetings.

"Sure," I reply, and we make our way to the bench without letting go. He sits down on the right side of the bench, hone leg bent and parallel to the wide side of the bench and the other straight, his foot tapping the floor. I sit between his legs, resting mine on the rest of the bench. He wraps his arms around me as I lean back into his chest. This is *way* too intimate for our relationship status, but I couldn't care less.

I tell him everything. I talk about my nightmares about Sylvia, the one I had this morning (without saying that he was involved), and just about everything else. I mentioned the stress about this weekend and classes and the fact that college decisions are coming soon. Everything spills out, even stuff I haven't told Vinny yet. While I spew my nonsense, he listens intently, not saying a word.

I finish my rant by complaining about my therapists' lack of availability for this week. "Sorry to dump all of this on you," I mutter.

"It's no problem at all! Do you feel better in any way after telling me?"

"I think so. Thank you for listening."

"Anytime."

I sit up so we're now at matching eye levels. "Spencer, you've done so much for me and I feel like I've done nothing for you. Is there anything I can do to pay you back?"

He blushes. "Uh, I don't think so, I didn't come here expecting to be paid back."

He's so pretty when he blushes. I want to kiss him. It made me feel better in the past, it'll make me feel better now, right? It can't hurt to try.

I want to ask him out. I want to confess to him right here, right now. I want to tell him to his face just how amazing and pretty he is and how much I want to be his *actual* girlfriend, not just the imaginary one I've been pretending to be for the past few weeks. I *should* just do it.

I *can't*. I'm too scared. I'll deal with those feelings later.

I'd rather do something easier, and arguably more fun.

I readjust myself so that I'm sitting on top of him. He stares at me with disbelief, his mouth agape. "Are you sure there's no way I can pay you back?" I ask with a grin.

He pauses. "Why do you always want to pay me back for stuff? I feel like I don't really deserve it right now. I just wanted to help. I don't want you to think I have bad intentions."

"Of course you don't It's just the best excuse I can think of."

"So you…aren't doing this to 'pay me back'."

"Guess not."

He sighs softly, a confused smile forming. "What if someone walks in?"

I stand up and lock the door I came in from. The door that leads to the parking lot is always locked, so I don't worry about that one.

I turn back to Spencer, who's in the same bewildered state I left him in. "Looks like that's not a problem, you think?"

"Is this something you want?" he asks.

I nod. "I do. Is this something you want?"

"Charlotte, I'd be the biggest idiot in the world if I said no."

I jump back onto him, my thighs completely surrounding his. I grab him by his hoodie and pull him into an awfully sloppy but needy kiss. I needed this. Jeez, I'm such a teenage dirtbag.

He wraps his arms around my waist, pulling me close as I run through his hair with my hands. The muffled sounds he makes control how fast and rough I kiss him. I am in my element. Sylvia who?

After a few minutes, he breaks free. "Can I pay you back for the hickey you gave me back then?"

My eyes widen. All I can muster is an excited "sure".

He slowly unzips my jacket, revealing my neck and collarbones alongside my tank top. "Let me know if I'm hurting you, I looked up how to do it when I got back from comp."

What a nerd. "I'll double-tap."

He pulls me back in, his lips pressing against the left side of my neck. I dig my face into his shoulder and bite down on his hood to avoid making loud enough sounds that anyone in the hallway could hear us. Thankfully, the room right next to ours is the band room, so it's more likely that they'll hear someone practicing something awful. After about thirty seconds, he lets go, and my neck begins to sting. After staring at my neck for a bit too long, he zips my jacket up enough to where you can no longer see the bruise.

I sit up and take a look at him. The light in his eyes makes him look starstruck. "Charlotte, you are so pretty," he mutters.

"I can say the same about you."

"You think so?"

"Definitely," I say as I pull him back into a kiss. I press my body into his and watch as his eyes roll backward. I keep my left hand pressed against his head, running through his hair, while my right hand begins moving on to bigger things, also known as the rest of him. He takes my movement as his cue to start rubbing my back.

Y'know, I think he's only doing stuff that I've done to him. He's never gone further than what I've done. It seems like he's scared to do anything I haven't proven is okay, which definitely seems like something he'd do. I really respect that; he's such a gentleman.

My stomach growls. I break free to breathe, and I check my watch. We have fifteen minutes until lunch is over, and I finally have a lunch to eat. He opens his eyes and stares in my direction, smiling toothily with glazed, starry eyes.

"I'd love to continue, but I should probably eat my lunch." I whisper.

"Of course," he replies as I get off of him. He adjusts himself and sits up, leaning on the wall, his legs turned and stretched across the rest of the bench. He pulls out his phone, happily typing away, the light in his eyes persisting.

I grab my lunch bag and pull out the sandwich my mom packed for me: pork roll, egg, and cheese on a plain bagel. A New Jersey staple as well as my favorite sandwich of all time. I don't care about how fatty it is; it's a delicacy that I will indulge in.

While eating my glorious sandwich, I use my non-eating hand to check any messages that could've accumulated over the time I've been busy. Nothing but a text from Vinny reading *"Looks like the robot is getting fixed,"* alongside a video of him trying to open the door to the robotics room, much to no avail. I reply with a quick *"You're a dog."*

Jade quickly responds with *"Are you feeling better?"*

"Yeah..."

"Then that's all that matters. If you're not going to do something about this little crush of yours, we will."

Vinny chimes in with *"Wouldn't call it little"*, adding a smiley emoji.

I finish my sandwich of pure bliss. I am incredibly full, so I don't bring out the baby carrots or apple slices my mom packed alongside my sandwich. I'll probably eat those during Stats today. That teacher couldn't possibly care less about what I do.

After a few more minutes of sitting in silence, the bell rings. I quickly sit up, close my lunch bag, and grab my backpack. Spencer stands up to grab his stuff as well. Before we leave, he asks, "I may be being greedy, but can I kiss you again?"

I nervously chuckle. "Gosh, I wish, but I probably taste like pork roll and egg."

"I don't care," he says, grabbing my shoulders and giving me a quick peck. "You taste like you, and that's all I care about."

That was smooth. Smoother than he presumably expected, because after saying that, he immediately turned away, his face flushed once again. I wonder what goes on in his head when he says something like that.

We unlock the door and leave the robotics room. We walk side-by-side in pure, mildly awkward silence. I find myself looking at him more often than I usually do. He's smiling for no reason at all, like he always does, but this time it's with a sort of shine I've never seen before. The glimmer in his eyes hasn't left. He looks like when you're trying to hide that your heart is beating faster than it's supposed to. It makes me think something I never would've thought of before.

I'm starting to think he might kinda like me back.

Chapter Twelve
Spencer

My love is like a poem. It's long, convoluted, awfully depressing, and too dramatic for my own good. It's hard to decipher but can be simplified to a short statement: I am head over heels for a girl who is confusing the hell out of me right now.

I mean, I can kinda understand the first time everything happened, as we were both stressed and in need of letting off some steam, but we've kissed more than a few times since then, and it's getting to the point where I feel like we've crossed the murky line of being friends and arrived somewhere before the line of a real relationship. I feel nothing but pure and utter confusion.

I think back to what she said on the Sunday of our last competition: *"you weren't the only one who wanted to kiss again last night...paying you back wasn't my only motivation"*. I get that it wasn't transactional, but I'm now left to wonder whether she actually likes me or just likes kissing me. I'm okay with both, but I'd prefer the first one a million times over. The latter would, truthfully, kill me.

If I had any ounce of confidence that she was doing these things because she was romantically interested in me, I'd ask her out immediately, but I honestly can't tell. Maybe I'm just the biggest idiot in the world, jumping to conclusions in the false hope that the girl I've loved for years could actually love me back.

Sitting in my car, waiting for Maggie to finish packing for our competition this weekend, I scribble away in my journal. I've been drafting poems that I would love to give Charlotte if I had the chance. I'm a huge poetry guy, so it would be doing myself an injustice if I didn't write her one…as if I've never written any poems for her. Almost all of the poems I've doodled into my notebooks have been about my love for her, with the rest about loneliness. God, I'm such a mess. Such a hopeless romantic. Nothing steals the magic from writing the way thinking about it does.

Well, I might not *actually* be hopeless, but I can't really be sure.

My passenger's side door swings open and I immediately toss my poetry book into the backseat. Maggie waves hello, a pink overnight bag in her hand and an absolutely stuffed grey backpack hanging on her shoulders. "Whatcha writing? Love letters?" she asks slyly.

"No." I pause. "Yeah."

She throws her backpack on the floor of the passenger's seat and tosses her overnight bag in the back, next to all my stuff. She sits down and closes the door as I turn my car back on and start my GPS to the hotel we're staying at this weekend. This venue is about an hour and a half away from our school, in some random town in Delaware, so we had to stay the night. I wasn't gonna drive back and forth the entire weekend, and neither was anyone else on my team.

"A little birdie told me you and Charlotte were locked in the robotics room on Wednesday," Maggie says as we leave her neighborhood.

My muscles instantly tense up. I grip the steering wheel as if I'm prepared to crash. "Who told you that?"

"Gabe was looking for a power tool to bring to his class, but the room was locked. He heard two distinguishable voices."

Gabe is a sophomore on the mechanical team, with piercing blue eyes and platinum blond hair. He's freakishly tall, tall enough that he probably gets harassed by the basketball coaches on the daily. He doesn't like sports, though; he'd much rather be in the robotics room. He's like me if I wasn't 5'9.

I recall what we did on Wednesday, but my thoughts are shrouded by the memories of the out-of-body reactions I felt. I was trying to be quiet but it was difficult. I specifically think of when we first started kissing and she pressed her entire body into me. I had an otherworldly reaction; I swear I went blind for a moment. "What did he say he heard?" I ask.

"He said he just heard you guys talking and packing up. It was about when the bell rang."

"Oh, good."

She pouts. "Why do you ask? What the hell were you two doing in there?"

"Nothing out of the ordinary!" I snap.

"Why was the door locked, then?"

"Must've been an accident. I swear, we didn't do anything gross."

She sighs into a quick laugh. "Honestly, I have to believe you, because I know damn well Spencer Laine wouldn't have the balls to hook up in the robotics room. Charlotte maybe, but not you."

Full name is a little much for a statement that vulgar. "I don't know whether to be embarrassed or proud of that."

"Well, just goes to show that you're one of the most normal guys at this school." She holders her fingers up and bends them at the word "normal". "If I was into guys, and maybe a few years older, you'd be my top pick."

What a compliment, I guess. "Why do you say that?"

"Well, you're a cute guy, you have good music taste, and you're not a creep *or* a loser. You know how hard it is to find all of those in one *person*, let alone a teenage boy?"

Second time being called by a girl, this time from a lesbian."I'm flattered."

Maggie is a great friend to have around. Even though her and I both play for the same team, she's not a threat to me, because she has her own girls to go for. In this sense, Charlotte and I are very similar, both having an opposite-gendered homosexual voice of reason.

"Anyways, are you two dating yet? I have a bet with, like, three different people."

"No, not yet, I'm waiting on the right time."

"Oh come *on,* Spencer. It's obvious at this point that the girl likes you, just tie the knot!"

"Wait, what are you betting on?"

"Well, Gabe says you're never gonna do it. Benji thinks you'll do it this weekend and Connor says it's gonna happen in December, right before World Champs. I, personally, think it'll happen *at* World Champs, if we qualify."

"I'll see what I can do, I guess," I chuckle, "how much are you betting?"

"Twenty bucks each."

“If you win, do I get half of your winnings?”

“You can get a third.”

“I’m fine with that.” $20 would get me a pretty bouquet of flowers for Charlotte.

Maggie’s phone starts to buzz. “Speaking of Connor, he’s calling me now. I wonder what he wants.”

Connor is a junior and another one of the mechanical team members. I’ve always found him pretty weird. He looks like what I’d imagine a cartoon stoner would look like, always wearing a beanie to cover his curly black hair alongside outfits that are about three sizes too big. I think he smokes cigarettes. He sure smells like something similar. I don’t know how the hell he gets access to them; I’ve been told he has a secret dealer who hangs out in the back of the Wawa by his house.

“Hell yeah. Gotcha. See ya later, bye.” she hangs up the phone.

“What’s up with him?” I ask her.

“Apparently Connor, Benji, Gabe, and Olly skipped their last period and just got to the hotel, and they’re inviting us to a little ‘hangout’ in their room tonight, if you catch my drift.”

“I don’t.”

“Whoops, I forgot you’re you. They brought booze and plan on consuming it in their room. Wanna come?”

“Oh, jeez, that’s not really my thing.”

“Vincent, Jade, and Charlotte are gonna go.”

“Really? I’ll pop in for a bit, then.” None of them really come across to me as people who would be interested in drinking, but I guess I assume the best out of everyone. Nothing wrong with it, I've just never thought about doing it.

"Think of it as a team-bonding exercise. Plus, being around drunk people is fun. They get all loopy and say things they wouldn't sober."

"I doubt it, but I'll go for a little while. As soon as I feel uncomfortable, I'm leaving."

"Fair enough."

The rest of the drive continues in silence, accompanied by nothing but the music playing on my speakers. I'm listening to a playlist Charlotte sent me when she drove me home from a competition junior year; I don't *love* any of the songs musically, but they all remind me of her, which makes me love them for differently. I don't think they're *bad,* it's just something I wouldn't listen to unless a pretty girl I knew liked it. Therefore, I listen.

After a grueling drive full of dealing with every driver's first day on Earth, I finally make it to our hotel. Vincent's car is already here, alongside what I assume is Gabe's mom's minivan. Our school's logo is stuck to the back windshield next to a honor roll bumper sticker from our local middle school.

The hotel is nothing special. It reminds me of about a million different other hotels I've driven past on road trips with family. It looks recently renovated, maybe in the past ten years or so. It has a nice lawn in the front. Nothing to write a poem about.

I put the car in park and read a text from Vincent telling me he left a copy of our room key under an exposed part of the carpet in front of the room and to knock five times to be let into Gabe, Connor and Oliver's room. I guess that means they're already there.

I turn off my car, hop out, and grab my stuff from the backseat, throwing my poetry journal in my backpack. Once Maggie has all of her stuff, I lock my car and we enter the hotel.

Vincent says our room number is 510 and Maggie's is 512, so we walk together to drop off our stuff. I grab the key from under the carpet, unlock my door, and toss my stuff next to the bed that has Vincent's backpack on it. When I'm finished, I wait for Maggie outside her room. She comes out after a minute, and we make our way to room 501, the room where this "hangout" is happening. I knock on the door four times, and Benjamin lets me in. They definitely haven't been here that long, but he's visibly buzzed. I can see it in his eyes.cha

"What's up Spence, glad you could make it," he says, closing the door behind us. Everyone turns to see who showed up, and I lock eyes with Charlotte, who is holding a pink shotglass. Upon seeing me, she immediately jumps up and runs to me, pulling me into a tight hug.

"Hiiii Spencer! How are youuu doing?" she exclaims, her words slurring together.

I look up and see Vincent, very obviously sober. He uses his hand to make a bottle and holds it up to his lips, shaking it back and forth with a concerned look to him. She's definitely had a bit, and she's pretty small in comparison to a lot of our other teammates. Out of all of her friends, I had a hunch that she would at least try drinking tonight. I've heard it can be good to alleviate stress, and I'm sure she's stressed as *hell* right now, with everything going on.

She lets go, and I sit down criss-cross on the floor in between Vincent and Connor. Charlotte runs up to me and sits right in my lap, much to Vincent's surprise. I don't think she understands what she's doing or who she's around. I don't push her off. It's probably fine.

Connor offers me a shotglass filled with something. I hold the clear liquid close to my face, examining it. It smells like straight rubbing alcohol with a hint of lemon-scented bleach. "You don't have to drink that, y'know," says Vincent.

"I've never drank before. Can't hurt, right?" I put the glass up to my lips and swing myself backward, swallowing the entire thing in one fell swoop. I immediately gag. This is absolutely disgusting, how does anyone become an alcoholic? Liquid confidence can *not* be worth having to drink window cleaner.

"Want another?" Connor asks.

"No, I think I'm good for the rest of my life. That was disgusting."

"Your loss," says Benjamin.

Everyone continues talking about whatever they were talking about before Maggie and I got there, which was apparently who would win a fight between Vincent and Jade. Personally, I'm on team Jade. She uses power tools on the daily, and Vincent is shaped like a twig. Anyone who says Vincent would win is sexist.

Although, I think Charlotte could beat them both. I'm not biased, I promise.

I rest my chin on Charlotte's shoulder as she continues to drink, to the point of mild concern. I don't know how much she had before I got there, but both Jade and Vincent are visibly worried. "Char, hun, don't you think you've had enough?" Jade asks.

"Prooobably," she replies, putting her glass down and leaning into me, "I'm starting to feel tired…"

She begins to doze off, collapsing into my chest. "We should get her back to the room before she wakes up and wants to drink more," says Vincent.

Jade turns to me. "Think you can pick her up and take her back? We'll come with you."

"Yeah, of course."

I sit up, picking her up bridal-style in the process.This is probably the best way to pick her up without waking her up. I'm holding her by her back and her legs, which are probably the safest places to touch without asking first. Jade and Vincent rise in unison, getting the door for me. Now outside, the two of them pause.

"If she's not too heavy, can we take a picture real quick? It's for the memory book."

I laugh. "Yeah, sure."

Vincent grabs his phone and takes a photo of me holding her as well as a selfie with him and Jade posed up next to Charlotte's sleeping face. "She's gonna be so pissed when she sees these tomorrow." Jade snickers.

I carry her to her and Jade's room, 507. Jade unlocks it for us and I lay Charlotte down on the bed closest to the air conditioning unit. As soon as we get up to leave, she instantly wakes up and rises to a sitting position.

"Holy shit, that was fast," says Vincent.

"You two go away. I want him," Charlotte says, pointing to me. Vincent and Jade burst into laughter, visibly bewildered at her bold statement.

"Are you alright with that?" Jade asks.

"Of course. You guys go have fun."

The two of them leave, and I'm left with a drunk Charlotte. I sit down on the cushioned chair in the corner of the room, directly facing the beds. She rolls out of bed and onto the floor, immediately springing back up. "I need to change. I've been wearing these clothes all day."

She grabs some clothes out of her bag and unzips her jacket, revealing a black tank top. She begins to pull it off, and as soon as I realize what she's doing, I immediately turn away and cover my face with my hand. "I'm in here, you know." I mutter.

"Oh, my bad. You can close your eyes if you want. I don't mind." she replies.

I don't *want* to close my eyes, but this is drunk Charlotte speaking, and I'm sure sober Charlotte wouldn't want me to watch her undress. Sober Charlotte would *definitely* mind. "I will be doing just that." I say.

After about a minute of rustling and bustling, I feel something tossed onto my lap. I pick it up, unknowing of what it is. "You can open your eyes now," she says coyly.

I move my hand from my eyes and realize that what I'm holding is a black bra. I shriek and immediately toss it on the bed, far away from me. If she threw her bra at me, that means...

I take a good look at what Charlotte changed into. She's wearing a pair of shorts that barely cover anything, an oversized t-shirt she's obviously not wearing a bra underneath, and perfectly cuffed white socks. Her shirt is hanging off of her in a way that reveals the neck bruise I gave her a couple days ago, now slightly faded and red. Her hair is frizzy but not unkept. Holy shit, she's absolutely stunning. I'd sell my soul to wake up to this every morning. If I keep looking, I'm going to start thinking things I definitely shouldn't.

She jumps onto the chair I'm sitting on, wrapping her thighs around mine and pushing herself forward on my lap. She kisses me, and I can taste the alcohol and desperation on her breath. She pushes into the kiss, pushing her entire body closer to me. This is bad. This is a drunk Charlotte decision, not a sober one. I shouldn't be letting her continue.

Before I can say anything, she breaks free, a devilish grin on her face. "I have something to tell you, and I'm going to tell you now because we will both forget about it in the morning."

Both forget? Does she think I'm drunk too? "What's up?" I say. She brings me closer, rests her chin on my shoulder, and whispers in my ear:

"I love you, Spencer."

What.

The.

Hell.

"What did you say?" I ask, as if I didn't hear her perfectly.

She leans back, our eyes locking. "I love you, Spencer. I really, *really* love you, but I could never say it to you without a bit of liquid courage in my system.

"You're an amazing person, and so, *so* kind. You're always willing to help me, regardless of how awful of a person I can be sometimes. You've done so much for me and for this team, and you're...also..."

"What is it?" I ask, my entire body shaking.

"You're also the prettiest boy I've ever seen...every time I look at you, something fun flutters in my stomach. You're so, *so* handsome. I don't want to pretend to be your girlfriend, I want to be your *actual* girlfriend...I want to go on fun little dates, and kiss you so many times...I love you, Spencer..."

This is my chance. I've been rehearsing this for years, never knowing I'd actually be able to say it in real life. *"I love you too, Charlotte."*

Her eyes widen and start to water. "HUH? I never would've expected that!"

I'm gonna full send it. She said she won't remember it in the morning, right? I should practice now. "Charlotte, I've loved you for years. Ever since we met, it's always been you. I've only ever had eyes for you. You're the most gorgeous woman I've ever laid my eyes on."

I give her the biggest hug I've ever given someone, and she gives me another huge kiss to the lips, this one more passionate than the last. "We should celebrate," she whispers, "I have a gift for you, for putting yourself out there like that."

While kissing me, her right hand travels down my chest and torso to the top of my jeans. She starts to pull the zipper on my jeans down, but I instantly double-tap her shoulder, and she stops.

"No, I'm not doing something like that while you're drunk. I don't want to take advantage of you."

"Aren't you drunk too?" she asks.

"I think I'm big enough that one shot won't do too much to me."

"Alright, fine. Thank you for being so considerate. I love that about you."

She kisses me on the cheek and stands up. I zip myself back up and stand up as well. As much as both my upper and lower half wanted that to continue, I could never forgive myself for taking advantage of someone I love while she's in this state. I guess one could say I took advantage of her drunkenness since she confessed to me, but she did that on her own. I didn't exactly coerce her or anything.

"I'm so cold," she shudders.

I pull off the hoodie I'm wearing and hand it to her. "Here, put this on."

She listens, and my hoodie is huge on her. She looks so pretty in it, too. "Thanks, Spencer. Should I go to bed now?"

"That sounds like a wonderful idea."

I walk her to her bed and open up the sheets. She hops in and lies down on her back, staring at me with a confused look on her face. "Aren't you going to join?" she asks.

"Not while you're drunk."

"Fair point–uh oh." She rolls back out of the bed and races to the bathroom. I run after her, but she's already hunched over the toilet, hands attached to the sides. I hold her hair back as she gags and eventually throws up. I'm glad she made it to the toilet. I feel like I wouldn't have.

After about a minute of heaving whatever she had for dinner, which was probably just alcohol, she stands up, washes her hands and brushes her teeth, and lies back in bed. "Thanks," she mutters.

"Anytime."

"Hopefully there isn't another time." she laughs.

She rolls over in bed and I sit back down on the chair. I don't feel comfortable leaving her side until Jade gets back. She rolls herself into a log with the blankets.

"Goodnight, Spencer."

"Nighty night, Charlotte."

"I love you."

I could get used to hearing that. "I love you too."

She instantly falls back asleep, and I'm left here to think about what just happened. Was her confession to me serious? Will she actually remember it in the morning, or will it just be a weird dream to her? Does she actually like me, or was it the alcohol speaking? I know people say drunk words are sober thoughts, but what if this is all one big prank pulled on me to convince me to confess my love to her?

I think back to the day the two of us met, all the way back in our freshman year of high school. We had a few classes together that first semester, but we had our first conversation before that, during a summertime interest meeting for our robotics team. While Vincent and Jade gravitated toward the upperclassmen, she broke off to talk to me, a lone programmer trying to catch Kamal's attention as he explained how the robot code worked. She pulled me aside and introduced herself.

"Hey, my name's Charlotte." I remember her saying. *"I like your glasses, they remind me of a bassist I like."*

"Thanks...I'm Spencer," was all I could muster.

I was entranced. She was so cute, with her pink braces and the red headband she stopped wearing in junior year. Before I met her, I hadn't believed in love at first sight, but that's exactly what happened when I saw her for the first time.

I've been madly in love with this girl ever since.

I throw my head back against the chair, staring at the popcorn ceiling above me. This is too much to think about at once; maybe I should've drank more.

Chapter Thirteen
Charlotte

I wake up with an ear-splitting headache that travels through my entire body as I adjust to being awake. None of my alarms are going off. *Shit*, I'm gonna be late for comp! I grab my phone from the charger I don't remember plugging in and turn it on. It's 2am, nowhere near the time I need to get up today. *Phew*.

How did I get here? Last thing I remember was sitting in Gabe's hotel room, drinking with my teammates. Did Jade bring me back? All of my stuff is here. I sit up, and my entire body aches. I look to the bed closer to the door, and a body a bit too big to be Jade's is sleeping in it. God, where the hell am I? All of my stuff is here, but this is not my room.

I slide out of bed and open the curtains to let some moonlight into the room. I slowly walk over to the person sleeping in Jade's bed, preparing to beat the shit out of them if I need to. All of Jade's stuff is gone. Is this even my room?

Upon closer inspection, I see that it's actually Spencer fast asleep in what I thought was Jade's bed. What is he doing in here? Is he in my room? Am I in his room? If that was the case, Vinny and Benji would be here, but if it was my room, wouldn't Jade be here?

I need answers and I need them now. I pull the covers down to his waist, revealing his red pajama shirt, and quickly shake his arm back and forth. After a few pushes, he slowly opens his eyes. "What time is it?" he asks, his voice hoarse and flat. It's cute.

"It's two in the morning. What are you doing here? Whose room is this?" I ask frantically.

He adjusts to being awake enough to comprehend my yelling. "It's yours. Jade and I switched places so I could watch you and make sure you were okay throughout the night. How are you feeling, by the way?"

"Pretty good, how bad was I? I don't remember a thing."

"Not bad at all. Are you going back to bed?"

I decide to shoot my shot. It's cold, and I'm wearing nothing but a pair of shorts and a green hoodie I don't remember putting on. Maybe I'll sleep better if I sleep next to him. Or, rather, I am just making up excuses so I can sleep with him.

"Yeah, can I join you?" I ask, pretending to act cool.

"If you're sober enough, sure," he smiles as he pulls the rest of the covers down. He's sleeping on the left side, so I walk around the bed and crawl into the right. I lay down on my left side as he pulls me into him, his arms wrapping around my waist as his face digs into my shoulder. He kisses my neck in the spot where it still stings from Wednesday.

"You look so good in my hoodie, Charlotte." he mutters, muffled by my clothes.

That's where this hoodie came from. When did this come on? Oh god, we didn't do anything bad, right? I really doubt it. Spencer wouldn't do something like that. He wouldn't take advantage of me like that, right? Jeez, what if he did? I feel the same externally; I feel like my body would feel different if something happened. He wouldn't do that to me, he's too pure of heart. I trust him.

"Thanks," I reply.

I wrap my ankles around his, managing to get as close as possible to him. I can feel him breathe in and out. I can feel every part of him move back and forth as he breathes. He keeps pressing me against him, as if there was more room to move around. I'm completely trapped, but I don't mind at all.

His breathing becomes heavier and more spaced out. I can tell he's falling back asleep. He cranes his neck and whispers in my ear: *"I love you."*

With three simple words, the entirety of last night floods back into my mind. Everything. The excessive drinking, sitting on his lap in front of everyone, waking up in my bed, changing in front of him, confessing to him– *oh my god, I confessed to him.* I confessed to Spencer Laine last night. I told him I loved him.

Oh my god, I *love* him.

What's even crazier is that he said he loved me back. Did he drink at all? I think I remember that he took one shot and said never again, but did he actually follow up on it? Oh god, please tell me he was drunk too and won't remember when he wakes up. I wish I didn't remember!

What the hell do I do from here? Can I even pretend like none of it happened, or do I have to face my fears and tell him the truth? No, I can't do that yet, I have a competition to do. I'll deal with my feelings later. It'll be easier to pretend like I forgot now and tell him later. I can't let this convoluted romance affect today's Rounds; everything that follows is a bit more expendable.

Vinny and Jade are never gonna let me live this down. Honestly, I don't even care. This will-we-won't-we saga is almost over. I'm, like, 90% sure he's in love with me.

Of course, that could've just been the alcohol talking.

He *did* just say I looked good right now, though.

He has called me pretty a few times in the heat of the moment. What if he only thinks I'm pretty when he's filled with intense hormonal boy feelings?

He *is*, by all means of the word, a teenage boy. Boys think with their latter half. I know I've turned him on a few times. It's...pretty obvious when he is, way more than I could tell with my ex-girlfriend. He gets this look to him that makes me want nothing more than to tear him apart and kiss every part of him.

Spencer doesn't seem like that kind of boy. I mean, what is a poet other than a convoluted lovesick mess? He's kind. He wouldn't lie to me, especially in the most intimate moment in our lives.

He's probably just tired. Usually people tell the truth when they're tired. It's like being drunk, except when I'm drunk I apparently can't stop myself from spilling *everything,* from my guts to my love for Spencer. Yuck.

I can't stop admitting that I love him. That *must* mean it's true, right? I mean, I've been telling myself that I liked him, and I've been convinced for about a month now, but I guess I've officially fallen in love with him. I mean, who couldn't?

"Ever since my freshman year, it's always been you" is a line that I am pretty sure he said last night, although I question the accuracy of my memory. He wouldn't say something like that and not mean it. Both of us were convinced I was going to forget everything. He meant it. He said it then so he wouldn't have to tell me now. I don't know if

he was trying to be considerate or if it was something he'd never have the courage to say to me if I remembered it. Knowing him, it's the latter.

"It's always been you" is the most prominent line from the first dream I had about him, where we danced and danced until our hearts and legs gave out. It's almost prophetic, if I really think about it. Since September, I've come full circle, and all of my dreams and then some have become my reality. I think I'm a lucky woman.

I can feel myself starting to fall back asleep. I'm not going to fight the feeling, as I'd love to fall asleep in the arms of the boy I probably love. God, it feels so weird to say that. I still haven't come to full terms with it, and I don't know if I will until I truthfully, soberly confess to him.

Soon, I swear.

* * *

I can't remember falling asleep, but I woke up to the sound of my phone alarm blaring two inches away from me. I honestly can't remember bringing my phone to Spencer's bed, but I'm proud of myself for doing so. My headache is mostly gone, the pain being replaced by the emptiness in my heart knowing I have to go on today knowing so many things I didn't think I'd remember.

I check the time. I like setting alarms way before I actually need to wake up so I can happily snooze without any repercussions. It's currently 6:15, but I don't *really* need to get out of bed until 7. Since the district championships are usually run better than local competitions, we found out our schedule last night, and our first Round isn't until 10am. Because of that, we shouldn't need to arrive before 9am. Two hours should be more than enough time to get ready and get to the venue.

"What time is it?" Spencer whispered in my ear. I realize that in the four hours or so we've been asleep together, he hasn't let go of me. He's barely tightened his grip.

"6:15, but we don't need to get up till 7."

"Thank goodness," he mutters. He pulls down my–well, I guess *his*–hood and gives me a slow, meaningful kiss on the back of my neck. The sun is peeking through the curtains, shining a soft glow on our room. I shift around to face him and kiss him on the lips. I didn't ask him if it was okay, but he kissed me first, so he's probably fine with it.

I guess men are hornier in the morning.

He pushes us counterclockwise about ninety degrees. He finally lets go of me, holding himself above me on his hands and knees while I lay on my back underneath him. I can barely see him, but his eyes are full of need and desperation. As if I don't crave him either.

"Forty-five minutes, right?" he pants.

I nod. "Are you sober?" he asks.

"I think I threw up everything last night. Plus, the headache is gone."

"Then is this okay? It might be good to...let some stress out before competitions today."

Whatever lets him sleep at night. He said he loves me. He's taking advantage of the stupid excuse I made last time. He must be half-awake, because he's usually not this direct. I've been the one taking initiative.

"More than okay," I smile, "can I take your hoodie off first, though? It's hot down here."

"One sec." He pushes himself up so he's kneeling straight, creates a camera with his fingers, and pretends to snap a picture. He smiles with the goofy smile I've grown to adore and crave.

"What was that for?"

"You look so pretty, and I want to be able to cherish this memory."

"How sweet." I sit up and pull the hoodie off. I throw it at the end of the bed. I wonder if he'll let me keep it. It smells like him and the faint scents of coconut and vanilla, similar to what Vinny uses in the shower.

Upon removing the hoodie, I realize I didn't really leave much to the imagination when I changed last night. I usually *never* sleep in beds that aren't my own without a bra and socks, and tonight I only have socks. I was really trying to seduce him apparently, with my drunk and stumbling self. What was wrong with me? One sip of alcohol and I suddenly can't control myself.

Well, it wasn't just one sip, now was it.

He goes back to where he was before, with his hands surrounding my head and his body towering over mine. "Just because of last night, I need to ask one more time, are you sober?" he asks.

"Completely and utterly."

"Perfect," he says as he presses his body into mine and kisses me again. I can tell he's still not fully awake, because he's sloppy, greedy, and needy. It feels like he wants to kiss me again and again and never stop, regardless of whatever competition we have today. Honestly, I would let him if he asked.

I grab his right hand and direct him to where I want him to touch me, which just so happens to be around my torso and chest. He breaks free from our kiss, visibly startled. "Are you sure?" he asks, seemingly worried.

"Yep. You don't mind, right?"

"I'd be an idiot to mind, Charlotte."

We've done a lot of things as "just friends". Although, I feel like we crossed the friendly line the first time we intentionally kissed each other. If that night wasn't an indicator that things weren't how they were supposed to be, the morning after definitely was. We haven't been "just friends" for a while, and I think the two of us are waiting for the other to make things official and just confess already.

According to last night, I was the one to make that happen. I confessed first, even though it was under the clause that I wasn't going to remember in the morning. He only told me he loved me because he had proof that I loved him, and Sober Me was waiting on the exact same thing. I would have waited *much* longer if I was clear-minded.

Man, women have to do *everything* around here!

Our mouths slightly open, and once I can confirm that I definitely brushed my teeth last night, our tongues collide as passionately as our hearts apparently do. I direct his hands one more time, this time closer to my upper thigh. The longer we kiss, the rougher his presses get, and the louder his noises become. I wrap my arms around his neck and my legs around his back, pulling him as close as possible. I feel like a monkey latched onto a tree, longing for a banana.

Wait, that's disgusting.

What has my life come to? I'm partaking in a passionate make-out session with a boy I'm not even dating. This isn't even the first, or second, or *third* time. If I found myself from the beginning of the semester and told her that this is what competition season was like, she'd laugh in my face.

I can't say I particularly mind, though.

Everything ensues exactly how one would expect; there's not much to leave to the imagination when it comes to two ravenous teenagers with unrestricted access to one another. It feels like the only thing stopping us from doing more is the restrictive barrier of relationship labels. I'm sure that if that wasn't an issue, we'd be in his car driving to the nearest convenience store to purchase who knows what.

I feel sick even thinking about something like that. Not sick in a "I'm going to throw up because that's something that disgusts me" type of way; rather, it's more in a "I'm a little nauseated because I will be thrown into an unfamiliar situation that may be painful, but will be wonderful and fulfilling at the same time" type of way. I may be experienced in some types of intimacy, but nothing as terrifying as anything that can happen in a heterosexual relationship. I've never been in one of those.

My alarm blares in our ears. Spencer lowers his body directly on top of mine and digs his head into the pillow next to my head. "Damn, it's seven already?"

"Unfortunately."

"Five more minutes?" he begs, his voice muffled from the pillow.

I unfortunately have to be the voice of reason. "No, we need to get ready. We both need to shower, right?"

He nods. "You can go first," I tell him.

"Ugh, okay." He slowly but surely gets up and drags himself out of bed. I sit up and watch him grab his stuff from his suitcase. Before entering the bathroom, he looks at me one more time.

"It's unfortunate," he sighs heavily.

"What is?" I ask.

"The universe is taking me from you with the excuse of limited time."

"How poetic." I laugh.

"I'm pretty fond of poetry." Before I can say anything else, he darts into the bathroom, quietly closing the door behind him.

While he showers and gets ready, I grab my phone and check all of the messages from last night, seeing exactly what I had suspected: Vinny and Jade snapping picture after picture of me drunk and passed out. The photo of Spencer carrying me to my hotel room stuck out to me. I'm surprised he was able to do it; I thought I was pretty heavy for a woman. While embarrassing now, I'm sure it'll be a photo I cherish in the future, so I save it to my phone.

I text the groupchat with a simple *"I'm alive, in case anyone is wondering."*

"You're up earlier than I expected," says Jade.

"How's the hangover?" Vinny chimed in.

"Practically nonexistent, I feel pretty good, although we have a lot to talk about when we get in the car." I replied.

"Guess you'll be riding with me today, because I will not *be missing whatever you're talking about."* says Vinny.

I turn off my phone and stare at the ceiling, thinking about every decision I have ever made in my life that's led me here. The world around me, my lived experiences, dreams, and everything in between, and the people I love and hate that have influenced me to become the person I am today. I feel awfully sentimental; I guess that's just how it is when you're in your final year of high school and final season of the program you've grown incredibly fond of over the years. I am in love with everything, everyone, and every era and period of my life.

That damn poetry class is influencing me too much. I feel like a pop-punk song title; my problems are a mile long and there's no real coherent correlation between any of them. I'm simply an emo loser with nothing to do but wallow in self-pity and complain about everything.

Is it really complaining if I love it all? Despite everything awful that has led me to this situation, I love myself, and I love the fact that I can finally say that. I'm finally in a state of believing that I am truly okay, truly human. Who let me be happy? Who let me think of myself as something other than a putrid piece of shit who isn't worthy of love?

Vinny, Jade, and…Spencer, of course. My friends, as well as my overcomplicated situationship, are the people who have allowed me to progress through this tumultuous terror tragedy that is– no, *was*– my life. I didn't think I would make it this far after I broke up with her. My life felt over. Everything was over. I felt like I was nothing without her. She *made me* feel like I was nothing without her, and I really wasn't until he came along.

It's never over, and never will be.

Tragedy and turbulence truly are beautiful, aren't they? Without these awful experiences I had to trudge through, my life never would have blossomed the way I believe it has. I would be stuck in the same awful relationship I was in for two whole years, with no way to get out and no way of convincing me to find a way to. In a sense, I have to thank her for doing the awful act that made me end things in the first place. It hurt like hell, *god it hurt like hell*, but it must have been worth it if it led me to where I am today. I am at an interesting midway between being grateful and hateful, and I think I'm okay with that. The world isn't black and white; sometimes it's red with devil horns and box-dyed black hair.

The bathroom door opens, and out walks Spencer, with freshly blow-dried hair and his competition clothes on. "All yours, Charlotte," he smiles, as if the past hour or so didn't happen.

"Thanks."

I scurry out of bed and grab the clothes I need to wear today and head to the warm and steamy bathroom. As I drop my clothes on the wiped-down counter, I poke my head out and ask "Are you a scalding shower guy?"

"You caught me," he laughs.

I close the door and turn on the shower, this time on the medium setting. As I strip down, the thought that Spencer just used this shower lands in my mind with a large thud. My thoughts begin to wander, but I quickly shut them off when I veer too close to thinking about what he was doing in here before me. I need to act normal for once; not everything needs to be perverted.

Once the water finally feels warm enough, I hop in and begin my shower routine so I can hopefully wash away the last of the alcohol-infused headache. As the warm water flows down my body, I imagine myself as a monkey basking in a summer's rain, still longing for a banana because I'm a sick and twisted freak.

I shampoo my hair and use about three times the recommended amount of conditioner, running my fingers through the lower half of my hair. When it's sufficiently conditioned, I rub my hands together, rolling the excess hair that fell out of my head into a little ball. I stick it to the shower wall to be collected once I'm done. My mom always tells me to brush my hair before I enter the shower so I don't have to deal with all the hair *in* the shower, but I always forget until I'm already in the shower and my hair's too wet for anything to matter in the end.

I hop out of the shower and apply my caffeine solution and moisturizer. Since the UV is less than four all day, I omit the sunscreen. I then throw on my competition clothes, consisting of my t-shirt, black jeans, and everything else I need underneath. My socks are perfectly cuffed as always. I blow-dry my bangs and put the rest of my hair into pigtail braids. I've never worn my hair like this until our last competition, and we did really well. I don't usually believe in luck, but it can't hurt.

I grab all of my stuff and walk out of the bathroom. I fold my pajamas and place them neatly on my bed. I grab my safety glasses and badge from last comp from my bag and put them on, with my badge around my neck and my glasses resting on the collar of my shirt.

Spencer grabs his backpack and hauls it over his shoulder. "Ready to go?"

"Yup."

I grab the room key and place it in my pocket. We exit the hotel room and make our way to the elevator. "I wonder what our teachers think our team gets up to in these rooms. Don't you think it's weird that we've never had any adult supervision?" he asks.

"I've never really thought about it, no," I reply, "although I never remember anything really happening."

"Remember Carla and Josie from our freshman year?"

"Oh shit, I forgot about them." In our freshman year, our team had just came back from an amazing season, so our teachers assigned two seniors to be Captains, and they had a very...*public* relationship, to say the least. They were the reason why upperclassmen were allowed to book their own rooms, mostly because Mr. D did *not* want to deal with them. They were already adults by then anyway.

"I feel like after that, they would've at least checked in on us at night, right? One of my friends does DECA, and they keep them under intense lockdown at night."

"I guess they trust us, for some reason."

"Sometimes I don't think they should," he laughs.

The elevator opens and I see Jade and Vinny sitting in the hotel lobby, discussing something quietly while Vinny eats a granola bar. Upon noticing us, they jump out of their respective chairs and run towards us. Vinny grabs my hands while Jade places her hand on my forehead. They sigh in relief after realizing I'm not completely sick.

"You seem sober enough to compete," says Jade.

"Yeah, I feel good," I reply.

"Let's go. Benji's already outside waiting for you, Spencer."

The four of us walk out to the parking lot, with Vinny and Jade leading the way, Spencer lingering in the back, and me sandwiched in the middle. Benji is leaning on Spencer's car, typing on his phone. I run to Vinny's passenger side door to claim shotgun like I always do.

Jade, Vinny and I say goodbye to Spencer and hop into Vinny's car. I click my seatbelt in and Vinny backs out of his parking spot and drives out onto the main road.

"Alright, Char, what the hell happened between you two?" Jade asks, startling me.

"What do you mean?"

"Spencer had this…look on his face. Kinda gloomy or something like that."

"Wow, Jade, you have such a way with words." Vinny chimes in.

"Shut up. What did you do to him?"

"I didn't do anything to him! I just…something happened last night."

"Oh dear," Vinny groans, "spill."

"God, where do I even start? Last night was kinda a blur. You know how drunk words are sober thoughts and alcohol gives you the confidence you may not actually need?"

"Holy shit, did you confess to him?" Jade exclaims.

"Sorta? Last night, I was convinced I wasn't going to remember anything I did or said, so I did what I had been wanting to do, and told him I loved him. I said it, like, four times. I told him I wanted to be his girlfriend. I said so many things."

"How did he respond?" Vinny asks.

"He...said he loved me too. He said he's been in love with me since our freshman year."

"But if all this happened, why did he look like that? You're leaving something out." says Jade.

"He thinks I don't remember it. I woke up at two in the morning, woke him up, and laid down next to him. He was half-asleep and said he loved me again, and that's when the memories came back."

Vinny gasps. "Oh my god, he doesn't know."

I shake my head. He stops at a stoplight, turns to me, grabs the collar of my shirt, and starts violently shaking me back and forth, yelling "Charlotte, I love you, but you're a fucking idiot!"

"Calm down, Vinny!" Jade exclaims.

He exasperatedly groans, letting go of my shirt and continuing with his driving. "Come on, Jade, I'm tired of pretending to be oblivious to this whole thing!"

"What are you talking about?" I ask.

"Why didn't you tell him?" he replies.

"What if I'm misremembering? What if he was just saying that to make me feel better?"

"Charlotte, you're both the smartest and dumbest person I know."

"Why do you say that?"

"It doesn't take a rocket scientist to figure out that he loves you! He's been so damn obvious about it for years! The way he's looked at you, the things he does for you, everything points directly to that! I'm not sure if you were oblivious to it or subconsciously pushed it away, but I've noticed for years."

"To be honest, Charlotte, I noticed it too, but I didn't have the heart to tell you." Jade interjects.

"What...how..."

Vinny sighs, seemingly calming down. "Spencer's a smart guy; you really think he consistently broke our robots multiple times a week for three years? Ever notice how the robot *didn't* break when you were sick or weren't around? He didn't want to directly ask you to hang out with him, but he knew you'd stay if he 'broke something'".

Jade chimes in. "He spent an entire summer building a driving simulator for you to practice on. Who does something like that for someone they're not in love with?"

"When Sylvia showed up at our last comp, he went with your silly plan without a second thought! And let's be honest, someone who 'just wants to be friends' probably wouldn't make out with you all of those times."

"He's been head over heels for you for years, but couldn't and wouldn't do anything about it because you were with Sylvia for most of high school." Jade says. "Real bad and ugly case of a hopeless romantic."

Hopeless romantic. That's such a notably familiar term. Did I write that somewhere?

W. H. Auden. "The More Loving One". The student-submitted poem in Mrs. M's class.

I'm brought back to the exit ticket I submitted. *"Seems like someone at this school is a hopeless romantic for someone they believe will never love them back."*

He loves poetry. He told me he loved Auden. He specifically mentioned "The More Loving One."

Oh my god.

"He was the one who submitted that poem!" I exclaim.

"That's all you got from this?" Vinny asks.

I feel like I'm sinking into the chair. I throw my head into my hands and lean forward, curling into as much of a ball as I physically can.

"I'm so stupid."

Jade grabs my shoulder. "Charlotte, you need to confess to that poor boy as soon as possible, for both his sake and ours. I'm sure his poetic little heart can barely handle all of this."

"I'll do it tonight. I can't take the chance of ruining our Rounds today."

"As soon as we get back to the damn hotel, you're gonna pull him into your room and tell him everything. When I say everything, I mean *everything*. Tell him you remember and that you meant what you said."

"If you don't have a boyfriend by 11:59pm tonight I'm gonna throw you at him." Vinny interjects.

"Jeez, this feels like homework," I groan, my voice muffled by my hands.

"We're doing this because we love you," Jade says, "this is what's best for you and Spencer. It'll make you happy and finally end this whole fiasco."

"Well *I'm* doing this because I love you *and* I'm tired of seeing that poor guy mope around aimlessly. You're doing *me* a solid."

I let out a small, embarrassed chuckle. "Good to hear."

Vinny parks in front of the venue we'll be competing at this weekend, a small public university in the middle of Delaware. We grab our stuff and make our way to the front door of the building titled "Park Gymnasium". We collectively put on our safety glasses as we enter the building, our heads held high.

Today is important. We've been to district champs before, but by the scrapes of our teeth. We've never actually performed well enough to be competitive at this level. We're coming in with a *lot* of Ranking Points from our last competition, as both winners and the second-seed team.

Each team that qualifies for district champs receives a certain number of Ranking Points, or RP, that determines your overall ranking, not just for certain competitions. Teams receive points based on both ranking before playoffs and performance *in* playoffs. We have one of the highest amounts of RP, especially because we were the Captains of our Group.

This doesn't confirm our standing when it comes to qualifying for world champs, though. RP obtained at district champs is *doubled*, so it's way more important to perform well here. This means we *need* to perform well if we want to even have a chance at worlds.

District competitions also have an award system. The same judges from last comp judge us again and determine if we qualify for certain awards pertaining to robot performance or technical skills. These awards give us Ranking Points, and can make or break a run to world champs. We've never been lucky with these awards, but Vinny has been working really damn hard on our presentation, and our robot looks *damn* good.

The Mid-Atlantic District sends eight teams to world champs every year. The winner and finalist Groups automatically qualify, followed by the four highest-ranked teams, all determined by Ranking Points. To have a chance at qualifying, we need to either win an award or make it to Finals. If neither happens, we're screwed.

I quickly make my way to our Zone to do my routine checks on the robot. I grab my checklist, go through every single menial task, and shake the robot a few times. I kneel down to check our battery charger, and every battery is nicely charged. Sometimes, the freshmen will forget to plug them in, but they did their job this time. Mr. D probably yelled at them to do it. He scares me, but he's damn good at leading a team.

I hear footsteps behind me. I look up and see Spencer holding his open laptop. He smiles, the same way he always does. Goofy, but incredibly cute.

"Hey again," he says.

"Hey. Are you about to do your tests?"

"Are yours done?"

I nod, and shuffle to the side of our Zone so he has ample table space to put his laptop down. He grabs a test battery, plugs it into the robot, and turns it on, connecting to the robot through his computer. I watch him as he types away, pressing the same buttons he's been pressing these past three seasons.

Mr. D enters The Zone, holding two granola bars and a bottle of water. He hands each of us a granola bar and places the bottle of water on the floor next to me.

"I need you two to be in your prime today," he says, "let me know if you need anything else."

With that, he walks away. In previous seasons, when something would inevitably be wrong with the robot, he'd always be in our Zone with his head in the bot, trying to debug. Since our robot hasn't really had any issues so far, he's been able to hang out in the stands without a care in the world. Hopefully it stays this way.

I twist the cap off the water bottle and take a swig. I lift the bottle up and ask Spencer if he wants any. He grabs the bottle and uses his shirt to wipe off where my mouth was.

"Dude, my tongue was in your mouth this morning, and you care about sharing a water bottle?" I blurt out. I didn't mean for it to be so harsh.

He nervously chuckles, his face turning pink. "The rest of the world doesn't know that."

"I promise, nobody's watching." I laugh.

"You never know."

After he drinks some of the bottle, he hands it back to me, and I take another sip. An indirect kiss. We literally kissed this morning, but this is making my heart flutter for some reason. Crushes are weird.

What even is a crush at this point? Crushes feel childish. I've said I love him, how am I supposed to describe *that* as something someone with a crush would do? It feels like way more than a crush, but the world never came up with the mature version of a crush. Would I really call myself *mature?*

I stare at the ceiling while listening to the noise coming from the fifty other teams surrounding us. The college gym holding all of these teams is absolutely huge; it needs to be for all of the equipment coming in. I catch a whiff of a motor smoking from a Zone two rows behind ours alongside a shriek from either a teenage girl or a pissed mentor. Glad it's not our robot this time. The motors we used in our sophomore year were awful and would almost blow up if we had less than an hour of cooldown time in between our Rounds.

The Zone during district championships tends to smell pretty bad. There's an unfortunate correlation between the skill level of a team and the average deodorant usage between the team members. With the amount of people here, it gets quite warm, and warmth brings odor. I'm just glad I'm not on a team that wears extensive outfits. A few of the teams here wear worksuits similar to a Formula One pit crew, and I always overhear them complaining about how hot it is and how bad they smell. I don't exactly smell like roses after competitions, but I've never noticed a funk between me or my teammates. Well, Kamal definitely had some sort of funk to him, but we only worked together for a year until Spencer replaced him.

During Rounds, I'm literally right next to Spencer, and I've never had any issues with him smelling bad. When we started competing as Driver and Controller together, we made a deal that we would tell one another if we smelled bad. Thankfully, neither of us have had to say anything.

He probably smells like coconut and vanilla right now. I wonder what I smell like. At competitions like these, the best thing to smell like is nothing.

Spencer shuts his laptop off. "Wanna watch a couple Rounds?" he asks.

I stand up. "Sure!"

We walk to the stands together. Upon entering, I immediately spot Spencer's mom chatting with *my* mom. I didn't know she was going to be here. When is she ever?

"Hey, do your parents still think we're together?" I whisper to Spencer.

"Yeah, do you want me to tell them we're not?"

"Nah, it's fine." No point in switching up now, especially since my *mom* is here, and everyone knows that Andrea Laine is a chatty woman. I'm sure the first thing she said to my mom was "hey, did you know our children are dating?"

I wish we actually were dating. We'll see what happens tonight. If it happens tonight. I'll do my best to make it happen tonight, but I can't make any promises.

My mom notices us walk in and waves us over, a puzzled look in her eyes. I grab Spencer's arm and walk up the bleachers to where they're sitting, which is directly above Vinny, who's probably working on a business proposal on his laptop. I know damn well he sat there on purpose. That boy lives for drama and knows exactly when and where he can get it. Love him for it.

"Who did your hair this morning?" was the first thing my mom asked. I feel like there's more pressing matters that she's definitely aware of by now.

"I did." I replied.

"It looks alright. Your braids are uneven."

"Thanks." My face is as monotone as a statue.

"Charlotte, dear, how come you never told your mom this wonderful news?" Spencer's mom asks, her beaming smile nearly blinding me.

I look at my mom, her confused expression maintained. I can tell she washed her hair this morning; her southern Italian genetics are shining through her incredibly curly hair. I, unfortunately, inherited my dad's northern Italian features and the super-curly hair gene missed me entirely. My hair is slightly lighter than my mom's and more wavy than curly. It curls as it dries, but they're not as prominent as my mom's, or the rest of her side of the family. I definitely have her nose, though.

"I've been busy…guess I never really got the chance to." I chuckle.

"I thought you were gay. What happened to that?" says my mom.

Vinny bursts into laughter behind us. I jokingly push his head forward. Mrs. Laine smiles again, this time intentionally.

"Y'know, Mary, I thought Spencer was gay too! What a match made in heaven!"

Spencer's face flushes red, his hand covering his face in embarrassment. Vinny leans on Jade's shoulder and continues to laugh. I notice a tear forming in his eye. What a goof.

I sit next to my mom while Spencer sits next to his parents. "I'm surprised you're here," I mutter.

"Isn't this your last competition? I wanted to watch you one last time."

"Hopefully it's not the last one. We might actually qualify for world champs."

The phrase 'world champs' sits in my stomach like a nausea-inducing meal. Worlds isn't a mysterious entity that feels completely out of reach anymore. We can actually qualify. It's going to take a lot of work, but we could actually do it.

"Even if you do make it, I wouldn't be able to go, and you know that."

"Yeah, you're right."

World champs have been in San Francisco for the past decade. Our school agreed to pay for a portion of our flights and lodging *if* we qualify. I've never been to California; hell, I've never been further west than Michigan to visit my grandparents.

I watch the field, where team Close-Call, from somewhere in Philadelphia, is going through their first practice Round. Pennsylvania has a lot of the top teams in the country, and their side of the district is far more competitive than most of New Jersey. A Pennsylvanian team has won district champs every single year since the Mid-Atlantic District has been a thing.

They finish their practice Round in two minutes and fifty-nine seconds, which is *really* good for a practice Round. I watch a few more Rounds, all equally as impressive as the first one. At around 9:45, Spencer stands up and signals for Maggie to get ready. I say goodbye to my mom and join the two of them.

The three of us silently walk back to our Zone to pick up our bot. Spencer grabs the controllers and his laptop as Maggie starts to pull the robot cart toward the field area. I hold nothing other than the lump of nervousness in the pit of my stomach and the weight of our entire team's performance on my shoulders.

"How are you feeling?" Spencer asks.

"Like I just got hit by a tiny car, carrying a bunch of clowns, ready to laugh at every move I make."

"How…awfully poetic." he laughs.

"My poetry class has really been throwing me for a loop."

"You don't like it?"

"I think it's a fine class, it's just a lot of work, and I've been too busy with robotics to create anything meaningful."

"Oh, are you guys working on your personal poems now?"

I nod, and he continues. "That was one of my favorite assignments in all of high school. I spent, like, an hour after school talking with Mrs. M about the poem I wrote. She said it was one of the best she's ever seen from a student."

"She's definitely not going to say that about mine. What did you write about?"

His cheeks redden. "Nothing in particular, really."

He's definitely lying. I feel the overwhelming need to pry him further about this class. "Hey, were you the one who submitted the poem we had to analyze earlier this semester?"

His eyes widen and his smile begins to fade. "…was it an Auden poem?"

"Yup."

"That wasn't even the one I officially submitted. She just knew I liked the poem. Jeez, I didn't want her to use *that* one..." he mutters.

He turns to me. "How did you find out? Did she tell you?"

"You said it was one of your favorites, and I put two and two together."

"Oh, jeez. This is really embarrassing..."

"How come?" I ask. "It was a good poem."

"Albeit a depressing one. I told her what that poem meant to me in confidence."

"What exactly does it mean to you?"

"Nothing in particular..." he repeats.

Even I can tell he's lying again. I feel a metaphorical click in my brain, and everything becomes sorta clear. *Oh dear.* He probably related the poem to me, didn't he. The poem's all about unrequited love, and if he was telling the truth last night, that's probably all he's known for years at this point. God, how depressing.

I still can barely convince myself that last night actually happened. He's acting completely normal, as if it never did. Either he's a good actor, or I'm an oblivious idiot, like Vinny said. Is he really willing to spend the rest of our time together pretending that nothing was said? I guess he's been pining for so long, what's a few more months to him?

If he was slightly more confident and asked me out before I dated Sylvia, all the way back in our freshman year, two harsh, agonizing years never would've happened, and I'd probably be in one of the happiest states of mind I've ever seen. I wish he would've done it. Everything wrong with me now would've simply never existed. I wish I had liked him before.

The best part about when awful things happen is that eventually they become the past. I need to stop letting my past corrupt my present.

While I missed the best time, the second best time for us to be together is now, right? I can't waste my time lamenting over the past when I have my future to worry about. All I have to do is get through the rest of the day, and we'll be golden. Well, I hope so. There's still technically a chance that everything goes wrong and I was mistaken. God, I hope I'm remembering correctly. Please let him love me. Please let that not be a dream.

We enter the field, which is absolutely huge compared to our competition two weeks ago. I feel so smaller, even smaller than usual. I'm a small fish in the biggest pond I've ever seen. I'm going to be devoured.

Maggie and I pick up the robot off the cart and place it exactly where it needs to be. I turn the robot on. Everything is green. Thank goodness.

Spencer sets up the laptop and our controllers at the Driver's Table. He hands me my black X-Box controller the same one I've been using since my freshman year. "Ready, partner?" he asks with a big fat smile.

"I sure hope so."

"Don't worry about it, it's a practice Round."

The game announcer introduces us to the audience. "Please welcome the winners of the New Jersey Conference, Team 904208, The Devils from Smithville, New Jersey with their robot Ross!"

The crowd roars as we stick our devil horns up. There has to be at least a thousand people in this audience. It's loud. I've never seen this big of a crowd at a competition before.

The buzzer blares in our ears, and it's time to perform. My hands move faster than my brain as I fly through the course. I haven't practiced in a few days, so I'm not as precise as I'd like to be, but that doesn't matter. This is just practice.

I yell to Spencer: "Shoot!" He listens as he presses his buttons and advances us to the next part of the course.

At the monkey bars, Spencer lets go of a button too early, and we nearly miss the final bar. Missing the final bar would cause us to fall and completely shatter. Thankfully, Spencer and our robot clutched, and we progressed.

We finally balance, and our round ends at two minutes and fifty-eight seconds, faster than the team we went after. Spencer and I put down our controllers and high-five, our hands lingering together for longer than a normal high-five would take.

"That was great for our practice round!" he exclaims.

"You did amazing!" I reply.

I always feel awful before Rounds and absolutely amazing right after. This probably isn't good for me. Seeing Spencer's smile after a Round makes me feel a lot better, no matter how we did.

Maggie and I grab the robot and begin to bring it back to our Zone. Out of the corner of my eye, I see a familiar-looking woman wearing jet-black box-dyed hair and a t-shirt with a shell on it. My heart drops to a pit in my stomach it is all-too-familiar with.

Not again, goddamnit.

I let out a large groan, and Maggie notices. "What's up?"

"Sylvia's here again."

"I saw her this morning. What's she doing with Shell-Shocked?"

"She must be mentoring them for this competition. Why did they pick *her* of all people?"

"I did notice one of their main mentors is missing. He's…memorable."

"What are you guys talking about?" Spencer asks.

"Dude, she's back, with *Shell-Shocked* of all teams." says Maggie.

"A match made in Hell, I'd say. Her college isn't even close to Point Pleasant."

"You think this was planned?" I ask, my voice shaky.

"Has to be," he replies, "don't let her get to you. They suck anyway."

"Yeah, you're right."

We arrive at our Zone and drop the robot off. Our first real Round isn't until 11:30, so we have a while to relax beforehand. All I want to do is curl into the corner of our Zone and stay there forever.

I sit down as Maggie leaves. Spencer stays put. "You should go to the stands and watch some Rounds." I say to him.

"You should come with me."

"I need to decompress. I don't feel well."

"Do you want me to stay with you then?"

I pause for a moment. "Yeah."

He sits down next to me, with his knees bent and facing the ceiling while his arms wrap around his legs. I dump my head into my knees and let out a few substantially large sighs. My mind wanders through a mix of nothing and everything all at once. We sit together in silence for about five minutes; the silence both excruciating and enlightening. Sometimes all you need is a moment to internally scream and cry while sitting on a foam mat next to your driving partner of three years.

I look up, readjusting to the light of the hospital-esque Zone. Spencer is staring at the wall, seemingly without a care in the world. He notices I've come back to the waking world and provides me with a small smile.

"How are you feeling?" he asks.

"A little better," I mutter, "I'm just really, really confused."

"Wanna try sorting it all out?"

I groan. "Nothing makes sense to me with this girl anymore. What does she gain from constantly following me to competitions, sending letters and emails and texts, and overall harassing me every chance she gets? Doesn't she have a life or something?"

"My guess is she's gaining the satisfaction of allowing her to stay in your mind."

"But *why?* I ended our relationship in May."

"If I may ask, why *did* you break up with her?"

"There were a lot of reasons…" I begin. "...way too many."

"You don't have to answer if you're not comfortable."

"No, I'll be alright. It's hard to talk about, but I can't get over it if I can't talk about it..."

May 17th of this year. I'm sitting through the longest graduation ceremony I've ever been a part of, my entire body aching. The blistering heat from the late spring sun caused the ice pack I held over my cheek to melt in fifteen minutes, to the point where I was essentially pressing a bag of liquid to my face. It stung. Everything stung.

Sylvia Duran's name is called on the speaker, and I'm forced to drop my bag of water so I can clap and cheer. I feel fake; I'm acting more plastic than the outside of the mushy ice pack. I don't want to be here.

Her parents scream her name from the bleacher right behind mine. I'm sitting with the company of none but myself. I don't think they ever really liked me. I don't think she ever let them like me. I barely remember what her family looked like, that's how irrelevant they were throughout our entire relationship.

The unbearable pain fills the right side of my face. I bring the icepack back to my cheek. The night before was a blur, to say the least. All I can remember is being pushed back into the passenger's seat of a Ford Focus. The driver parked the car in my driveway, unbuckled her seatbelt, and jumped across the middle console to sit above me.

I can't remember any of the words. I don't really remember what I did. I probably didn't do anything, but according to her, I did everything I could've possibly done, and it was all wrong. I think I made a joke in front of her parents or something. All I can remember is that she wouldn't stop swinging.

She couldn't stop herself this time. She didn't want to stop herself this time. She pushed me down by my neck with her left arm while her right hand kept punching and smacking and everything else. I couldn't move. I was too scared. I wish I could've stopped her, but I took it like a complete idiot.

I always took it.

Her screams stung my ears nearly as bad as my cheek. When I looked in the mirror the morning after she physically threw me out of her car and onto the pavement, I noticed a giant bruise near my jaw and hand marks on my neck. It was then when I called Vinny and Jade and told them I was finally going to do it.

"I really thought I loved her, but I think I was just infatuated with how cool I thought she was before we got together. It was my first relationship; I was inexperienced. She wasn't, and knew she could take advantage of me and do literally anything without any repercussions. I thought that was how love worked. I was so, so wrong. She didn't love me. She used my naivety to get what she wanted, which was a girltoy to play with and throw around as she liked. She did so many things I felt like I couldn't say no to.

"Hopefully my next relationship isn't like that." I force myself to chuckle.

I turn to Spencer, his jaw dropped, tears spilling down his pretty face. My heart sinks. I said too much. I hurt him. "Oh my god, I'm so sorry, I shouldn't have said all that–"

He interrupts me by pulling me into a deep hug. "I'm so, so sorry that you had to go through that, Charlotte. I wish I knew what was going on. I wish I could've helped you get out."

"Vinny and Jade tried their hardest to force me out, but I didn't listen to them. I appreciate the offer, but it wouldn't have helped. I needed the learning experience."

"Learning experiences shouldn't tear you down like this did. Learning is supposed to be beautiful, not agonizing."

He breaks from the hug and grabs my shoulders instead. "Charlotte, you are one of the strongest and most perseverant people I know. The fact that you're able to stand here and compete after all of that says so much about how tough you are. I don't think I'd be able to handle it."

I feel myself smile. "It's really great to hear that. It gets hard, but I'm glad I have such amazing people like you by my side to get me through it."

I hug him back. "Don't worry, I'm only interested in kind, respectful partners from now on."

"Good to hear."

I lean on his shoulder as we continue to sit on the floor together. We have about forty minutes until our next Round, but I don't feel like leaving our Zone. I don't want to go back to the stands, just in case she's there to torment me once again. I need a Sylvia-less mind for once in a while.

I pull out my phone and begin mindlessly reading through my spam emails. Spencer grabs his and turns on the livestream playing the Rounds going on outside. "Y'know, you can go out there and watch if you want."

"I'd rather watch here and sit with you. Are you okay with that?"

"Of course I am. Can I watch?"

He nods, and I press my head against him while he holds the livestream in between the two of us. His right arm travels around and wraps itself around my waist. I try to imitate his breathing as he intently watches robots move. This isn't the first time we've hung out in our Zone together instead of going to the stands with our team, but I appreciate how special it feels this time. The butterflies in my stomach, once shot dead by my ex-girlfriend, are flourishing in a tiny garden created by the most poetic boy in the world.

After a few Rounds go by along with discussions in between about team performance, I look up from Spencer's phone to see Maggie walking back into The Zone. He turns off the livestream and the two of us stand up. I've been sitting for so long that my legs feel wobbly. Either that, or I'm about to start sobbing. At this point, I don't think I'll ever know at any given time.

I plug a battery into the robot as Maggie pulls the cart toward the field. Spencer trails behind with his laptop and our controllers. Once everything's plugged in and working fine, I slow my pace so I can walk with him.

"I might already know the answer, but how are you feeling?" he asks.

"I appreciate you keeping tradition. I'm feeling…alright, actually."

"That's a step above what you normally say! I'm really happy to hear that."

Spencer is one of the coolest people I've ever met. I appreciate how joyful he tries to be all the time. No matter how awful I'm feeling, he somehow always knows how to make me feel better. He's a great asset to have around.

I love him.

Jeez, I can't stop throwing that damn L-word around. I used to throw around a different L-word back when I was dating an L-word.

We enter the field, with stands that are somehow even more packed than last time. A team from Delaware is currently running through their Round. Delaware teams are usually decent and on-par with the Jersey teams most of the time. They're not as much of a threat as the Pennsylvania teams, though.

As they finish up, we bring our robot toward the field. The crowd cheers for both us and the Delaware team that just completed their Round. To the audience, we must be one of those 'good' teams. Winning a competition really *does* make you look better.

I glance over to where Shell-Shocked is stationed in the stands and see Sylvia staring directly at me, her face red with anger. I give her a soft, intentionally uninterpretable smile.

I'm not your bitch anymore. I promise.

Maggie and I quickly drop off the robot. I walk over to Spencer, who hands me my controller.

"Ready, partner?" he asks.

"More than ever. Let's do this."

Two minutes and fifty-three seconds passes faster than you could say "robot". I couldn't believe my eyes when I saw it. I look at the scoreboard and see that our performance placed us in first. First place at district champs. Even though we're still in the beginning of the day, this isn't something I thought I'd ever see before. I refuse to believe it's real.

Spencer throws his controller on the table, grabs my shoulders, and begins to jump up and down like a neurotic dog. "Do you see that? 2:53!" he exclaims.

"Great job!" I reply, matching his energy without jumping.

"Oh please, it was all you!"

* * *

The rest of Saturday was all but normal. We kept on improving without a peak in sight. Our second Round was still 2:53, but we had decreased by about a third of a second. Round Three was 2:52, and Round Four barely hit 2:51. Our fifth and final Round ended at a monumental 2:50, a time never before seen in this team's history.

While we've performed well enough to attend world champs in previous years, way before I entered high school, Rounds have become way more optimized than they ever were, mainly because of new, updated motors and electronics. A 3:30 ten years ago is equivalent to a 3:00 now.

Our last Round ended at around 6pm. Once everything was checked and accounted for, we left the university and began our drive back to the hotel. We left a few minutes later than Spencer and Benji did because we spent an extra ten minutes waiting for Vinny to take a shit in the bathroom right next to The Zone. I sat in the backseat this time, despite my love for shotgun in Vinny's car. I knew shit was going to hit the fan as soon as we drove far away enough from the school.

"So, Charlotte," Vinny says, "what are you going to do as soon as you get back to the hotel?"

"I'm going to confess to Spencer..." I mutter.

"Louder, hun." says Jade.

"I'm going to confess to Spencer." I reply, slightly louder.

"Say it like you mean it!" Vinny exclaims.

"I'M GOING TO CONFESS TO SPENCER!" I scream, probably loud enough for the car next to us to hear.

"That's the spirit! We believe in you."

"You better update us as soon as it happens, okay? I wanna have my own bed back." Jade shudders.

"Jeez, sleeping next to me isn't *that* bad." Vinny retorts.

"Vinny, nobody wants their arm grabbed at random points in the night. I'd rather sleep next to a kicker. I'd even rather sleep in the same room as those two lovebirds."

"Hey!" I interject as Vinny and Jade laugh.

I scroll through my phone as Vinny and Jade bicker about sleeping arrangements in the front of the car. Sometimes, these two feel like the parents I never thought I needed, but ones I'm so glad I have. Even though they've seemingly made it their lives' goals to make fun of me for eternity, they always have my best interests in mind, regardless of the methods used to deliver their advice.

Vinny enters the hotel parking lot and parks directly next to Spencer's car, right in the front near the sidewalk. He turns off the car and turns around to meet my gaze. "Go on, get your man!" he exclaims. I immediately unbuckle my seatbelt and run into the hotel lobby, my heart beating faster than my brain can think.

I dart to the elevator and press the up button. After thirty seconds of waiting, I run to the stairwell and sprint up five flights of stairs. I don't think I'd ever be able to do something as stupid as this if I didn't have adrenaline running through my veins. I feel manic. This works better than alcohol!

I run to room 507. I fiddle in my pocket for about twenty seconds before I find my room key. I'm both physically and mentally shaking. I am ready. I am ready. I am ready.

I open the door and see Spencer sitting in the desk chair, typing away at his computer. All of my built-up adrenaline immediately melts away. I'm not ready. I'm not ready. I'm not ready.

Who knew this would be so *hard?*

I quickly say hello to him and enter the bathroom, slamming the door behind me. I splash water on my face and quickly wipe away a combination of sweat, tears, and hotel tap water. How am I supposed to do this? Everything that happens right now is real, and I can't use the excuse that I'm drunk. I'm terrified. Horrified, even.

It's go time. If I don't do it now, I'll never do it. I need to do it before it's too late and I'll never know if he truly likes be back or not.

I walk out of the bathroom as nonchalantly as I possibly could pretend to be and lay down on the bed next to where he's sitting. I lay on my stomach, my feet swinging in the air as I look at him.

"You guys must've left a while after we did. I've been here for ten minutes already." Spencer says, apparently completely unbothered by my exasperated expression.

"Yeah, Vinny took a while in the bathroom."

I need to full send. It's now or never, and I'm not a fan of never. Come on, Charlotte, you've been in stressful situations before. Hell, you've been in six stressful situations *today*. You can do this. Just say it.

"Hey, I have a question." I say.

He swivels around in the chair, now facing me. "What's up?" he asks with a smile on his face.

"What happened last night after we left Gabe's room?"

He pauses, a pinkish hue dusting his face. "Well, you fell asleep, so Vincent, Jade, and I took you back here. You woke up again, threw up, and fell back asleep again.

"Why do you ask? Did Vincent show you the photo of me holding you already?"

It's go time. "I knew you were a poet, but I didn't know you were also an actor."

His eyes widen. "What are you talking about?" he asks, his voice shaking.

"You're a good liar, y'know."

He stares, shocked, mouth agape, completely speechless. I get up from the bed and grab him by his shoulders. "Be honest, Spencer. Did you mean it?"

After about three seconds of silence and tension so thick you could cut it with a knife, he stands up, his face now completely red.

"You weren't supposed to remember that." he whispers, breaking free from my grasp.

He runs out the door.

Chapter Fourteen

Spencer

Run.

My internal world begins to crumble into nothing as the external world rocks back and forth. I've never been much of a runner; every time I ran the mile in my freshman year, I became nauseous to the point of nearly throwing up. Back then, running had no purpose other than to torture me and the other hundred kids in my gym class. Now, I'm running away from my biggest fear and my worst nightmare.

She knows. My cover's blown.

I tried to hide my dissatisfaction all day. Throughout comp, I had come to accept that what happened last night was going to be left in the past, as a mystery solved by no one other than me. I was content with my life continuing as normal. She broke a promise she never made.

I don't know why I ran away. Confronting people is hard. Running is an admission of guilt, although it was evident that she was convinced she was right, and she is. I thought she wasn't going to remember.

I should be happy for myself, but I can't bring myself to be. I've wanted her to know this for years, but this isn't how I wanted to tell her. I wanted it to be more…romantic, with a magical evening of dance and laughter accompanied by a poem or two. I've been dreaming of this moment for so long, but those dreams have crashed down in front of me and turned into nightmares.

She's running after me to reject me and tell me it was all a lie, isn't she. Of course that's what she's going to do. She would've stayed put if this wasn't the case, right? God, I can't think straight. All I know is I screwed up *bad.*

My therapist has said a dozen times that I need to face my fears with confidence. Here I am, running away from my problems like a little baby. I don't *want* to be a baby, but sometimes we don't get what we want in life.

"Spencer, please!" Charlotte exclaims, trying to catch up with me. "Stop running!"

I can't say anything. I dart to the nearest stairwell, swing the door open, and race down the stairs, jumping down two to three at a time. She follows, the sound of her yelling echoing off the walls and following me like a dog.

Five flights of stairs feels like twenty. I feel like I'm stuck in an infinite time loop. When I finally reach the ground floor, I feel awfully dizzy, mild nausea creeping in. This is when I should stop, but I can't physically prevent myself from running. It's as if my legs grew their own legs and ran off, leaving my mental state in the dust behind them. As if *that* makes any sense.

I run down the ground floor hallway and into the lobby, my legs moving faster than my mind. The sliding doors to the parking lot slow me down and allow for Charlotte to slightly catch up. Where do I even go from here? What could possibly be my next move? I can hide in my car. I can run and run and run forever until I shrivel up and die. That doesn't sound too bad right now.

I hunch forward on the sidewalk near a grassy field people use to walk their dogs to catch my breath. Before I can think of what I'm going to do next, I turn around and see Charlotte lunging forward at me. She makes contact, and the two of us fall down and into the grass. I hit the dirt with a thud.

She kneels above me, her hands pressed against my arms in a way where I can't move. "I'm so sorry," she whispers, "but not really."

My tense body begins to slow down and relax, and I start to sob. A real ugly cry, full of sniffling, wincing, and embarrassment. I stare at the sky above me to avoid making eye contact. I can't look at her right now.

She lets go of one of my arms to push my head down so I *have* to make eye contact. "Spencer, what the hell was that for?"

I'm so filled with fear that I forgot how to speak. I force myself to look at her, and her entire face is red, tears streaming down her cheeks. She's panting, probably from the running. My heart feels like it's about to explode.

"Spencer, please..." she pleads, "why did you run from me..."

"I don't know..." is all I could muster.

"Was everything you said last night true?" she asks, her voice trembling. "Was all of it true?"

I slowly nod, trying to stop the tears from flowing down my face and onto the pavement. "Verbally, goddamnit!" she exclaims.

"Of *course* it's all true!" I blurt out.

She steadily lets go of me and stands up. "Let's sit on the sidewalk. We need to talk."

I get up and wipe the dirt off of my pants. We sit on the curb of the sidewalk, right next to my car. My head falls into my hands as my entire world seems to fall down. We sit here for about a minute before I begin to speak again.

"Were you telling the truth?" I ask.

"Yeah. All of it. I was fully convinced the alcohol would make me forget everything."

"Oh."

"Why did you run away?" she asks. "You scared me real bad, y'know."

"I…didn't want to face my biggest fear so quickly."

"Fear that I reciprocate?"

"No," I lift my head, "I was convinced you were lying to me and this was all one big game to mess with me."

"Why the hell would I do that?"

"I just…I thought there was no way you actually liked me back. After all this time…it didn't make sense."

"Well, there *is* a way. I really, really like you."

She grabs my hand and interlocks my fingers. "Look, Spencer, I don't know what else to say that I didn't say last night, but I really, *really* do. You're one of the kindest souls I've ever met. I wish I fell in love with you sooner."

I can't believe my eyes, ears, and every other body part for that matter. I feel like I'm dreaming. It's true. It's all true. She's not playing with me. She likes me back. Holy shit holy shit holy shit.

She continues. "Also, seriously? Since our freshman year? I don't know how I never noticed."

I attempt to laugh, but it comes out awkward. "Not sure, maybe you were just too busy."

"I wish I wasn't. Y'know, you're the most perseverant person I've ever met. Being able to crush on a person for so long…it's impressive. You have a lot of resolve."

I can be cheesy now, right? The cat's out of the bag. "Well, you'd have as much resolve as I do if you got to see the prettiest girl in the world every single day. I would've been content with just that."

"But you don't have to be *just* content." She grabs my cheek and turns my face toward her. She's smiling, dried tear marks covering her cheeks. Her eyes are still watery, but nothing's coming out. Her hair is still perfectly put together in her braids, and her bangs look nothing but amazing. She's gorgeous, as always.

"Spencer, will you be my boyfriend? Like, my *real* one."

Even though I had a hunch that it was coming, my heart still felt like it exploded into a million little pieces inside my chest. My face feels hot; I can't even imagine what shade of red I am right now. My hands are shaking out of both excitement and leftover fear. The scared feeling still lingers in my mind, but my heart is full of love.

"Of course I will!" This is the greatest day of my life!

I pull her into a deep, heavy hug. "I'm glad you asked, I don't think I ever would have had the confidence to."

"Believe me, I know." she laughs as she hugs me back.

She lifts her head up to where she's looking at me while we continue to hold each other. "You really thought I was lying last night?" she asks with a grin.

"I thought it was too good to be true."

"Let's be honest, people who 'just wanna be friends' don't make out with each other as many times as we did."

"Or at all." I add.

"Yeah, probably. I think we were a little bit *too* passionate with each other for our lack of relationship status, but I can't complain, now can I?"

"I never did." I chuckle.

She pauses. "Can we watch the sun set before we go back inside?" she asks. "It's so pretty out here."

"Of course we can!"

She grabs my hand and leans on my shoulder as we face the setting sun in front of us. The wind slows down, and it feels like no one else is in this parking lot other than us. The sunset is pretty, sure, but I find that I keep turning around to stare at her pretty eyes. In normal lighting, her eyes look simple and brown, but when facing direct sunlight, they have a beautiful glow to them, mixing different shades of green and brown. I love her eyes. I love *her*.

She loves me.

Holy shit, she loves me.

The sunset includes multiple hues of red, orange, yellow, and pink. A cloud, kinda shaped like a heart if you squint hard enough, slowly floats across the sky, as if purposely placed there. Sometimes, it feels like everything is perfectly placed together as if it was made to push me along. Every piece has slowly fallen together over this strikingly obscure competition season. I wouldn't have it any other way.

I feel like I'm dreaming, but I've already pinched myself enough times to know that it isn't. My back end also wouldn't hurt from this curb if I was dreaming. Everything is real. She's real. She's real, and she loves me. My life sure is full of surprises. Perhaps this isn't really as much of a surprise as I thought. Everything happens for a reason, right? Maybe this was coming all along.

The sky is becoming dark, and the night becomes cold. We're wearing nothing but our team t-shirts and jeans. I can feel Charlotte begin to shudder from the temperature. "Do you want to go back inside now?"

"Yeah, the pretty part's over anyway."

The two of us stand up, hand in hand, and walk back inside the hotel. I glance at the hotel desk employees, who give us a weird look. They're probably confused about the two kids who just ran out of the hotel after each other that came back just fine. Either that or they don't care and give that look to everyone. Regardless, it doesn't really matter.

We take the elevator this time. I really don't want to walk up the same five flights of stairs I just ran down a little while ago. The elevator is slow and long, and with the two of us being alone in it, all I want to do during this short ride is pin her to the wall and kiss her.

Unfortunately, it would take a lot longer to muster up the courage to do that than it takes to finish our elevator ride.

The elevator door opens, and Charlotte skips to our room. She unlocks the door and we enter. I notice something on Charlotte's pillow that wasn't there when we left, and I let go of her hand to examine it. Upon closer examination, I see a small box with a giant bow on top alongside a note that says: *"Just in case. Good luck! Love, Vinny and Jade."*

I remove the bow to see that what I am holding is actually a condom box. I let out a yelp and quickly throw them to the edge of the bed, right where Charlotte is. She picks up the box and laughs.

"They're such assholes," she smiles, "I love them for it."

"They definitely know how to scare the shit out of me."

"Speaking of Vinny, he told me a little secret of yours."

I pause, thinking of what I could've possibly told him. It clicks. "He told you I got a speeding ticket?"

"No, he said–wait, what? *You* got a speeding ticket? You drive like you're eighty!"

Shit, I'm wrong again. "What did he tell you then?"

She walks up to me, placing one hand on my chest. Our eyes lock. "He told me that you didn't actually break the robot all those times."

Aw shit. Gotta come clean now. "Yeah, I'd say almost every time was fake."

"Oh come on, I stressed myself out a few times over fixing that damn robot over and over again! It *was* a pretty smart move on your end, though."

"Can't blame me for having to find different ways to see you more often. If I asked, it would've been weird."

"I guess so. Is it okay if I change real quick? I need to get this damn comp outfit off ASAP."

I nod and turn around. I listen to her fumble through her bag. Once the sounds cease, she turns me around with a grin. "You don't *need* to turn around, y'know."

"I don't want to make you uncomfortable."

"I appreciate, but I don't mind. I'm not stripping *completely* naked."

"Alrighty then. Should I change too?"

"Only if you want to." she winks. Of course I do. If I change into lounging clothes, we can lounge *together*, as boyfriend and girlfriend. I still don't believe I'm not dreaming at this point.

I grab a black t-shirt and a pair of blue sweatpants from my bag and take my team shirt off. I turn around to see Charlotte pulling hers off, revealing a black bra and a dark red mark on her neck. I didn't know hickeys were supposed to last that long. Holy shit, she's beautiful. This must be how the ancient Greeks must have felt when they saw Aphrodite. I believe Charlotte's prettier than her.

"Don't stare for too long," she smiles, "you should put a shirt on before I forget about changing and pounce on you."

"Gotcha," I reply as I quickly put my other shirt on. She slips on a purple baggy t-shirt, hiding everything I couldn't stop gawking at.

I quickly take off my jeans and replace them with my sweatpants. These pants are a little big, so I tie the waistband tight. I turn back around to Charlotte sitting on her bed, removing her braids. She's wearing a pair of black running shorts as a replacement for pajama shorts. I'm seeing a lot of her I haven't seen yet. I'd be a fool to complain.

She slides off her bed, grabs my shirt, and pulls me close. "Let's celebrate, for real this time!"

She pushes me onto my bed, and I turn myself around so I'm parallel to the bed, leaning against the headboard in a sitting position. She hops on top of me, tying her hair into a cute little bun. I feel like I'm in heaven.

"Darling..." I blurt out. Upon hearing myself, my heart drops. I went too far immediately. God, I'm such an idiot!

She covers her mouth with her hands, surprisingly visibly excited. "Oh my gosh, I've always wanted to be called that! Can you keep calling me that?"

Not the reaction I expected, but one I definitely appreciate. "Of course, darling."

"Yay!" she squeals.

I can't help myself. I *need* to kiss her. I grab her by her waist, pulling her down to my level, and kiss her. She seems to melt into it while wrapping her hands around my shoulders. As she breaks free from the kiss, all that's left on her face is a giddy smile.

"Our first kiss in our relationship!" she exclaims.

"One of many." I smile.

"Gosh, I just *need* to hug you." she mutters as she wraps her arms around my neck, digging her head into my shoulder. I wrap my arms around her waist as she pushes herself even closer to me. Too close.

She lifts her head up enough to make eye contact with me while she laughs. "Jeez, you're poking me already."

I cover my face with my arms and shrink into the bed out of embarrassment. "I'm so sorry..."

She moves my arms away and kisses me again. "I wasn't complaining."

Passion. Bliss. Vehemence. Love. All of those words could describe the romantic tension in the room between the two of us. We haven't done anything we haven't done before yet, but it very noticeably feels different. It's not a dirty little secret between us anymore; we're allowed to pursue each other with the avidity we've been quietly craving this entire time. Nothing's limiting us anymore.

She slowly moves back and forth, inner thighs pressed against my waistband, as I pull her hair with one hand and tug at her shirt with the other. I'm starting to get used to doing the things she likes, when she likes them. Honestly, I could care less about what she's doing to *me* as long as I know she's enjoying what I'm doing to *her.* Hearing her audible approval is all I need.

While I am a big fan of her sitting on me, I'm feeling the sudden urge to get on top of *her*. Like, an uncontrollable urge that I crave, as if I need to do it or else the entire world is going to collapse. Is this what teenage boys are supposed to be like? In the first three years of me crushing on her, I never had any…impure fantasies about her. The most scandalous dream I had was holding her hand and kissing her. It wasn't until after we started fooling around that my mind started wandering into different, more adult realms. I guess we *are* technically adults now, so it's fine, right? It still felt weird to think about those things, but it's much less awkward now that the barrier of relationship titles is gone.

I break free from our warm, wet embrace, pick Charlotte up by her waist, and slowly push her onto her back, making sure she's not too close to the edge of the bed. I lean on top of her, my hands next to her shoulders, digging into the comforter. She stares at me with glossy eyes. I love the face she makes when she *needs* me. God, I need her too.

"Don't just sit there," she pants, "come down here."

"Of course, darling." I reply as I bring myself down to her level, my face darting to the left side of her pretty little neck that I want to put more bruises on. I push my head up to her ear and whisper "is this okay?"

"Please."

I spent close to two hours one time researching exactly how to give someone a successful hickey, among other relationship must-haves. I wanted to make sure that I knew how to do everything and be the perfect man for her if the time came. I read dozens of relationship forums an deven took notes on how to please a woman in every single way.

I use my right hand to grab the collar of her shirt and pull it down so whatever I do is easier to hide. The first time we made out, the hickey she gave me was in the middle of my neck, and my mom chewed me *out* as soon as I got home. I think she was more pissed about the location than the act itself.

I'm definitely doing something right, according to her loud groans filled with obscenities. She's pulling on my hair and pushing me deeper and deeper into her. I'm enjoying every second of it. My eyes, ears, and hands are in pure ardor. I would do this forever if the world let me. I love this gorgeous woman.

I slowly travel to the other side of her neck, adjusting my arms accordingly. I am craving the idea of seeing her completely covered in kisses and bite marks. I'd be worried that she's in pain, but from what I can tell, she's feeling every emotion *but* pain.

Once she's completely covered, I sit up to take a good look at her. She's staring at the ceiling, eyes widened, breathing heavily as if she had just run a mile. She uses her thumbs to pull her collar back down so I can see the damage I've done. Wow. Her shoulders and upper chest are smothered in red and purple marks. I make a camera out of my hands and pretend to take a picture. I need this in my memory book. I want to look back at this moment for years to come.

I lean over to the nightstand and grab my water bottle. I'm completely parched from all of the everything I've been doing over these past few minutes. My mouth is awfully dry.

"Guess I won't be able to wear tank tops for a while..." she laughs.

"It's nearly winter, so you don't have anything to worry about."

"My mom likes to keep the house at seventy-six! I'm so screwed when I get home!"

"My bad."

"No, it's a good kind of screwed, I promise."

With that clarifying comment, I lean back in, kissing her on the lips this time, wasting no time before sticking my tongue back into her mouth. I watch as her eyes roll to the back of her head. I was initially worried that she wouldn't like me being so direct, but it seems like she liked it. Honestly, I think I'm just paranoid. She's so obviously enjoying it.

After about thirty seconds, she grabs my hand and directs it under her shirt. I pause and break free. "Are you sure?"

"Please," she pleads, "I want it so bad. I'll stop you if I have to. I feel like I *need* you to do this. Please touch me."

She lets go of my hand, leaving mine to rest on her bare waist. Her hand travels to the back of my neck and pulls me down to continue kissing her. I comply as my hands explore the newfound territory I've unlocked. Touching her is like pressing my hands against a pure cashmere sweater in a fancy clothing store. Smooth and soft, as if she's way too expensive for me. She's priceless, in my eyes.

My hand slowly crawls up her stomach, ribs, and eventually her chest. Her bra has a velvety feel to it. I cup my hand around it and press down, slightly squeezing. My thumb grazes her bare skin that isn't covered by the bra. I'm the luckiest man in the world, by far.

She continues to make loud, passionate noises that are barely muffled by my mouth being on top of hers. Music to *my* ears, but I hope these walls aren't as thin as I think they are. I'm sure hotels are used to things like this happening all the time, but a noise complaint would absolutely kill me.

I am in pure, unadulterated bliss. I feel like I'm in a dream. The only thing making this different from a dream is that I can feel *everything*. Every touch, every grab, every dig into my back from her nails, every throb in my lower half. It's all real, and I can't believe it. This must be how it feels to win a million dollars, but even better.

I'm being greedy. My squeezes are getting tighter, my kisses are getting rougher, and the beads of sweat falling down my face and body are flowing faster. All I want to do right now is rip both of our shirts off and push our bodies together, skin to skin...

Jeez, I'm disgusting.

Well, anyone else would want to do the exact same thing if they had the chance. She's the most gorgeous woman in the world, how could I possibly hold back now? She's officially mine; I can kiss her as many times as I want to, as long as she's okay with it, with absolutely no repercussions.

Charlotte breaks free and playfully pushes me off of her. I fall onto the bed with a soft thud as she sits up and kneels in front of me. "I'm feeling kinda warm…" she mutters with a grin, "is it okay if I take my bra off?"

"Yes," I say without thinking. If I did think about it first, I would've said the exact same thing.

She turns around so her back is facing me. "I have a hard time taking this one off, mind disconnecting the hooks for me?" she asks with a wink.

"Of course I don't mind."

I sit up and lift up her shirt, revealing her bare back and her bra band with four hooks that need to be unclasped. My hands take their sweet time, slowly traveling from her waist to the band. I disconnect the hooks pretty easily; I've seen women online complain about their husbands not knowing how to take it off, but frankly I think those men are just incompetent. A monkey could take a bra off.

As the band falls, she fumbles around with her shirt and pulls her bra off in one fell swoop. She turns around to face me again, tossing the bra to the side of the bed. She stares at my lower torso as she unties the knot I tied in my sweatpants. I pull back, shocked.

"What are you doing?" I ask. "They're gonna fall off."

"Making you more comfortable. It looked like you were going to stretch a hole into these."

"What a compliment."

Her hand travels down to places I couldn't fathom while her eyes maintain eye contact with my lower body. I can feel my body writhing underneath her, yearning to embrace whatever she's planning on doing.

“May I?” she asks, her fingers grabbing my waistband.

“Do what?” I reply, frozen solid.

“Y’know, help you alleviate some stress before tomorrow.”

Same excuse she used when we kissed for the first *real* time. I push myself back toward the headboard, and she follows. “Are you sure that’s the reason why, or is it just an excuse?”

She laughs. “You got me there. I just wanna do it. So, may I? I did an internet search on how to do it. I’ll be gentle, I promise.”

“I would never say no to that,” I say, as whatever was left of my adolescent naivety combusts into flames, never to be seen again.

* * *

I feel like a brand new person. I feel like a *man*. I feel like I could take on the world in a boxing match and win without receiving a single punch. I’m on top of the world. This is the greatest night of my life.

The two of us are now in the bathroom, washing away our communal sins. I’ve already cleaned up my lower half, and now I’m washing off my pruned middle and ring finger. Charlotte is next to the toilet, cleaning herself up, slightly off balance. She almost fell over when she tried getting out of bed for the first time. I’d say I did a pretty good job.

While we didn’t have sex, primarily because we’re not ready yet, secondarily because I’m way too terrified to commit to that right now, we basically did everything else that’s close enough. I feel like a sponge that just got all of the soapy water squeezed out of it. Ecstatic because I served my purpose, but completely exhausted and wrung out.

I've taken so many mental pictures that my storage is nearly full. My brain's voice recording box is bursting at the seams with moments I'll treasure. I've learned how to do so many brand-new things; I've had so many "first-times" over the past two hours that I feel like a brand new person. I don't know why men complain about doing stuff like this; I could serve this woman for days without a care in the world.

Once I'm done drying my hands off, I walk over to Charlotte and give her a quick peck on the forehead. She smiles as she throws the toilet paper she was using to clean herself up into the toilet and flushing it down. She slowly makes her way to the sink to wash her hands. I wrap my arms around her waist and lean my chin on her shoulder as the sink water hums.

"This reminds me of a hallucination I had once." she laughs.

"Come again?" I ask, bewildered.

"I had a dream about you back in September, and the morning after, I saw you in my bathroom mirror, resting your chin on me the same way. Crazy how everything comes full circle."

"How many Red Bulls did you have the night before?"

She smirks. "Not enough, apparently."

Hand in hand, we exit the bathroom and lay down under the covers of the bed we did...everything on. I set my alarm for tomorrow morning and wrap my arms around my brand-new girlfriend. She kisses me on my cheek and curls up in my arms.

"I love you, Spencer."

I thank whatever deity that is above me for allowing me to get used to hearing it.

"I love you too, Charlotte."

Chapter Fifteen
Spencer

"Good *mooooorning*, sunshines!" a shrill, mildly masculine voice exclaims, pressing their hands against my back.

I open my eyes, only to be blinded by Jade opening the curtains, spreading the warm light of the waking morning sun into the room. I turn and see that Vincent was the one who pushed me.

"Welcome back to the land of the living, Spence." he smirks.

"What time is it?" I ask, my voice hoarse.

"Six in the morning on the dot," Jade replies.

"Oh come *on*," I groan, "we don't have to be up for another two hours at the earliest."

"Nonsense!" He pulls the comforter off of us, and the world suddenly becomes freezing cold. I look down, realize my hand is still under Charlotte's shirt, and quickly remove it. He laughs.

"Looks like youse had a long night." he snickers. I quickly pull it back before Charlotte wakes up, but it's too late. She squirms from underneath my hold.

"What's going on?" she mutters.

"We've been woken up." I reply. The two of us sit up and lean against the headboard.

"We're here to celebrate! We even bought you two a little something last night."

Jade brings over a box with a mini cake in it. It's a white cake with what looks like buttercream frosting. Written on it is the word "virgin" written in black with a giant red X over it. Charlotte laughs as she pushes the box back toward Jade.

"I'm sorry, but we can't accept this," she says, "that didn't happen."

"Wait, Jade, the box is unopened." says Vincent, holding the condom box they graciously gifted to us last night.

"Virginity is just a social construct anyway. Some people think it's one thing, some people think it's another, all that matters is that they did *something*. Let's have it with lunch today."

"Mr. D is gonna kill us if he sees that."

"All the reason to bring it."

"Can we go back to bed now?" Charlotte asks. "I'd like my extra two hours before playoffs and judges and all that."

"Sure, but your breakfast's gonna get cold. We drove back to Jersey to pick up some bagel sandwiches for you two."

"Jeez, you guys really wanna make this morning wonderful." I say, finally adjusting to being awake.

"Well," Jade smiles, "we want to go to worlds, and you two are the only people who can make that happen. Plus, what's better than a cigarette after sex than a pork roll, egg, and cheese after sex?"

"I told you, we didn't ha–" Charlotte begins, but Vincent presses a finger to her lips and makes a shushing sound with his.

"Believe whatever you wanna believe, hun. Now we gotta go, but be ready by 9:30, alright? I'll leave without you if you're not."

"Okayyyy."

The two of them leave, and Charlotte turns to me and gives me a big kiss. "I wish this morning would've started different."

"Honestly, I wouldn't want it any other way." It was a dream of mine to wake up next to the girl of my dreams as her–well, *our* friends wake us up with silly gifts. How else would I want to spend my mornings?

She hugs me, melting into whatever warmth is left on my body. My arms instinctively wrap around her waist as I kiss the top of her head. This is so surreal. Every time I blink, I feel like I'm dreaming again, and this is all one big dream. I have to keep reminding myself that this is real, she is real, I am real.

"How are you feeling after last night?" she asks, drawing a line with her finger on my chest.

"I felt things last night that I never knew were possible."

She laughs. "Good, then?"

"Ethereal."

"I swear, you're like an English major in a Computer Science student's body," she says before kissing me.

"I'd do myself a disservice if I didn't do both. Picking one major sounds awful."

"Isn't it called a 'concentration' at Harvard or something?" she asks.

"Yeah, but no way I'm getting in today," I chuckle.

This evening is when most top universities release their Early Action and Decision results. Thankfully, I'll be too busy with competitions today to think that the trajectory of my life is going to be determined by one click of a button. It's better to not think about it.

"I have faith," is all she says before kissing me again.

I lay back down, and she slides back under the covers next to me. I grab her once again, pulling her as close as physically possible. "When we lay together, I feel like I'm in a straightjacket." she snorts.

"In a good way or a bad way?" I retort.

"A good way. It's comforting, I think."

"You're comforting."

"Ugh, you're just too sweet."

We lay together, side by side, for a while. I trace around the parts of her body I can reach, fiddling around with her clothes, memorizing every component's feel and location. This keeps my hands busy while my face covers her neck and cheek with kisses.

"You're awfully touchy this early in the morning, Spencer Laine." she whispers.

I let go. "Is that a problem?"

"Not at all," she replies, and I continue.

I don't know how many times I can say I'm the luckiest man in the world, because it feels like I become luckier every waking moment of this divine life of mine. Love is a dangerous drug, and I'm high as a kite.

"Part of me still wants to convince myself that this is all a dream," says Charlotte, in between short breaths, "but, thankfully, the soreness in my neck and lower half keeps proving me wrong."

"Whoops." I reply.

"No, it's a good kind of stinging feeling. Proves I'm alive, human, and madly in love with the person who made me sore."

"Y'know, you're a lot more poetic than you make yourself out to be. Have you tried writing a poem before?"

"I've never tried, and frankly, I don't think it's my thing. I'd much rather leave the poem-writing to the professionals, and I'll just wallow in myself through some other form of media, like screaming at music in my car."

"Professionals, huh?" I chuckle.

"Yeah, like you."

"Woah, I'd never consider myself to be a professional."

"Come on, I know you've been writing for years. Will I get to see them at some point?"

"Um..." I pause, "they're sorta– well, *incredibly* depressing. A lot of pining and yearning. I really could only write love poems with you as my muse, and you know how I felt about the possibility of us being together."

"I kinda catch your drift."

"Well, imagine Morrissey and Pete Wentz had a child who got really into poetry. That's the best way I can describe the vibe my poems had."

"Two of my favorites! Jeez, that *does* make them sound depressing," she laughs.

"Don't worry, I'll write you something new soon, now that I can see you as my lover instead of an out-of-reach enigma."

"Can't wait!"

I've never really put a name to my writing style before, and comparing it to a British vegetarian and an allegedly bisexual bassist was nowhere near what I thought I'd describe it as. I've listened to her playlist for hours on end, looking into the lyrics to see how she's feeling. She likes to add and remove songs from time to time, so there was always something new to search. A lot of her songs are kinda whiny, but the lyrics are really beautiful, and I like reading them and analyzing their flow. I never would've known of the world of Pete Wentz lyrics without her, but I'd rather read his band's songs than listen to them.

I need to write her a poem. One that's not heart-wrenchingly bleak. She deserves a million poems, and I'd be willing to spend the rest of my life writing them all until my hands fall off.

I'm a hopeless romantic who isn't hopeless anymore. Go figure.

"How do you think today's going to go?" she asks.

"Who knows? We're ranked third. All we need is to do well in playoffs and we'll qualify. How do you feel?"

"Well, there's a lot of pressure on me to win."

"Pressure on *us,* you mean?"

"Yeah, but if something goes wrong, they're blaming me before they blame you, since I'm Captain and all."

"You know full well that I'm going to defend you if something goes awry. Jade and Vincent will too."

"Yeah, but seeing the looks of disappointment on their faces if we don't make it is going to hurt so much more than it has in previous years. We're *actually good* this season; I can't let them down when this is the best we've been in years."

"Everything is going to go as planned, I promise."

"I really hope I can believe that." She kisses me, opens the comforter, and hops out of bed. My world is suddenly cold again. "That workout we did last night is finally catching up to me. I'm starving."

She grabs the bag of bagel sandwiches on the TV stand, pulls both of them out, and tosses one at me. I slowly pull myself out of bed and embrace the freezing atmosphere. Grabbing the sandwich, I sit down on the chair in the corner while Charlotte swirls around in the desk chair, happily eating. I unwrap the foil only to be pushed back by the strong yellow hue of an egg bagel. They're my absolute favorite of all time, but I have no clue how they knew that. I swear I've never told anyone.

I take a bite. It's cold, but the saltiness from the pork roll and the cheese are still strong. Despite my love for hot showers, I prefer my food to be cold or cooled down at the least. I don't like burning my tongue as much as I like burning my skin. With this in mind, I also have an outrageously bad spice tolerance.

We eat in silence, checking our phones for the first time in a while. I haven't looked at mine since everything went down last night, and the only time Charlotte checked hers was to put on music while we...hung out. Something about making out with the girl you love while listening to The Cure is truly heavenly. I don't even like The Cure all that much.

"Yo, take a look at this."

Charlotte tosses her phone at me with the screen open. I pick it up with the hand I wasn't using to eat and I see a photo of us sleeping, taken this morning by Jade. My face flushes with embarrassment, but this isn't nearly as embarrassing as when we got caught kissing at our last comp. *That* was a terrifyingly embarrassing video, from what I've heard.

"At least you look pretty in it," I say as I toss the phone back to her. I appreciate that I'm allowed to say stuff like that out loud without it being weird.

"Oh, shush," she smiles, and we continue to eat.

Charlotte tosses her empty wrapper into the trash can and quickly jumps out of the chair. "All that grease makes me crave a nice, warm shower. I'll be back."

She quickly grabs her stuff and walks over to the bathroom, closing the door behind her, keeping it unlocked. I didn't plan on going in there anyway, but it's nice to know that she trusts me enough to not lock the door.

I grab my notebook and a pencil and begin to jot down ideas while listening to the shower water crash into the bathtub. I want this poem to be the pinnacle of my writing prowess. Simple, legible, easy to understand even if they have never read a poem in their lives. I want to be blunt when I tell her how much I love her and *why* I love her. I need to tell her how gorgeous she is.

Unfortunately, happy poems have never really been my thing, because there's never been anything poem-worthy for me to write about. I don't gain writing inspiration from winning competitions or programming.

Writing poetry is kinda like coding . Lines of code, lines of a poem. There's different styles, genres, subgroups, and languages. The main difference is that poetry doesn't have comments to explain what's going on like code does. Poetry and programming are two things you'd never expect to be super alike, but here I am. Maybe all programmers are poets utilizing their potential in a more practical manner.

The thing is, I've been wallowing in my self-deprecating love for so long that these newfound emotions are impossible to write about. I've only felt entirely happy about this relationship for about twelve hours; that's not nearly enough material to write a cheerful romantic poem. I also can't write a depressing love poem, because I have no reason to be depressed about my love anymore.

The bathroom door opens, and Charlotte walks out with freshly braided hair, her team t-shirt, and a pair of black jeans. "Is it just me, or is it cold in here?" she says, shuddering.

I grab the same hoodie she put on two nights ago and toss it at her. "You can wear this until we have to compete."

"Perfect, thanks." She throws the hoodie over her head and puts it on. "This smells just like you."

"What do I smell like?" I ask.

"Your body wash. Coconut Vanilla Crush, right?"

"How do you know?"

"Vinny uses the same thing."

Sometimes I wonder just how close Vincent and Charlotte actually are. Will she tell him all of the naughty details of what we were up to last night over pizza today? I guess I don't really mind, but I sure hope I'm not in the room while she does it. I'd probably die of embarrassment. Vincent seems like the type of guy to ask for *all* of the nitty gritty details, and Charlotte's the type of girl to tell him.

I grab my showering equipment and walk into the bathroom. It's not super steamy in here; I wonder how hot

Charlotte likes her showers. Probably not as hot as I do. I've never met another person who has the same preference as me. I wonder what temperature she prefers.

Now I'm thinking of her showering. How adolescent of me.

I turn the shower water back on and strip down to nothing. While waiting for the water to heat back up, I stare at myself. Nothing has changed since the last time I showered, but I look and feel different. I feel older, more mature. My expression is different. People joke that you look different after you've had your first time, but we didn't even go that far, and I'm still noticing differences. Maybe other "first-time"-esque moments speed up aging in some way. I need to stop staring at myself before I have an existential crisis again.

I quickly cleanse my body, washing the last of our combined sweat down the drain. The scalding water feels so good, burning the memory of her touch into my skin. The hot water makes me feel awake, aware, and ready for today.

I shut the water off, and the world becomes cold again. I wrap my towel around my waist and begin my skincare routine. I rub everything in faster than usual so I can have more time to spend with my pretty girlfriend. I'm being greedy, but I don't care; I want to be near her as much as I physically can.

I quickly get dressed, grab my stuff off the counter, and exit the bathroom. I drop all of my things into my suitcase and zip it up. I'd like to be fully packed a while before we have to check out of the hotel today. Again, I'd rather get this done now so I can hang out with my gorgeous girlfriend for longer.

I look up, and Charlotte is sitting on our bed, staring at me with what I know now are her "I want you" eyes. "What's up, darling?" I ask, knowing exactly what she wants.

"Come here," she says, signaling with her finger. As any smart man would, I listened, and laid down next to her. She crawls over me and sits down on my stomach, one braid laying over her shoulder and one pressed against her back. She has a devilish grin plastered onto her face.

"What time is it?" she asks.

"About eight," I reply, "we have an hour and a half before we should leave."

"Perfect. Wanna go for round two?"

"Excuse me?"

"I mean, we have the time, right? Do you want to?"

"I'd be a fool if I said no."

* * *

Imagine if you took a sponge, squeezed out as much water as you physically could, and then flattened it with a hydraulic press. That's exactly how I feel right now, and it's somehow the best I have ever felt in my life. I didn't know I could feel this way.

I never want this honeymoon phase to end.

The two of us lay side by side, disheveled, belts thrown into the corner, pants unzipped, a paper towel roll by our bedside, with balled up pieces scattered across the floor. Charlotte's pigtail braids have fallen out and been reduced to a singular ponytail. Her face is pink with orgasmic relief, and our deep, raspy breaths match each others.

Is this how adults feel? Is this what adults do? Put their mouths in places they shouldn't and swallowing their fears of maturity alongside the release of orgasmic ecstasy? I shouldn't care about that; all I really want to think about now is how good she feels and how all I can taste is her.

She went first. All I can remember is involuntarily closing my eyes, running my hands through her hair with one hand and gripping the mattress with the other, and my mouth groaning every curse word known to mankind as well as her name about half a dozen times, all while my legs vibrated like a cell phone and my back arched into a nearly perfect parabola. I wish I could've looked at her longer and taken more mental images, but I physically couldn't stop myself from shutting my eyes and digging my head into the pillow.

After we cleaned that up, it was my turn. My ultimate goal is to give her the best experience of her life, but since I don't have the skills to do that yet, a mind-altering experience will have to do. I kinda knew where I was going after last night, but I made sure to ask for her input every so often. Though, every time I lifted my head up to say something, she pushed it back down.

She tastes how I assume a cigarette feels: warm, comforting, and incredibly addictive. I kept looking over her body to stare at her eyes, but they were facing the headboard, and all I could see was her neck, covered in the bruises I made last night.

Thirty minutes of pure, unadulterated euphoria passed. I held onto her hips with my free hand as her lower body convulsed for nearly fifteen seconds. I felt everything as she felt it, but I could tell she felt it even harder. She pulled on my hair so hard I thought she was about to rip it out and give me a bald spot. If we didn't receive a noise complaint last night, we were about to now. People ought to be awake now. I could never complain, though. I never thought I'd enjoy hearing my name out loud as much as I do. It's such an exhilarating feeling.

I feel so dirty, but in the same way that a vintage painting feels old. Not in a bad way, just a way.

"I feel like my whole body is throbbing," she whispers.

"Same," I reply.

I pull her toward me by her waist and bring her into a big kiss. Her mouth slightly opens, which is my cue to press my tongue in. We taste like each other. Every part of each other. I don't care where her mouth was just a few moments ago. If anything, it makes the overall experience even more intimate.

I wish I could spend the rest of my life kissing her. I want her to be the only person I interact with, talk to, and coexist with. I want her so bad. I need her so bad. Yet, somehow, I *have* her. In my arms.

After about ten minutes of the sloppiest, messiest makeout session of my life, my alarm goes off, meaning it's 9:15 and we have to leave in fifteen minutes. I planned accordingly, just in case we needed to clean ourselves up. I let go of Charlotte and she rolls out of bed, pulling her hair out of her ponytail.

"Damn, now I have to redo my braids," she groans.

"Want me to braid your hair?" I ask.

"You know how to braid hair?"

"I have two little sisters," I smile, "of course I know how to braid hair."

She sits back down and I grab her hair tie from her hand. I wouldn't say I'm the best hair braider in the world, but I know how to make it look nice and tight without hurting her. My sisters would cry to my mom if I tugged even a little.

Charlotte grabs her phone and takes a selfie of me braiding her hair. I see the angle she's holding it at and drop everything, realizing I left my pants unzipped. "Hey, you can see my underwear in that!"

"Whoops, I'll crop it."

I finish braiding her hair in a single braid, and she runs over to the mirror on the wall to check it out. "Wow, this is really good!" she exclaims.

"Much appreciated."

I zip up my pants and throw out our used paper towels into the small trash can in the bathroom, extensively washing my hands after. I shut off the bathroom light and grab my suitcase. Charlotte is spraying perfume, probably to hide the immediate smell of whatever we just did. She sprays me as well. I now smell like cotton candy, roses, and other femininely floral scents. If I smelled like this in front of my mom without proof of having a girlfriend, she'd automatically confirm her previous assumptions of my sexuality.

"Ready to head out?" she asks.

"Whenever you are."

Hand in hand, we grab our luggage and exit the hotel room we had so many shared first-times in. I kiss her forehead a few times as the elevator slides down to the ground floor. We walk through the hotel lobby and leave through two sets of sliding doors, typical for most hotels. As the business guy, Vincent generally checks us out of our hotels through an app on his phone, so there's no need to talk to anyone.

"Jade just texted me. They left already and took Benji with them." says Charlotte.

"I was gonna drive you regardless, so no worries." I reply, unlocking my car's trunk. I grab her suitcase from her and toss it in the back alongside mine. My trunk is a mess, I haven't been able to clean it for weeks. My toolbox, just in case I break down again, is laying wide open instead of being strapped to its typical spot.

We hop in the front seats of my car and I turn everything on. She immediately connects her phone to my car and starts to play her music. Listening to men whine about being unlovable is not exactly how I would prepare for a competition, but it being *her* playlist of men whining makes it all okay.

Her left hand latches onto my right as I exit the parking lot and begin our drive to the venue. The path to get there is mostly linear, so I don't mind driving with just one hand. I'd rather hold her hand than the steering wheel.

"Honestly, I am beyond excited for today." I say as we stop at a light.

"I feel like I should be more stressed, but my body is still in paradise. The only thing that's affected from stress is my mind; physically, I'm still in the same state of euphoria."

"Wow, I didn't know those feelings lasted that long."

"I didn't either. How do you feel?"

"Completely emptied, in some ways."

She laughs. "I guess I kinda wrung you dry."

The rest of the drive is silent, other than Charlotte's music playing on my radio. I use this time to think about the competition ahead, our potential to qualify for worlds, and what that would mean for our team. Going to worlds in my senior year would be an amazing opportunity, and I'd get to skip the first week of next semester. It also means, every night after we compete, I get to be completely alone with Charlotte without a chaperone in sight, unless Vincent and Jade count.

Jeez, I need to get my mind out of the gutter.

I park next to Vincent's car and turn off my car. Taking off my seatbelt, I lean over the middle console and kiss Charlotte's cheek. "Ready to go, darling?"

"Yup. Man, I love it when you call me that."

"I'll keep doing it, then."

I check my car's clock for the time: 9:43. I hear a knock on my window and see Vincent and Jade's faces plastered onto it. I unlock the door and they hop in the backseat.

"Let's talk strategy real quick." says Jade.

"I talked to both the number one and two seeds at different times last night, and they said they both wanted to pick us." Vincent chimes in.

"Holy shit," says Charlotte, "Grouping with them would practically confirm our spot for worlds."

"Who says they won't pick each other?" Jade asks.

"The top ranked teams have a bit of a rivalry with each other." I add. The top ranked teams, The Saints and York County Robotics, are two well-established teams from the Pennsylvania area, and from what I have heard, absolutely hate each other. Apparently, after some sort of logistics argument, students and mentors from Saints broke off and created the county team. Teams breaking up to create new teams isn't super common, but this happened nearly twenty years ago, and they're still salty with each other. They've been consistently top five for the latter half of a decade now, and they've never even considered Grouping together.

"So one of them is bound to pick us." Charlotte muttered.

"We don't have any issues with either team, right? Please, Charlotte, don't reject them." Jade begs.

"Nah, there's no bad blood. I wouldn't reject either of them, they're two viable options. Plus, if we don't get picked, the next best team is Shell-Shocked, and there's no way in *hell* I'm picking them. I'd rather drop out."

"Frankly, it's too late in the season to pull some bullshit like that. We may need to put our differences aside if necessary."

"I guess, but I hope it doesn't come to that."

"Well, that was easy," says Vincent, "ready to go inside?"

The four of us hop out of my car, our stuff in hand, and walk inside the venue for the last time. Jade grabs Charlotte's hair and examines it. "I thought you didn't know how to braid like this. It looks really good."

"I don't, Spencer did it for me."

Vincent and Jade turn to me with a puzzled look. "I have sisters," is all I said, and it seems like they understood.

I hold the door open for everyone. The three of them thank me in varying levels of enthusiasm. Mr. Davis is waiting by the door for us. He sees Charlotte, still wearing what is very obviously my hoodie, and gives me a weird look.

"You two ready for today?" he asks.

"Yup." Charlotte smiles, and he walks to the stands.

Charlotte and I break away from Vincent and Jade and enter The Zone to prepare for Group Pairings. Upon coming closer to our Zone, we see two students in blue t-shirts with shells on their backs standing inside. Charlotte grabs my arm and pulls me closer to her. Sylvia isn't there, but she's a part of their team, which is even worse.

"I don't wanna see her today," she whispers, "I don't wanna sour this wonderful morning."

"I won't leave your side, I promise."

"Please don't."

We approach our Zone and discover that the two Shell-Shocked drivers are the ones in our pit. "Hey Spencer, hey…*Charlotte*. Sorry, I forgot your name."

"Hi, Shawn. What are you doing in our Zone?" I ask him.

"Rumor says that Saints and York are gonna Group together at this comp. If they do, you guys should pick us. We're close enough in times that I think we can beat them, or at least make it to finals."

"You're on our list." Charlotte lies. She would rather choose anyone else.

"Good to know. See y'all later."

They walk away, and she turns to me. "I've never hoped that someone was lying to me more than I do now."

“I really doubt they’re telling the truth. No way they’ve fixed a twenty-year argument today. I saw the way their mentors looked at each other yesterday.”

“If they *do* pick each other, I’m gonna have to pick Shell-Shocked, aren’t I? I *can’t*. Not while she’s with them.”

“You don’t have to do anything you don’t want to.”

“I think I’d *have* to, though. There’s so much pressure for us to do well, and if I make a smartass decision, Mr. D’s gonna have my head shoved in the robot. I would be more okay with picking them if she wasn’t with them, even though I can’t *stand* Shawn. Never have.”

“Fair. I trust that you’ll make a smart and self-motivated decision.”

“That makes one of us.”

The intercom turns on, and the announcer exclaims that it’s time for teams to head to the field for Group Pairings. Charlotte pulls my hoodie off and drops it next to my backpack on the floor. We hold hands as we slowly walk through The Zone, making eye contact with every Zone except a certain coastal team’s. We line up by rankings, and we stand in between Shell-Shocked and Saints. The drivers on Saints keep staring at us and jotting stuff down in a notebook I can’t quite see clearly. All I can see is “904208” at the top of their paper. Hopefully that means something good.

The announcer begins his spheal. “It’s 10am, you guys know what time it is! All of our top sixteen teams are on the field, so let’s see who’ll be paired with who! Starting off with our number one seed, 603104, York County Robotics!”

York’s two drivers, both female, enter the main field. The older-looking girl is handed the microphone. I’ve seen her compete before. “We’re team 603104, York County Robotics, from…York County, Pennsylvania, and we’d like to invite team 511317 to Pair with us today.”

Charlotte and I stare at each other, absolutely flabbergasted. No way they picked Shell-Shocked before us! We’re ahead of them by two seconds! What do they have that we don’t?

Shawn and his Driver walk up to the field and quickly accept. After handing the microphone back to the announcer, Shawn turns around and gives me a mean grin. What a dick.

“Our next Group Captain is team 213864, The Saints!”

Their drive team walks up to the field and grabs the microphone, hesitating for a moment. If they pick the fifth place team instead of us, I genuinely have no clue who we’re gonna pick. It’s over if this happens. It’s so over.

Charlotte grips my hand tight enough to cut my circulation off as they begin to speak. “We’re team 213864, The Saints, from York County, Pennsylvania, and we’d like to invite team 904208 to Pair with us today.”

We’re saved!

Charlotte and I quickly walk to the microphone. She breaks free from my grasp and grabs the microphone, her hands shaking. “Team 904208, The Devils, from Smithville, New Jersey, accept this Pairing offer.”

The crowd cheers, and I can hear Mr. Davis shouting “LET’S GO!” from the stands one hundred feet away. The microphone is taken from Charlotte and we begin to chat with Saints.

“You’re probably wondering why Shell-Shocked was picked before you guys,” says their Controller.

"I was wondering that exact thing," I reply, "what's that all about?"

"I hate to break it to you, but it's legacy. Shell-Shocked has a history as a well-known and well-respected team. This is the first season in a while that youse have been good. York is probably playing it safe."

"That's dumb," Charlotte mutters.

"No, it actually makes a lot of sense," I add, "thanks for filling us in."

"Of course, man. How's your robot doing? Do you guys need us to check anything?"

"We should be alright, thank you. I would ask the same about your robot as well, but I'm sure you're fine."

Their Driver chimes in. "Actually, our robot has been drawing a *lot* of current recently, and I heard from the grapevine that you guys have a really good electrical team and haven't had any errors this season."

Man, do these kids have info on everything? "You're looking at the electrical lead right here." Charlotte concedes.

"Oh shit. Can you take a look?"

"Sure!" she beams. For her, being asked to help a prestigious team is probably ecstatic. She looks so excited; her eyes are gleaming.

After the Group Pairing Ceremony ended, we walked back to The Saints' Zone, which is fortunately right across from ours. We have a lot of time before our first playoff Round, and we'll be going against Group Seven. No biggie.

As Charlotte runs off to help Saints, I stay back at our Zone to do my routine checks on the robot. Nothing should have changed since last night, but it doesn't hurt to check.

Upon turning the robot on, I notice a red glow from the sensor lights. That's not good. I check the hardware client on my laptop to see that none of the motors are showing up. This isn't good.

I check the robot and see that a sensor wire is sticking out of the frame. How did we not notice this? Charlotte wouldn't let something like this happen. Maybe she wasn't feeling well? Maybe she was busy with dealing with me. Regardless, this is incredibly unlike her. I'll tell her when she comes back.

"Your batteries look pretty old, I think that's gotta be the problem." I hear Charlotte coming back to our Zone with the Saints' drive team. "I don't think you guys are charging them long enough in between Rounds, which makes them lose current faster."

She grabs one of our plug-in voltage and current displays and hands it to them. She built them with Mr. Davis over the summer, and they have a little screen that shows exactly how much power our rechargeable 12V batteries have. We've had battery issues in the past, so while I spent my summer building a driving simulator, she spent her summer building a doohickey that ensures we never die on the field again.

"You guys can borrow this until the end of the day, and take one of our batteries for our first Round. Sign this paper so we can remember you took them."

Their Driver smiles with relief. "Wow, thanks! This is really cool. You guys have really stepped up your game since last season."

She points to me. "Spencer and I spent a really long time fine-tuning our skills. He built a whole driving simulator for us to practice on!"

"Woah, you guys need to upload that and make some serious money!" their Controller exclaims.

The two Saints walk away, and I turn to Charlotte. "Hey, there was an open sensor wire over here, did you check something last night and forget to plug it back in?"

She grabs the wire, her smile fading. "No, I didn't touch the robot after our last Round."

Her hands and legs shake as if she's about to collapse onto the floor. "No, I wouldn't let something like this happen…I didn't touch the robot…I didn't do anything that would've constituted this…oh my god, we could've had so many issues…"

I grab her and pull her into a hug. "Hey, it's okay, we all make mistakes."

"No, I don't make mistakes like these. Jade took a photo of the robot before we left this school last night while we were waiting for Vinny to get out of the bathroom. I'll ask her to send it to me. We'll see if it was unplugged last night."

She breaks free from our hug, whips out her phone and calls Jade. "Hey, can you send me the photo of Ross you took last night? There might be an electrical problem."

She hangs up and opens her text messages, where Jade immediately sent a photo of the robot. Charlotte zooms in to the exact spot the exposed wire was, and lo and behold, it was perfectly plugged in. She drops her phone onto the foam mat floor and quickly plugs the wire back in.

“I didn’t do that. Someone else did.” Her expression is cold, emotionless, and terrifying.

“What do you mean?”

She turns to me. “We’re being *sabotaged.*”

My heart drops. “*Sabotaged*? Are you sure?”

“I think so, and I think I know *exactly* who did it.”

I think back to Shell-Shocked standing in our Zone. What were they doing in there before we got to The Zone? Wait, I shouldn’t jump to conclusions. Maybe it was an accident. Maybe *I* unplugged it for some reason. Seems unlikely, but not impossible. I tend to ‘break the robot’ a lot, but not this time. I would *never* do something like that during competitions.

“I think you’re right, but I don’t want to jump to conclusions before we have more proof.”

“Yeah, but hopefully there *isn’t* more proof.”

I hug her again. She digs her head into my chest, and I can feel her eyes starting to water. “It’ll be okay, Charlotte. She can’t do anything to you while I’m here.”

“I hope so.”

We sit down on the floor of our Zone in silence for a while. I’d watch playoff Rounds right now, but I’d rather sit here and console her. She needs it more than I want to sit in the stands.

After about thirty minutes, Maggie walks up to us and grabs the robot cart. “We gotta queue in a minute.”

“Heard.” I say as the two of us stand up. Charlotte quickly does her routine electrical checks, even more carefully than she usually does. I just know she feels awful right now.

Even if she's convinced she didn't unplug it, she's still blaming herself for it somehow. I really wish she wouldn't.

We begin our trek to the field with our robot, Maggie holding the cart handle and me holding Charlotte's hand. "How are you feeling?" I ask her.

"Like a sponge crushed under a hydraulic press and set on fire."

"It'll be alright. We're in a great Group. We just need to do what we always do."

"Which better be enough to win."

"I promise it will be."

Since we're the pick of the highest seeded Group, we have the luxury of going first. Some would say it would give them performance anxiety, but I would argue that I'd rather get it over with and watch everyone else.

"Let's relax a bit this Round, okay?" I whisper. "We're going against Group Seven, nothing special."

"Hey, I'd still like to do well," she counters.

Her and Maggie drop off the robot onto the field, while I set everything up on my end at the Table. Fear is settling in, but deep down, I know we're going to do well. We have a great robot, no issues, and we're with another great team. The odds are in our favor.

Charlotte comes back and grabs her controller, fiddling with the joysticks. "Ready, darling?" I ask.

She immediately turns her head, eyes widened. "I'm 'partner' here, remember? You can call me darling later. Don't break tradition after all these years."

Silly me. "Alrighty. Ready, partner?"

"I am now." She kisses me as the announcer screams our team number into the microphone. We put down our controllers to stick up our devil horns. We have lots of traditions, and while they might have seemed goofy when we were sophomores, it feels nostalgic now. I can't believe there's going to be a Round where I stick my horns up for the last time. I don't want to even *think* about that right now. We have a competition to win.

The Round begins. Nothing else matters except for pressing buttons and listening to Charlotte's commands. When she says shoot, I shoot. When she says extend, I extend. I listen to her every word. Competing is the only time I'm around her when I forget to think about how drop-dead gorgeous she is. All I can focus on is doing great.

Our Round ends at 2:52. Slower than last night, but fine for our first Round of the day. I'm not worried too much; the Captain of Group Seven maxed out at 2:54, and I know Saints are gonna do great.

"Nice one," I say to Charlotte.

"We can do better," she mutters. "We *will* do better."

Charlotte and Maggie grab the bot and we make our way back to our Zone. In our Zone, four grown adults are seemingly interrogating Vincent and Jade. Uh oh, judges are here.

Vincent turns to us and smiles with relief. "Great, you guys are here! Spence, this wonderful lady had a question about our codebase."

"Yeah, sure, lemme just open it up."

I open my laptop and begin to explain particular components of the codebase, specifically why I decided to put different branches in different places and where I was able to optimize space. All of the countless hours of tidying up the codebase were worth it. Honestly, it's so well commented that anyone could understand it, even a child with no programming experience at all. The whole reason I did that was to win awards, but it taught me a lot about how to not make my code look like hieroglyphics. I'd feel awful if I graduated and left and Maggie couldn't comprehend a thing I wrote.

Being a writer of poetry also makes writing code comments a lot more natural. I'm good at providing context and explaining things thoroughly. Who would've thought that the humanities are incredibly important, even in Computer Science?

I finish my spheal about the code and the woman thanks me for her time. A different judge turns to Charlotte and asks about some electronic-related questions. She answers them as if she's been practicing for years. She practically has been, with how many judge interrogations she's been through. She talks their ears off for about ten minutes about different signal wiring practices we implemented and how we haven't had *any* electrical errors this entire season. She even begins to draw circuit diagrams to explain further. The judge is having a ball with her, and seems genuinely interested in what she has to say. She worked hard to optimize electrical, and it's paid off like crazy. She's probably the most knowledgeable person here.

Man, competitions are a *great* opportunity to admire my incredibly intelligent, immensely capable, and absolutely jaw-droppingly beautiful girlfriend. I get to stare at her while she talks and talks and, even though I don't understand all of it, I'm proud of her nonetheless.

"Now that the robot is in front of us, I can continue talking about the different mechanical components of it," says Jade, and the conversation moves to her. The three of us listen intently as she explains the physics behind every move she's made this entire semester. Again, I don't understand most of it, but I am well aware that it's impressing these judges.

The judges leave nearly thirty minutes after we got back from our Round. I see Saints come back, their drivers holding expressions that mean nothing but pure happiness. "How did it go?" I ask them.

"We hit a PR! 2:45!" their Controller beams.

Woah. 2:45 is insane. "Congrats! I'm assuming we've advanced to the next bracket, right?"

"Of course. Neither team broke 2:55."

"Phew."

I get a text from our team chat that pizza has arrived. Charlotte opens her phone, reads the text, and immediately turns to me. "Let's get going!"

We walk out of The Zone and make our way to the cafeteria. Before we open the doors, I hear a faint yelling sound coming from an all-too-familiar middle-aged sounding man. I wonder if they brought the cake.

The door opens, and lo and behold, Mr. Davis is standing over Jade and Vincent's giddy smiles as they're holding a small container. Yeah, they brought the cake.

"Are you two serious? What if a judge walks in here and sees this? Are you two twelve or something?"

"Relax, Big D, it's just a joke." Jade snickers.

Mr. Davis' head turns red. "How many times have I *told* you not to call me that, goddamnit!"

He turns around and sees Charlotte and I walking up to the table. "I don't even wanna *think* about you two right now. Just keep winning, okay?"

We nod in unison, and he lets out a large sigh and begins to mutter. "We need chaperones at these damn events again...I've been way too lenient with these dumbass kids..."

The two of us sit down, across from Vincent and Jade. I sit next to Maggie while Charlotte sits at the end of the table. Maggie turns to me with a disappointed look on her face. "You're a dick, Laine."

"What do you mean?" I ask, as if I don't know exactly what she means.

"You made me lose twenty bucks to *Benji* of all people!"

"A 'congrats' would've sufficed, Lin." I retort.

"Wait, there was a *bet*?" Charlotte asks.

"Yeah," Benji interjects from the other side of the table, "we made a bet on how long it would take for you two to get together."

"Damn, it was obvious to everyone but us, huh."

"Well," Vincent chimes in, "I mean this with love, but youse are the dumbest people in the universe."

Charlotte leans over the table and jabs Vincent in the shoulder while he laughs his ass off, similar to how I'd assume a hyena would act. I'm a big fan of their friendship.

I pull out my phone and watch the current playoff Round. Shell-Shocked completes their Round perfectly, followed by a PR by Group Four's second team. They nearly matched times, with Shell-Shocked being slightly ahead, but it's close. A fumble by York could destroy Group One once again.

"Do you do anything other than watch Rounds?" Jade asks. "I feel like you're always watching some team play on your phone."

"I write on occasion. Plus, either of these teams could be our opponents. I'd like to be aware of any shortcomings before going on the field."

"You're gonna have such a fun time if we qualify for worlds," Vincent adds, "there's gonna be so many new teams to look at."

"You don't even *know* how excited I am for it."

He snickers. "Believe me, I have a bit of an idea."

I put my phone down while Jade cuts through the cake they bought for us. She cuts tiny slivers so our entire team can snag a slice. I'm not exactly sure how much of a fan I am of the apparent state of my virginity being put on display for the team I've grown up with to view, but at least the cake tastes good. It's a strawberry cake with a jam filling inside. Looks like an aesthetic portrayal of a period.

We eat cake and talk about the inevitable doom that we call our classes. I mention a calculus homework I haven't started that's due Tuesday, and the three in front of me all groan in unison. At least they all forgot about it too.

I hear a crash coming from my phone, and yelling from the stands. I instantly grab my phone and see that York fell off the monkey bars. Their frame is bent and their elevator is still hanging on the top rung.

"Group One is going to be out again." I mutter.

"Holy shit, we have a chance again!" Charlotte exclaims, her face brightening. Her smile could light up this entire dingy cafeteria if she opened her mouth enough.

"We just have to beat Group Three, who just blew Group Six out of the water." Vincent adds. "Shouldn't you guys get ready for next Round?"

"Yeah, let's go, guys." Maggie stands up, and Charlotte and I follow. We quickly throw out our paper plates and walk back to The Zone, with a little bit more of a pep in our step than last time.

A faint vibe of dread, regret, and evil emanate through the Zone. The air is heavier. Something's wrong, I can feel it.

"I don't feel right." says Charlotte.

We enter our Zone, and everything is an absolute mess. All of our sensor wires have been disconnected and thrown around into a jumble of cables. My heart drops. I guess this is the undeniable proof I needed that Charlotte didn't mess up last time. Someone is doing stuff to our robot.

Charlotte immediately jumps into action, grabbing her wiring diagram and plugging stuff back in quickly. "Spencer, go stand out there for us. We're gonna be late," she says.

"Are you sure? Do you need any help–"

"*Now!*" she snaps. I know this version of Charlotte all too well. This is how she becomes when something is wrong and it's her job to fix it. She may look mean and rude on the outside, but she's having a full on panic attack on the inside. She's about to crumble into pieces and collapse to the floor.

I give her a quick kiss on the cheek. "Got it. See you there."

Since we're not allowed to run in The Zone, I walk with purpose to the field. On the way there, I accidentally lock eyes with Shell-Shocked's Zone, and specifically Sylvia. She grabs my arm, stopping me in my tracks. Her sharp, freshly manicured nails dig into my arm.

"You did this to yourself, Spencer."

"What the hell are you talking about, Sylvia?" I ask.

"This is what you get for stealing my girl from me."

"She's not 'your girl' anymore. She's *mine*. Now let go of me." I break free from her grasp and keep walking. As much as I enjoy calling her mine, now isn't the time to revel in happiness. I need to get to the field as soon as physically possible.

I make it to the field and the lead queuer meets me with a glare. "Hello, 904208. Where's your robot?"

"It'll be here soon. We're experiencing some technical difficulties."

"You know that'll be a ten-second penalty, right?"

"Yep." Shit. I forgot about playoff penalties. If you're late to a normal Round, you don't get much other than a slap to the wrist and a warning. On the other hand, being late to a playoff Round means extra time gets added to your total. It's five seconds for the first Round, ten for the second, and fifteen for Finals.

I drop my stuff off at the Driver's Table and wait patiently for Charlotte and Maggie to arrive. They enter the field after two minutes of pure torment to my mind and quickly drop off the robot. Charlotte comes up to me, visibly exasperated.

She updates me. "Robot's fixed. Saints helped me plug stuff in. I asked them if they saw anyone come by our Zone, but neither of them were there. I think they could tell we didn't do that."

"I hope so."

"Ten seconds, right?" she asks.

I nod. She sighs. "It just means we need to finish ten seconds faster than we normally do."

"We've got this. How are you feeling?"

"An overwhelming urge to strangle someone who isn't you has come over me. Don't let Shawn or Sylvia come near me, or I swear–"

She's interrupted by the announcer calling our names once again. Out of habit, we stick up our horns. "Ready, partner?" I ask.

"Something like that, yeah." We begin.

I become an entirely different person when I Control. I enter a completely clear state of mind, hard as diamond. Nothing gets through to me other than Charlotte's commands. All I know is my X-Box controller and my robot's location on the field. I've studied this game for so long that it's almost second nature to me. I am in my element. This is what I'm meant to do.

I can feel sweat dripping down my face. I don't care how disgusting I look. I need to perform. I'm putting on a show to the audience, full of people who probably couldn't care less about my team. Regardless, *I* care. I care about where we're going and where we'll end up. We determine the paths of nearly a dozen talented students.

It's a lot of weight on my shoulders, but I believe we can do it.

We balance. The timer stops. We finish at a record-breaking two minutes and forty-three seconds, shaving *six whole seconds* from our previous record, and crushing the records of every other team around us. I inadvertently begin to jump up and down, grabbing Charlotte to pull her with me.

"I'm so proud of you!" I exclaim.

"We did amazing! Too bad we have the penalty."

"Another great Round from team 904208! Without that penalty, they would have broken the championship record!" the announcer booms into the mic.

We quickly pack up our robot and drop it off at our Zone. Hand in hand, Charlotte and I make our way back to the stands to watch the rest of the teams in our playoff bracket compete. We sit next to Vincent, Jade, and Benji. Mr. D, alongside some other teachers from our school, sits behind us.

The second team of Group Three, a Pennsylvanian team named Close-Call, absolutely demolishes their Round, finishing in two minutes and fifty-three seconds, exactly the same as our post-penalty time. This isn't good. They're supposed to do slightly worse. Hopefully Saints can clutch again this time.

The Captain of Group Three is a team from Delaware named The Lions after their school's mascot. Their Driver and Controller kiss before their Round begins. I guess Charlotte and I are not the only romantic pair out of the drive teams here. I'm surprised that most drive teams *aren't* dating, with how close you have to get with your fellow driver. It feels inevitable, but I probably wouldn't have thought that just a few days ago.

The Lions crush their Round as well, completing the track in a whopping two minutes and forty-three seconds, matching our pre-penalty record. This isn't good. I swear they weren't that great during qualification matches, so what the hell happened between yesterday and now? They did better than Saints did last Round, and Saints is the number two seed.

"Please, Saints, please..." I hear Charlotte mutter.

I grab her hand and squeeze tightly. "They've got this."

As The Lions leave the field, The Saints enter with their robot, their faces grim. Their Driver is holding their stomach, as if they're pressing against a stomachache. This isn't good. The worst part about competing is that you have to depend on other teams to not have issues on top of ensuring that *your* team doesn't have issues. It's a good example of how teamwork can be both influential and detrimental, but not much else.

They begin. I watch as, despite the apparent stomach issues their Driver is facing, they instantly cool down and focus on the task at hand. Unfortunately, it's not enough.

It's never enough. There's only so fast you can drive, so fast you can press buttons. Your robot's peak is determined by mechanical, electrical, programming *and* business components. If you build it a certain way, there's only so fast you can go without reaching the human limit.

The Saints' battery begins to go out as they reach the seesaw, and they barely make it and balance. I look at the clock, and my heart drops to my shoes and onto the floor.

Two minutes and forty-four seconds.

We lost.

By one second.

I turn to Charlotte. Her head is hung low. I can see tears falling down her cheeks and onto her jeans. She chokes on her slow, deep breaths.

“It’s over,” she whispers, “I have failed.”

Chapter Sixteen

Charlotte

Fuck.

Breathe in, breathe out. I can't breathe. Every breath escapes my mouth as if it's stolen from me. I feel weak. I feel like nothing. I *am* nothing.

An all-too-familiar feeling rises in my throat. I need to run. Now.

I stand up faster than I should have. My entire world becomes dark and blurry for a brief moment. Without giving myself time to recover, I run out of the stands, jumping over seats and slipping through the audience. I can hear yelling behind me, but it's incoherent. All I can focus on is getting to a bathroom as soon as possible.

I arrive at the main entrance and dart toward the women's bathroom. Completely empty, thank goodness. I swing open the middle stall door, lock it behind me, fall to my knees, and lean my head over the toilet, bracing for impact. Everything comes out: my breakfast, lunch, cake, and anything else I happened to swallow over the past eighteen hours. All of it escapes my stomach in a frenzy as a combination of vomit and tears mixes into the toilet bowl. How disgusting this must look and sound doesn't even cross my mind.

It stops and starts again. I feel weak. Every time I think it's over, I gag once again, and I keep going. My hands grip the toilet seat as if I'm holding onto the handlebar on a rollercoaster, except this is the exact opposite of fun and exciting. This is depressing, dreadful, embarrassing. *I* am depressing, dreadful, and embarrassing.

I deserve this and everything else coming to me. Or out of me.

I wait a full minute after the rest of whatever I've consumed in the past day has exited my body. Once I can confirm that I'm finally done, I lean back against the stall door and begin to sob. It's all my fault. My final season is over. We're done. I'm done.

How could I let this happen? I shouldn't have left the robot unattended. I shouldn't have sacrificed our entire season so I could eat some stupid pizza and cake. If I wasn't such a fat piece of shit, this wouldn't have happened–

No, this has nothing to do with my weight, and everything to do with how much of a goddamn idiot I am. I *knew* someone was messing with our robot; it was clear that *someone* wanted us to lose. Why would I let them do it again? If I didn't get that penalty, if I had just stayed with the robot instead of eaten, none of this would've happened. We would've advanced. I would've made my team proud.

But no, I prioritized socializing over making sure that we had a clear shot of qualifying for worlds. If I didn't get that penalty, we could've *won.* If I was smart for once, we would've progressed further. God, I'm such a *selfish idiot!*

Sylvia's words ring in my ears. *Stupid. Worthless. Horrible. Waste of space, air, and everything else.* God, it hurts. It hurts so goddamn bad to know that she was right about everything she said about me.

They all hate me. I hate myself.

I try to stand up, but I didn't take into account the sudden weakness of losing so much body weight at once. My knees lock, I collapse, and everything goes dark. I open my eyes, and I'm back on the floor, my legs straight, brushing against whatever grime and dirt plagues this bathroom. I'm disgusting.

There are certain parts of you that are inherently there, forever. For me, it's the inevitable release of complete and utter failure. I am nothing but a mindless, dim-witted failure.

I feel and hear a knock on the stall door, slightly shaking me with the vibration of the collision. I thought the bathroom was empty. "Occupied…" is all I could muster.

"Charlotte, darling, are you okay?" It's Spencer. This is the women's bathroom, how did he get in here? Didn't someone stop him?

"No…" I reply.

"Are you in a state where you can open the door?" he asks.

I slowly lift my arm up and unlock the door, which swings open from the outside. I lock eyes with him; he looks like a nervous wreck. His eyes are watering, tear stains covering his face, but he's not currently crying.

"How long have I been in here?" I ask.

"About six minutes. I had to convince a security guard to let me come in here."

"Oh." I try standing up on my own again, but Spencer grabs my underarms and lifts me up on is own.

"You're pale as a ghost," he mutters.

"I think I threw up everything I've eaten today."

"Oh dear, I'm so sorry. Here, let me bring you to the sink so you can wash your mouth out."

We slowly walk to the sinks together, him holding his arms around my waist for support. He lets me go as I wash my hands first, since they directly grabbed a toilet seat. Then, I cup water in my hands and shove it in my mouth, swishing back and forth for about twenty seconds. I spit it out and repeat the process.

"Y'know," I laugh, trying to make light of the situation, "this isn't the first time you've rescued me from a school bathroom."

Junior year, local competition. We had just come back from lunch, and my robot was completely broken. Electrical errors galore. Spencer tried to help, but he didn't know what to do. I was the only one who worked with the electronics at this time, meaning I was the only one who knew anything about it. We ended up making it to our first playoff match, but the penalty on top of another electrical error on the field made us lose in the first Round of playoffs. Spencer and I were blamed for the loss, and I spent an extra three hours at our next meeting proving to Mr. D that I was still a viable Driver and Electrical Lead. I still don't think he trusts me. He definitely didn't want me to be Captain this year, but that was a student vote without major mentor input.

She broke the robot on purpose. She said it was payback for getting 'too close' to my driving partner. We weren't that close at the time; we were just friends and partners. We worked well together, and she didn't like it.

"That's what you get for talking to that fuckwad too much." is all she said. After that, I remember running to the

bathroom, throwing up my breakfast, and walking out to Spencer waiting for me, worried sick. After a quick debrief, we walked back to the stands together to continue watching Rounds. Spencer never knew why I threw up that time, and I never wished for him to know.

I didn't know it at the time, but I should've talked to him more. So much more. He would've helped me break free from her. Why did I ever love her? All she did was hurt me. All she did was punish me for things that were either out of my control or not a big deal at all. I'm so stupid.

A sense of dread fills in the pit of my stomach, now made readily accessible from the amount of liquid I just vomited. That memory had been hidden for months, and it just now decides to be brought back when I'm being sabotaged yet again. She made me lose. Again. *She did it.*

I dry my hands and my mouth off with a stiff and nearly useless paper towel. I hold onto Spencer's arm as we exit the bathroom. I can hear Vinny and Jade chatting in the distance. Shit, they must be pissed. They're gonna yell at me and tell me that I'm a worthless Captain, Driver, *and* Electrical Lead. My friends are going to abandon me.

We walk out of the bathroom and I'm blinded by the sudden fluorescent light of the lobby. Spencer lets me go as two people of similar stature grab me and hug me. I adjust to the light and see that it's Jade and Vinny.

"Oh my god, Char, are you okay?" Vinny asks.

"Hun, we were worried sick! Why did you just run off like that?"

I'm bewildered. Why are they worried about me? They should be pissed right now. I should be getting yelled at.

"Guys, I lost." I sniffle as the tears keep flowing down my face.

"That's not important!" Vinny snaps. "Are you okay? You look sick."

"I'm not okay at *all*, Vinny. I lost! I completely decimated our chances of qualifying for worlds! It's over! *I* made us lose!"

"Stop with all this 'I' shit! This was a group effort. *We* lost. You're not the only person on this team who has to carry that weight."

"Spencer filled us in while we ran after you," says Jade, "you think you've been...sabotaged?"

"She did it. She did it last year, she did it again. She's made it her goal to torment me for the rest of my life, and I keep falling for it."

"What do you mean last year?" Vinny asks.

I explain what happened in our junior year. "Why is this just coming to light *now*? Why didn't you tell us last year?" Jade exclaims.

"I didn't want to get her in trouble...you know what would've happened..."

"Trouble is nothing compared to what I want to give her," Vinny mutters.

The announcer exclaims that it's time to hand out awards. I don't want to listen. There's only four awards to give out, and forty-eight teams here. If we win one of the awards, we'll automatically qualify for worlds, but if we don't, we're done. Usually, being third place at the end of qualification Rounds would be an automatic qualifier, but since both first and second place were kicked out of playoffs in the second Round, we don't have that kind of buffer. I don't want a false sense of hope.

"Can we sit here for a bit?" I ask. Without saying anything, everyone else sits on the bench outside the women's bathroom. I sit next to Spencer and lean on his shoulder.

Why did I think my friends would hate me? They're my friends. Even if they think I'm an awful person for losing this competition, they wouldn't say it to my face. They wouldn't hate me. We love each other; we've been through so much worse together.

Why do I automatically resort to the worst possible outcome? Why would my friends hate me? Why would they scream at me? They would never do that. Why must I always jump to the worst conclusions possible?

Despite wishing to avoid the awards ceremony, I can hear the announcer loud and clear. "Our first award is the Mechanical Award. This award goes to the team that displays an accelerated level of mechanical knowledge and skill. This doesn't exactly go to the best built team; rather, it's an award for the team that has a deep understanding of their hardware.

"With that in mind, congratulations to team 603104, York County Robotics from York County, Pennsylvania!"

The crowd cheers. Of course they win that one. Their robot is beautiful. So well designed and implemented that you'd never believe that a group of students built it. Honestly, I didn't believe them either until I heard them talking with the judges. Those kids know their stuff.

"Next is the Programming Award. This was a close one, let me tell you that! This one goes to a team that blew us away when explaining the nitty gritty details of their codebase. Their code was so simple that even a monkey could understand it!

"Again, this was an extremely difficult decision, but we chose to give this team this award, as the runner-up qualifies for another award. Congratulations to team 511317, Shell-Shocked from Point Pleasant, New Jersey!"

No. They can't win again. They're gonna go to worlds, and we're not. I curse under my breath, apparently loud enough for my friends to hear. "It'll be okay." is all Spencer says.

God, I wish I could believe him.

"Our third award is the Electrical Award. This award goes to a team that knew more about the electronics they were using than the electrical engineer judging them. One judge highlights that a student of this team talked his ear off for nearly ten minutes, showing exceptional knowledge of the ins and outs of their robot. This award was a no-brainer.

"Congrats to team 904208, The Devils from Smithville, New Jersey!"

Did I hear that right? Are my ears deceiving me? Did we just win an award?

Spencer grabs my arm and lifts the two of us off the bench. I suddenly gain the ability to run onto the field to accept the award. The judge I conversed with held the award and handed it to me with a smile.

"Congratulations," he says, "you deserve this."

I look in the distance and lock eyes with Mr. D's glare. It's softer than I expected, with us being booted out of playoffs and all. I hope he's proud of me for once.

Benji runs up to me and pulls me into a huge hug, almost making me drop the trophy. "I just ran some numbers, and we qualify for worlds! We're the second ranked team after the Finalists, right in front of Shell-Shocked!"

"We beat them?" I ask, my voice quivering.

"Barely, but we beat them! By one ranking point!"

Holy shit. We qualified. We're going for worlds, for the first time in more than half a decade. We're. Going. To. Worlds.

And I won the award that's getting us there.

The competition staff takes our team picture and we're sent back to the stands. The adrenaline of qualifying has begun to wear off, and I become weak once again. I should drink some water, maybe eat something.

I sit down in front of Mr. D. I match his gaze. "Congrats," he says, "you guys barely made it. No more penalties now, alright?"

"Yes, sir." I reply, my beaming smile misrepresenting my response.

I take a swig from Spencer's water bottle and eat a granola bar from Vinny's backpack. I would've packed snacks, but I've eaten a lot today and didn't expect for it to be all gone by afternoon.

Watching Finals calmed me down. There's no more pressure for me to perform. We're set for the rest of the competition. All I need to do is sit back, relax, and watch a few teams stress over winning. While I enjoyed winning once, I'm glad there's no pressure for me to win anymore. I like not hating myself every once and a while.

Group Three beats Group Four by four seconds and wins the competition. This makes our Group technically third place. Unfortunately, there's no bronze medals in robotics, only silver and gold. At least we have an electrical trophy to make up for it; it's arguably the most important trophy I've ever held.

Once the Final Round is over, my friends, Spencer, and I exit the stands and enter the lobby. I've never been more glad that I'm an upperclassman and don't have to take apart and pack up our Zone. I did my time, now it's time for the freshmen and sophomores to do it.

"I'm going to use the bathroom before we drive home, is that okay?" Spencer asks. I guess he's driving me home. I wouldn't want it any other way.

"Of course! I'll wait by the door for ya."

I lean against the wall next to the bathroom and check my phone. All that appears is a "Congrats" text from my mom. She couldn't come today because of work or something. Honestly, I'm still surprised she was here yesterday.

Yesterday feels like forever and a day ago. The past twenty or so hours have felt like twenty or so *days*. I feel like I've lived three additional lifetimes. I even have a *boyfriend* now. Who would've thought I'd get this far?

An almond-shaped acrylic nail flicks me in the forehead. I lift my head and lock eyes with Sylvia, whose face is mere inches from mine. "I need to talk to you." she snarls.

"What now, Sylvia? You torment me for months, you break my robot not once, but *twice*, AND you stalk me at my competitions. What else do you want from me?"

"You're such a little shit, you know that? None of this would've happened if you stayed away from that backstabbing blond freak. I knew he wanted you from the very *beginning!* Now you're *using him* to get back at me. I'm doing this because I love you, and *you're* doing this because you *still* love me!"

I do something that I would've killed myself over a year ago. While she's staring into my soul through my eye sockets, I lift up my right arm and smack her right across her face. She pulls back, holding her cheek, visibly disgusted.

"I *don't* love you like I did. You *never* loved me, you loved the idea of *controlling* me."

She grabs my shoulders and starts violently shaking me back and forth, banging my head against the wall. It hurts so bad. I was already severely lightheaded from the vomit; now I feel like I'm going to pass out again. I close my eyes, fading in and out of consciousness. Even when I stand up to her, I'm still outpowered.

At least we're in public this time. Doesn't anyone notice?

"You–you little bitch! You cocksucking, slutty whore! I swear to God, I'm going to *kill–*"

An arm grabs her by her shirt collar and drags her off of me. I open my eyes as Spencer grabs me and pulls me into a hug. "Are you alright, darling?" he asks, rubbing the spot on my head that was banged against the wall nearly a dozen times.

He turns to Sylvia. "Are you *serious*? What is your *problem*?"

"You goddamn homewrecker! You *stole* her from me! You forced her to break up with me so you could steal her from me! You're a rat bastard, Spencer Laine!"

"I guess you never noticed this, but she's her own person who can make her own decisions on who she loves. I guess the word 'no' doesn't really have a definition in your dictionary, now does it? Get the hell out of my sight, and leave my girlfriend alone, or I *will* press charges."

He points to a security camera directly above us. Spencer's dad is a well-known lawyer in our area and could easily get her arrested. Her expression fades into fear as she begins to understand the possible consequences of her actions. She can't hide in her car this time. She can't pretend it never happened. There's irrefutable proof that she's hurt me.

"Fuck. You." she mutters as she storms off, hopefully never to be seen again.

"You wish," I call after her. I break free from the hug and turn around. Spencer is trembling, eyes wide open with an expression that mixes fear with anger. "Are you okay?" I ask him

"That's not important. Are *you* okay, Charlotte?"

"Yeah, bit of a headache, but no big deal. She's gone. Thank you."

"Looks like she's gonna be gone for a while. Let's go home before she changes her mind."

We catch up with Vinny and Jade in the parking lot. For the sake of time, I decided I would debrief on the whole Sylvia situation after we got home. I didn't want them to be pissed on the drive back. For all they know, nothing happened, and everything is hunky-dory.

Spencer begins the ninety-minute drive home from the college as I choose the music. I forget the day's lows as I sing along to the songs I queued. As sick and twisted as my life is, at least I'm not as depressed as a Smiths song. I don't think I could ever reach that kind of low.

When I'm not singing, I'm watching as Spencer drives a single mile over the speed limit on the highway. People are passing him from all sides and one car even goes through the shoulder to pass him. Usually, I'd make fun of his driving, but at least we're safe. That's all I wanna be right now.

I wish I knew how safe Spencer made me feel years ago. I would've never gotten with Sylvia if I did. Spencer is one of the kindest, greatest people I've ever met, and I regret not falling in love with him sooner. I guess to really appreciate certain things, you have to spend a lot of time lacking it. I wish I never lacked him.

I really need to appreciate the present more. I did everything I've aspired to do over the past few months: I won a competition, I got rid of Sylvia, I qualified for world champs, and I confessed my love to the boy I had some well-strung dreams about. I've gotta thank my brain for planting those in my mind at just the right time. Crazy how things just happen, right? Maybe it was fate all along.

Spencer breaks the silence. "Did you know that the verb "cleave" is the only English word with two synonyms which are antonyms of each other: adhere and separate?"

I immediately burst into laughter. "Where the hell did *that* come from?"

"Nowhere in particular. It just came to me."

The drive continues with nothing but the round of the car running and my music playing. I notice a soft smile on Spencer's face that doesn't fade for the rest of the drive. He's so cute. I'm so glad he's finally mine.

After what I wish was forever but was probably only the allotted time our GPS gave us, he pulls into my driveway and puts his car in park. I suddenly get a call from Vinny. I pick it up and hear him scream like a little girl.

"What's your problem, Vin?" I ask him.

"Char, all of the colleges released admissions results! *I got into Brown!"* he exclaims, loud enough to blow my ear off.

"Oh shit." I check my email, and lo and behold, an email from MIT appears.

"Dear Charlotte, your admissions decision is available in your portal."

"I just got an email too." Spencer shudders.

We open the admissions portals for our respective schools and pause before the "open decision" button. I hand Spencer my phone. "You open it for me." I mutter.

He hands me his. "You do the same."

My hands shake like crazy as I press the button on his phone. I'm instantly met with confetti.

"Dear Spencer Laine,

Congratulations! I'm delighted to inform you that the Admissions Committee has admitted you to the Harvard College class of 20XX."

I hear his seat belt unbuckle as he pulls me into the biggest hug I've ever felt. This seems...good.

"Charlotte, you got in! You're going to MIT!"

I can feel my heart skip about five beats. "Wait, really?"

"Yeah! I'm so proud of you!"

He looks over to his phone, but I interrupt him with a kiss. "How does it feel knowing we're going to be neighbors next fall?"

He grabs his phone from my hands and immediately tosses it back. "Holy shit, holy shit, holy shit! We *both* got in!"

I take my phone back and see the acceptance letter along with Vinny's face on a video call. "Jade just got into Stanford! We all did it!"

I pause to take a deep breath. I feel like I'm about to pass out again, this time in a good way. Everything is tying together in a little pink bow, as if things are going to work out for all of us. I didn't think I'd be able to top the news of us qualifying for worlds, but here we are. I can't believe I've cultivated such an intelligent group of friends…and boyfriend.

"I'm so proud…I'm so proud of all of you…" I begin to sob.

"Hey, don't cry! This is only the beginning!" Spencer exclaims, grabbing my hands so tight, they feel like they're about to pop off. Despite the tears falling down my face, I can't stop smiling.

"We'll let you two lovebirds go and celebrate on your own, okay? Send me your acceptance letters later! Love you, bye!"

"Bye, Vinny!" I reply. He hangs up, and I'm left with my future Harvard boyfriend.

"What an ending to our insane day." he smiles with the same goofy smile I love and cherish more than anything else.

"What a rollercoaster of emotions!" I laugh.

I see my mom waiting by the window, watching our every move. "I should probably get going, though. We should call tonight."

"May I walk you to your door?" he asks.

"Of course you can!"

Spencer opens his trunk and grabs my luggage, carrying it up my driveway for me. As we walk together, I notice a piece of paper sticking out of his pocket that wasn't there before. I don't say anything, because it's probably not my business.

We walk up the steps to my front porch. He drops off my suitcase and gives me a big kiss goodbye. "I have something for you," he says, pulling the paper out of his pocket and handing it to me.

"What's this?" I ask.

"I wrote you something," he smiles, "read it when you get inside, and let me know what you think."

I wrap my arms around him and squeeze him tight. "Thank you so much. Drive safe, alright?"

"I always do. See ya tomorrow, darling."

"Bye, I love you!"

His smile widens. "Love you too. Bye-bye."

I stand on my porch as he gets back in his car and slowly drives away. My mom opens the door for me and I bring my suitcase and backpack upstairs. I'll worry about unpacking later. I need to read whatever this is.

I jump on the bed and open the piece of paper. It's a short poem, hand-written with what looks like a fancy pen:

I love you with a focus and resolve that will never slip,

Through every conversation, every meticulous quip,
You're the moon to my overwhelming sun,
I want you to know that you're the only one.

I will never forget the color of your eyes,
Wide-eyed browns that made me realize,
A girl like you is rare to find,
And I thank the world I get to call you mine.

I quickly place the paper on my desk so I don't cover it in happy tears. I've never been much of a poetry fan, but damn is he going to make me one. He's the sweetest boy in the world, what kind of karma did I obtain to deserve him? I'm so lucky to be able to call Spencer my boyfriend.

I have all of this love in my heart, and it's evenly distributed through the people I love the most. I'm filled with a sense of contentment. I am happy. I feel human. My heart happily aches with undying love for my friends, family, and *everything* in between.

Everything's going to be alright.

THE END

Acknowledgements

This has been a project that I've held close to my heart for such a short amount of time compared to the years it's felt. I wrote my first draft in a little more than two months, all while finishing my first semester of my mechanical engineering degree. It's been a fun ride, and I'd like to thank everyone who has helped me get through it.

I'd like to thank all of the people I cherish and who either directly or indirectly helped me write this story. Many of the characters are similar to current and previous friends. For example, Charlotte is a carbon copy (albeit genderbent) of my boyfriend.

Special thanks to my best friend Adrianna, who has been reading and critiquing my work since middle school. I should also apologize to Adrianna for having to read the stories I wrote at age 12.

I'd also like to thank the two robotics teams I was on in high school (you'll never know their names since I do not technically exist). While this competition format is completely different to what I did back then, the passion and dedication held by The Devils parallels how my teammates and I were. I loved being a part of robotics in high school, which is mainly what led me to create this project.

I remember winning my first competition, progressing through playoffs wondering "how the hell did we make it this far?" I coached my drivers; basically, I told them what to do during matches and strategized with other teams. I conveniently omitted the Drive Coach role from this competition system for that specific reason. We did damn good, and the adrenaline rush of my first win will never be forgotten.

Lastly, thank you for reading. If you're like Spencer, and have been in love with someone for a while, tell them. Seriously, do it. Regardless of any factors stopping you, it never hurts to say something. You might make their year. Things will all work out in the end, I promise. Write that love poem. Drive that robot straight into their heart. It'll be worth it.

www.ingramcontent.com/pod-product-compliance
Lightning Source LLC
LaVergne TN
LVHW100517110826
845146LV00002B/677